THE DIAMOND FUND

THE DIAMOND FUND

Philippa Annett

Matador
9 Priory Business Park,
Wistow Road, Kibworth Beauchamp,
Leicestershire. LE8 0RX
Tel: (+44) 116 279 2299
Fax: (+44) 116 279 2277
Email: books@troubador.co.uk
Web: www.troubador.co.uk/matador

ISBN 978 1783065 141

British Library Cataloguing in Publication Data.
A catalogue record for this book is available from the British Library.

Typeset by Troubador Publishing Ltd, Leicester, UK
Printed and bound in the UK by TJ International, Padstow, Cornwall

Matador is an imprint of Troubador Publishing Ltd

MIX
Paper from
responsible sources
FSC® C013056

In memory of my father, David, whose initial research led me to this story.

ACKNOWLEDGMENTS

I am hugely indebted to my husband Stuart, for his endless patience, support and assistance throughout this lengthy adventure. Also to my mother Ethie, my brother Mark, my children, my cousin Wendy, and some very dear friends (you know who you are) who kindly read various versions of this book and gave encouragement and valuable criticism along the way. Finally to my son Daniel, for the perfect photograph that brought Murad Amrad to life on the cover, and to Marina for helping with the design. Thank you all for your help and enthusiasm. I doubt I'd have finished this book without you.

DISCLAIMER

The Diamond Fund is a fictional story, inspired by the extraordinary journey made by my ancestors nearly two centuries ago. The historical events are factual, as might have been seen through their eyes. Although I have loosely modelled the Galperin family on that of my forebears, names have been changed and any similarities to others with the same names are accidental. Characterisations, conversations and most of the events in *The Diamond Fund* are from my imagination. Some, however, are not. I leave it to the reader to decide which!

CONTENTS

THE GALPERIN FAMILY TREE

ABRAM GALPERIN (1776 – 1848) married in 1796 to **SZEJNA (1777 – 1832)**

Son: **MURAD AMRAD (1800 – 1871)** married in 1819 to **TAMARA (1801 – 1830)**

    Progeny: HANNA   (1820)

                 ELZBIETTA   (1821) married in 1841 to JOSEPH LAROSA

                 TOMAS (1822 – 1889)

                 UTAH   (1823)

                 DINAH (1826 – 1830)

SONJA (1794) married to ISAAC (1793 - 1830)

Progeny: **FANNY** (1823 – 1891)

    TOMAS married in 1842 to **FANNY**

    Progeny: JAMES 1844

                 NATHANIEL 1847

                 ABRAHAM 1848

                 SARAH 1852

                 ANNA 1854

                 DAVID JAMES 1860 – 1918

                 LIZZIE 1861

                 FANNY 1862

                 ESTHER 1865

    DAVID JAMES married in 1890 to MARIA

    Progeny: **WILFRED (1891 – 1973)**

                 Edith

                 Mary

                 Freda

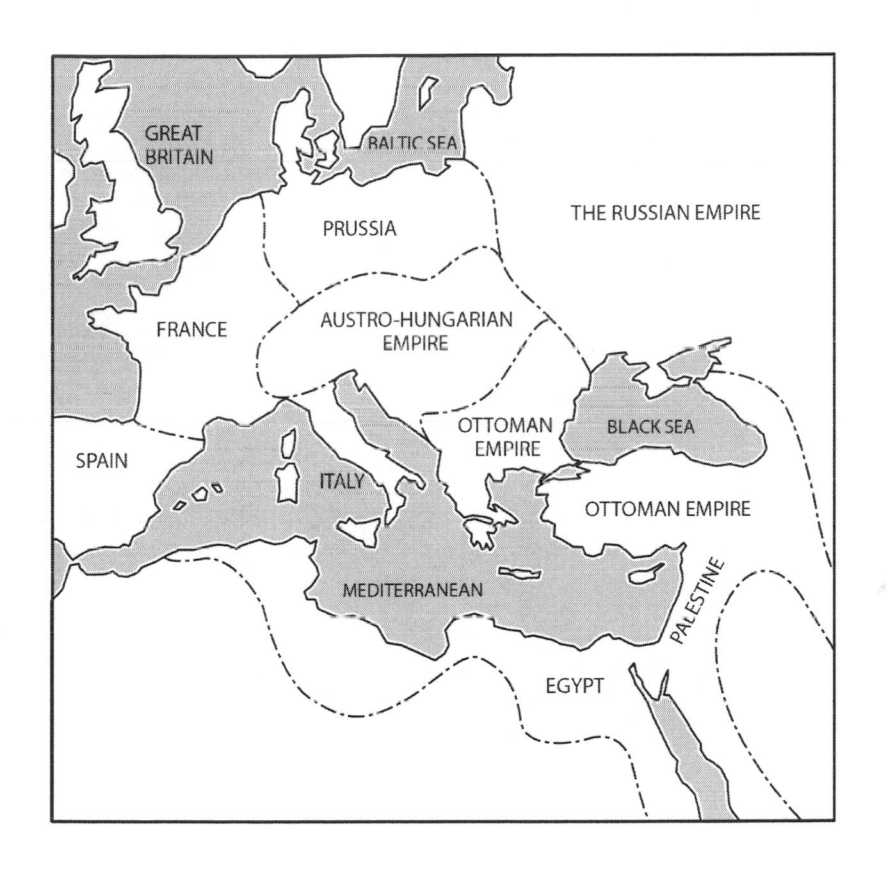

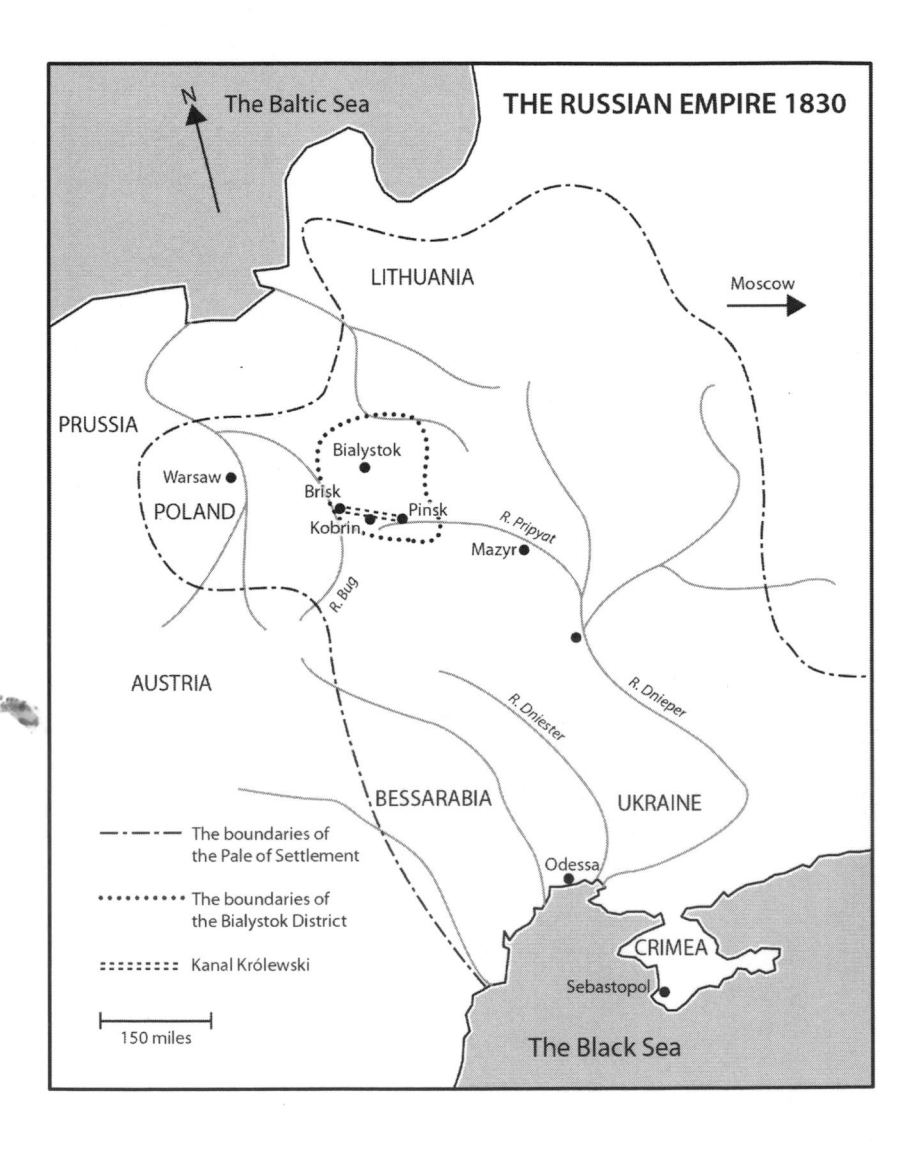

THE RUSSIAN EMPIRE 1830

The Baltic Sea

N

LITHUANIA

Moscow →

PRUSSIA

Warsaw ●
POLAND

Bialystok ●
Brisk ●
Kobrin, ● Pinsk ●
Mazyr ●

R. Pripyat

R. Bug

AUSTRIA

R. Dniester

R. Dnieper

BESSARABIA

UKRAINE

Odessa

CRIMEA

Sebastopol ●

The Black Sea

–·–·– The boundaries of
the Pale of Settlement

·········· The boundaries of
the Bialystok District

:::::::: Kanal Królewski

├─────┤
150 miles

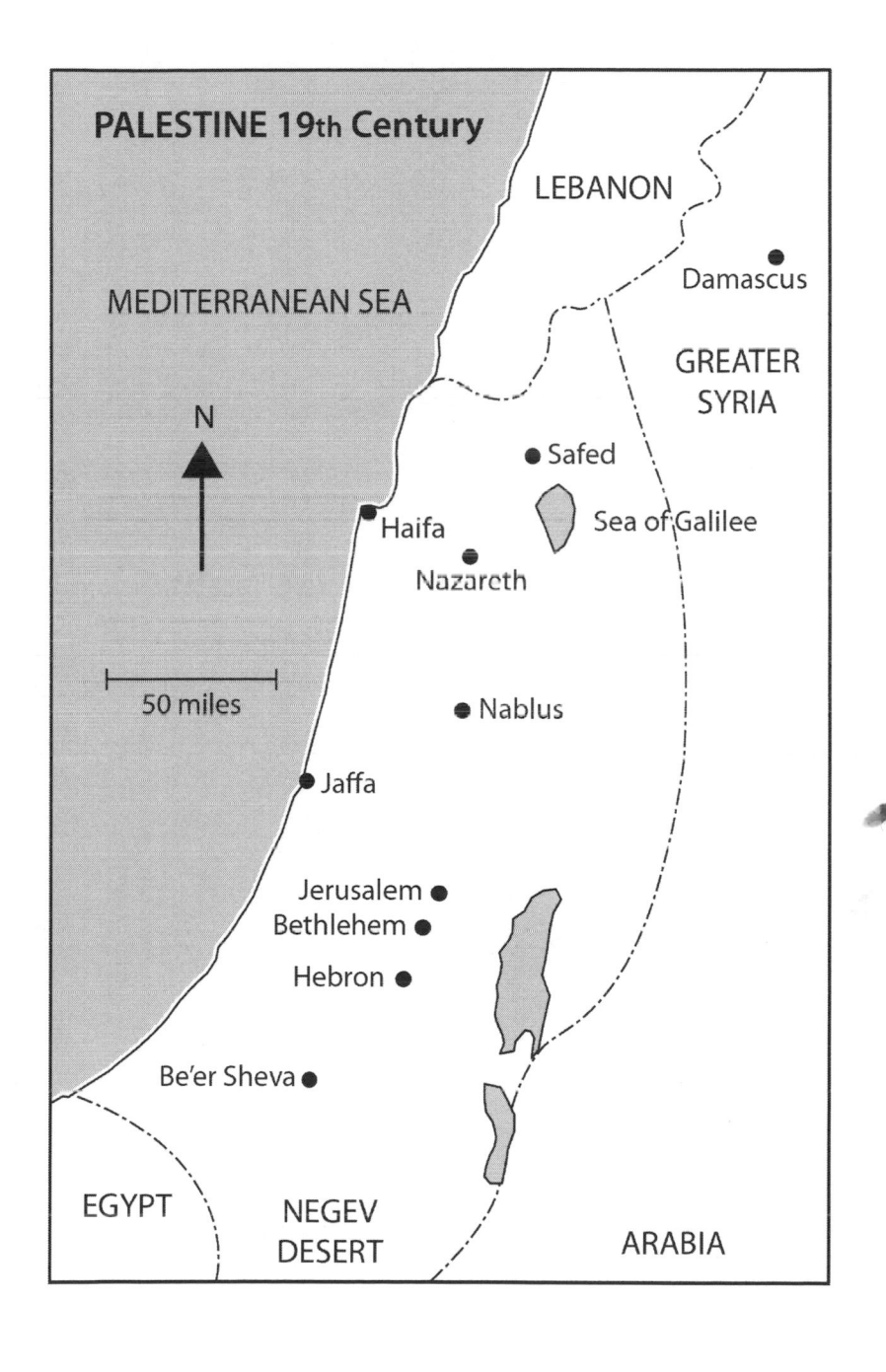

PALESTINE 19th Century

LEBANON

MEDITERRANEAN SEA

Damascus

GREATER
SYRIA

N

Safed

Haifa

Sea of Galilee

Nazareth

50 miles

Nablus

Jaffa

Jerusalem
Bethlehem

Hebron

Be'er Sheva

EGYPT

NEGEV
DESERT

ARABIA

PROLOGUE: BENI SUEF, EGYPT: 1918

The house in Jaffa was large and cool, built around a courtyard out of which grew a gnarled, old olive tree. Outside the house, a track led in one direction down to the honey-coloured, flat-roofed buildings of the city. In the other direction it led up a gently sloping hill to dusty fields intercepted by rough stone walls. At the top of the hill, the land opened out onto orange groves where, under the shade of the waxy leaves, the grass remained a soft shade of green all year round. From here you could see all the way to the coastline and out to the blue of the sea beyond. He and his sisters had run up the hill and collapsed laughing and panting at the top. He remembered lying on the ground to get his breath back and looking up at the clear blue sky beyond the startling orange fruit.

The old man smiled at the memory and began to write his letter.

Beni Suef, Egypt, 31st January, 1918

My dearest son,

Your letters to us all are read so much and I am happy to hear that you are keeping well and as cheery as possible. I wait for your homecoming with open arms and my daily prayer is for this war to soon be over and for you to return safely. I too have had some rough times of late, as I have been unwell. But I get through and it is enough to know what a glorious time awaits us both. Many changes have occurred here during the past few years and we will both have a great deal to talk about.

I have been giving much thought recently to all the changes endured by your Grandfather, Tomas, and your Great Grandfather, Murad Amrad. I don't believe you know much about them, and for that I must take the blame. I have decided to remedy that by writing down what I can remember of their story for you to read. It is one which may surprise you but one, I hope, in which you will one day take pride. I will keep it here, with the family papers and photographs, to wait on your return.

Keep happy my boy and take care of yourself. Drop me a PC if you can.

Your loving father,
David James Galperin.

BIALYSTOK, POLAND: 1830 – 1832

The day in early October 1830 that marked the beginning of change for the Galperin family started much like any other. But by the time it was over, nothing would ever be the same and the fortunes of the family would be set on an altered course. In later years, Murad Amrad would tell of a brisk cold wind that blew through the streets of Bialystok that day, bringing with it much more than the first taste of winter. He would wonder whether lives might have been saved or subsequent events been any different had he stayed at home that day instead of going out, or indeed had he never responded to the message given to him the day before. But by then, his hypothesising was discounted merely as the preoccupations of an old man. And on the morning in question, the wind was nothing more than cause for him to raise the collar of his fur-lined coat and to push his felt hat further onto his head as he bade his family good morning and closed the door of his home behind him. There had certainly been no foreseeable reason for him not to proceed with the planned events of the day.

Murad Amrad Galperin had every cause to feel good about his life that morning, and he whistled contentedly through his teeth as he walked along the dirt street towards the centre of town. He was blessed with a loving and healthy family, his business was thriving and, at thirty years of age, he was still in love with his wife. This last observation would have caused him to chuckle to himself. He often wondered how many other Jewish men in Bialystok were lucky enough to be able to say that. It was true that his marriage to Tamara had been arranged by both sets of parents. That was the way it was done. But he never ceased to give thanks for the wisdom of their choice. That Tamara possessed all the humility and piety expected of a good Jewish wife was without doubt. That she was also a fine looking woman, a gift not considered worthy of notice in Jewish

1

society, was a secret pleasure to him. That she had a shrewd and businesslike brain and was an invaluable help to him in all aspects of his business dealings was something he now took for granted. But after eleven years of marriage, his relationship with Tamara had developed into something far greater than the sum total of her assets. She had quite simply become his '*Bashert*', his soulmate, lover and friend. He thought of them as the perfect team, working hard to ensure that their family lived a Godly life: their daughters would eventually choose wise marriages and their sons would inherit a good business. By this time they had five children. Hanna at ten was the oldest, followed by Elzbietta who was nine, then Tomas eight, Utah seven, and finally Dinah who was four.

Thinking of the children caused him to take out his pocket watch and check the time. He gave a little grunt. Tomas and Utah would be setting off from home shortly, walking into town to attend their lessons on the *Torah* (sacred scripts) and in the Hebrew language with other boys of their age. He smiled. They were good boys. He imagined Tamara making sure they were clean and dressed correctly before they left. Hanna and Elzbietta would probably be helping their mother with Dinah while she sorted the boys out. The little girl had not been herself that morning. He'd thrown her into the air before leaving and instead of shrieking with pleasure as she normally did, she just gave him a rather patronising smile. He gave another chuckle. It was extraordinary how adult his youngest child sometimes appeared to be.

"Good morning to you, Murad Amrad." The greeting called out from the doorway of a neighbour brought his mind back to the present, and thoughts of what his family was doing at that time began to recede. He tipped his hat and lifted a hand in reply.

Murad Amrad was a small and wiry man whose fine features and sharp blue eyes were accentuated by the generosity of his beard. He walked everywhere at great speed and with considerable purpose, but still made time to smile or exchange a few words in greeting to those he passed in the street. Sometimes this made the journey through town take longer than it should. He had been born and raised in Bialystok and there weren't many people among the resident community with whom he wasn't acquainted. But he was happy to leave home earlier than he needed each morning and was never late opening up his store in the market hall.

He walked passed single storey wooden dwellings separated by rough fences. Each had a garden behind where vegetables grew in neat rows and chickens and geese were fattened in pens. They were much like the one in which he had been brought up. He had fond memories of his childhood home and knew that should he step inside any one of these simple houses, he would be greeted by warm cooking smells, welcomed with Jewish hospitality and invited to sit and share the food on the table. His stomach rumbled at the thought. He hadn't eaten much before leaving his house. Anxious not to be late for his forthcoming meeting, he'd made an effort to leave even earlier than usual. He would buy a pastry later. For now, he wanted to remain as clean as possible and he took care to keep to the planks that were placed along the street. There'd been a great deal of rain recently and the ground was pitted with water-filled hollows and churned into a muddy quagmire by the horses and carts.

As he neared the market square, the streets were, thankfully, cobbled. Here the buildings were two or three storeys high and built closer together. Many, like his own home, were fronted by workshops and small businesses and, at that time of the morning, butchers, bakers, tailors, brewers, winemakers and innkeepers were all opening their premises ready for the day's trade. The majority of the merchants in the town were Jewish, like himself, and all were men Murad Amrad knew well.

"Good morning, Izidor Zablludowski," he called out as he passed the Jewish print shop in the town.

"Good morning to you, Murad Amrad. I hope your family is well?"

"Thank you, yes. And your wife and baby?"

"They are thriving, thank you."

Murad Amrad was as always, grateful for his wife's regular reminders as to who in a family had been ill or whose wife had just given birth. Another man stopped him in the street. He looked preoccupied and rather harassed.

"Ah, Murad Amrad. Good morning to you. Will I see you at the

Batei Midras (meeting hall) tonight? We need your advice. I know you're always very generous in your support of our organisations, but with the numbers of refugees arriving in the town almost doubled in the past few weeks, we need to find a way to increase our funds. You are just the person to come up with some ideas on how best we can do this."

"I'll be there tonight as usual, Noakh. We can discuss it then."

"I always know we can rely on you, Murad Amrad." Noakh gave a relieved smile, tipped his hat and walked on.

Murad Amrad needed no reminding of the refugee problem in the town and wished he could do more to help. The plight of the homeless and unemployed was very evident, despite the best efforts of men like his friend Noakh Blokh and the several welfare institutions in the town. They all did what they could to help the sick and elderly among the refugees. He felt that familiar surge of rage against the Russian authorities. It was they who had forced so many thousands of Jewish peasants to leave the countryside and head to the towns to live in squalid ghettos and depend on charity. He had heard that Bialystok wasn't the only town finding it difficult to accommodate the consistent increase in population. He shook his head in frustration. It would do him no good to rage against the Russians.

"Murad Amrad!" A young man hailed him from outside a store across the street and interrupted his thoughts. Murad Amrad walked over to join him.

"How is business, Eliezer?" He asked.

"It's good, thank you. And that's what I wanted to say. I wished to thank you again for all your business advice. You were most generous with your time."

"I'm always happy to help, Eliezer Perlis. And I congratulate you on your success. Now you must forgive me. I am going to be late for my meeting." Murad Amrad touched his hat and walked on. But he was pleased to learn that his young friend had benefited from his help. Their town needed as many successful businesses as it could get. Despite the hardship endured by many in Bialystok, he had great hopes for the future of the town in which he lived, as indeed he did for the continued success of his own family's business. It was for this reason that he believed it was important to make time to talk to people, to offer his business expertise should it be asked for, and to get involved in as many aspects of the town's daily affairs as he could. He liked to think that the difference between a good business and a bad one could be as little as being in the right place at the right time or the wrong place at the wrong time.

The Galperin family business had begun over thirty years earlier, when Murad Amrad's parents Abram and Szejna had first arrived in Bialystok in the spring of 1796. They had walked from their home village of Marijampole in Lithuania, leaving behind them everything they had ever known; a close community contained within a collection of small wooden houses, where living conditions were often harsh, but where the Jewish tradition of charity was nurtured and a unique family way of life preserved. Life had always been hard for the Jews of Lithuania but increasingly so since the country had become part of the Russian Empire. When that happened, Empress Catherine II had drawn up a defined geographical area she called the Pale of Settlement, outside which Jews were not permitted to live or work. Within the Pale, the men and women who lived in the small Jewish towns and villages, called *shtetles,* were most often small time traders and street sellers who struggled to make a living. Abram had seen how hard life was for his friends and family. He was young and ambitious and knew that there was little scope for a newly married Jewish couple to build a good future inside the Russian Empire. So he and Szejna had decided to travel in search of a better life. Bialystok was more than one hundred and twenty miles to the south of Marijampol, situated in the dense forests of northeastern Poland, which at that time was part of the Kingdom of Prussia. They had heard that Jews were not only given the opportunity to prosper in Bialystok, but were traditionally welcomed, and to this end they were prepared to travel far and work hard.

One hundred years earlier, Bialystok had been owned by a Polish nobleman, Count Jan Klemens Branicki. Hoping to gain the Polish Crown, Branicki had decided to build Bialystok into a grand city, and his modest manor house into a residence as befitting a future king. In return for land and building materials he'd invited anyone to the town who was prepared to help him work to this end, and among those who arrived to take up his offer were a great number of Jewish tradesmen and their families. Branicki had been inspired by the French architecture of the times and designed his magnificent palace to have lakes and water features all around it. Branicki had also designed Bialystok's distinctive triangular market place as a centre for trade, with a large hall at its apex to house shops solely for Jewish businesses. He also built churches, a monastery and Bialystok's first two storey brick buildings. Commerce had flourished and Bialystok had quickly become a town of some importance. In 1746 Branicki had obtained the rights to transform it to the status of a city and a year later he granted the Jewish population of Bialystok equal rights to those of the Christians. Branicki never did achieve his dream of becoming king, but the legacy he left was of a thriving town where Jews were welcome and to which migrants from all over Europe continued to be drawn.

Abram was a silversmith, and once he and Szejna arrived in Bialystok, he set up a modest forge and began to produce the set ceremonial pieces of Judaica silverware that were essential to every Jewish household. He had learned the basic skills of beating silver from his own father in Marijampole, where he used to help out as a boy, and from an early age had demonstrated a distinctive artistic style of his own. Now that he had his own forge, Abram was able to develop his talent further. He leased a shop in the market hall from which to sell his silverware and, as his business began to grow, he and Szejna became active members of a town in which Christians and Jews worked together, making it a good place in which to live. And when the great powers of Europe, Russia, Prussia and Austro-Hungary decreed that their Jewish citizens were required to adopt surnames, Abram chose to take the name Galperin for his family and Galperin Silverware for his business. Galperin was derived from the name of a town in Germany where his Ashkenazi forebears had come from and it had seemed the right choice.

Ten years later however, Poland too was absorbed into the Russian Empire and Abram, together with the other Jewish merchants of the town, expected the worst. Bialystok and its surrounding area had become a separate administrative district within the Russian Empire, with Bialystok as its capital city, and life for Jews under Russian jurisdiction had become no easier. There were countless stories of Jewish families like themselves being made homeless by the growing number of governmental dictates. The boundaries of the Pale were constantly being changed and Jews were now forbidden entry into many cities. The Russian Government had even introduced legislation limiting Jews in their choice of work. As a result, thousands of Polish and Lithuanian Jews, forbidden to continue in their trades and professions, had been forced to leave their homes in search of employment. Their *shtetles* lay deserted and life for most of them was quickly reduced to a matter of survival.

But as it happened, Abram's fears were ungrounded, and Bialystok's predominantly Jewish population was given something of a reprieve. Although the Russian Government abolished their equal rights and introduced a tough new tax system on their businesses, the town's Jewish merchants were at least permitted to continue trading. Noting the success and growing wealth of many of the Jewish run businesses in the town, the Russian authorities had seen a useful means of boosting state revenues through taxation.

Over the next thirty years, as commerce in the area continued to grow and Jewish businesses to prosper, so too did the popularity of Abram's silverware. And before long, every successful Jewish family in Bialystok aspired to own at least one piece of Galperin Silverware as evidence of their growing wealth. Whether it was an item of Judaica silverware or a piece of silver jewellery, Abram's unique talent made each item instantly recognisable. His Chanukah lamps were more intricately engraved than any other; the decorations on his Kiddush wine goblets for use on the Sabbath were executed with such skill that the pictures embossed into them seemed to come alive in the evening candlelight; and if his delicate silver jewellery pieces were displayed on any woman in the town on festive occasions, it was a testament to her husband's success. But the single most sought-after pieces, in great demand from the wealthiest businessmen of Bialystok, were his spice towers. A symbol of his Ashkenazi roots, these containers for ceremonial aromatic spices were the ultimate showcase for his art; the exquisite filigree work and minute carvings for which he had become so well known, perfectly displayed in one piece of work.

Abram had taught Murad Amrad much of his skill, but he was pleased to discover that his only son also possessed an excellent business brain. Always the first to get his hands on a good financial deal or a good sale, once he had joined his father in the business Murad Amrad began to diversify. He saw that the town could not continue its growth without the aid of a local monetary facility and, like many others of the more established and wealthy Jewish merchants in Bialystok, he began to offer a money collecting and lending service to assist developing businesses. In this way, Abram and Murad Amrad expanded Galperin Silverware to such an extent that by 1830 they had moved to larger premises, one of only a handful of stone built two storey properties outside the centre of the town. Murad Amrad and Tamara lived with their family behind and above a large workshop and forge that opened onto the street, while in single storey houses built on either side, both accessible from the central workshop, Abram and Szejna lived in one, and Murad Amrad's cousin Isaac and his family in the other. Isaac also helped in the business. And on that October morning when this story begins, life was looking good for the Galperin family. As Murad Amrad made his way across town, Abram was working on a specially ordered piece of silverware in the forge, Hanna and Elzbietta were helping their Grandmother Szejna in the family's kitchen, and Isaac was in the workshop speaking to a young man about a gift for his new wife.

However, Isaac was beginning to feel unwell, and was praying that the young man would make his decision soon. And in their apartment on the floor above the workshop, Tamara was fretting over her youngest daughter, Dinah, who had taken a turn for the worse. Tamara did not feel that well herself but was putting it down to sympathetic symptoms. She had often found herself suffering in some small way from whatever her children were feeling when they were ill, and knew it was common for mothers to do so. But unknown to her, the cholera epidemic that had been born in the sewers and water supplies of the overcrowded slum areas had started to creep through the streets of Bialystok and now, invisible and deadly, it was showing no deference to the better-off households.

Murad Amrad meanwhile continued on his way. The streets were filling with people now as men, women and children headed towards the marketplace to open up their stalls for the day. They carried with them every kind of merchandise, from cooking pots to flimsy cages packed with live geese. Some rode on horse-drawn carts, others pulled handcarts or were bent double with heavy loads on their backs. Murad Amrad dodged through the crowds, occasionally nodding his head in greeting or tipping his hat at people he knew. A group of chickens scattered in front of him. In trying to avoid them he nearly collided with a young water carrier running down the street with two full buckets hanging from a yolk over his shoulders. The boy was scantily dressed and filthy. Murad Amrad shivered. The weather was beginning to turn cold and as he entered the market square a collection of autumn leaves scuttled dryly in front of him as he walked. He took out his pocket watch again, checked the time against the clock tower above the market hall and gave a satisfied grunt. He wasn't late.

His destination was the splendid Branicki Palace that dominated the centre of town. He had been brought up on the story of its creation and felt the palace to be part of his heritage. It was testament to all that Bialystok had once stood for; to the hopes and dreams of another age, when its grand style, beautiful gardens, pavilions and sculptures had earned it the title of 'The Versailles of Poland'. He had probably taken its presence for granted lately, for as he approached he noticed for the first time that its yellow painted walls were flaking and the once glorious gardens surrounding it were somewhat overgrown. Like the town, the palace now belonged to the Russian Empire and was the temporary home of a Russian nobleman, Count Alexei Petrovitch, who was rarely in residence, favouring as he did his estates near St Petersburg. Today was no exception and Murad Amrad was meeting his son, Viscount Viktor Petrovitch.

The previous day, Murad Amrad had been surprised at being stopped in the street by a man in the dress of a Russian servant who, after a formal greeting, handed him a sealed note. On breaking the seal, he had read that his presence was required at the palace the following morning on a matter of personal importance. The sheet of paper was headed with the family crest and was signed by Viscount Viktor Petrovitch himself. Now passing under an ornate archway and approaching the side entrance in the palace to which the servant had directed him, Murad Amrad checked an unaccustomed feeling of nerves. He drew back his shoulders and smoothed down his beard. He'd never been inside the palace before but knew he needed to keep the upper hand in the forthcoming interview.

He had his suspicions about what the Viscount might want from him. He'd seen Viktor Petrovitch riding out from time to time and heard enough talk in the town to know that the Viscount enjoyed a somewhat dissolute lifestyle, and one that evidently incurred considerable expense. When his father, Count Alexei Petrovitch, was away Viktor was left ostensibly to run the Branicki Palace and the affairs of the town. But the Viscount preferred to spend time with his friends, hunting in the surrounding forests during the day and revelling during the night. With so many small breweries and winemakers in Bialystok there was never any shortage of alcohol. Murad Amrad had heard stories of how the young man was occasionally seen in one of the town's many drinking houses in an intoxicated state, surrounded by immodestly dressed young women. Other stories circulated of excessive parties in the palace with visitors from the households of local Russians, and of nights spent gambling. Gossip was rife in Bialystok and everyone knew everyone else's business, so it was inevitable that among the heated political topics regularly aired by the population of Jewish men in the *Batei Midras* discussions sometimes included the goings on at the palace. And it was the general opinion that Count Alexei Petrovitch kept his son on a very strict budget. Why else would he be in so much debt to most of the Jewish innkeepers and brewers in the town, they argued. However, Murad Amrad knew there was little any of them could do about the situation. Viscount Viktor Petrovitch was, after all, the man representing the Russian authorities and it would be unwise to deny him the credit he demanded. But if his father was due to return to Bialystok before the onset of winter, the Viscount might now be wanting to borrow money to help repay his debts and he, Murad Amrad, as one of the leading moneylenders in town, was an obvious choice.

A servant – he couldn't be sure if it was the same one – escorted Murad Amrad down a corridor with a domed ceiling and black and white tiles on the floor. Passing through a felt covered door into what was presumably a central hallway in the palace, Murad Amrad had a brief glimpse of a wide staircase carpeted in red and flanked by gilt statues. The walls were richly decorated in brightly coloured patterns, and vast crystal candelabra hung from the ceiling. There wasn't much time to take it all in, however, before he was shown to an ornate door where the servant paused and knocked discreetly. A voice from inside gave a command and they entered a small room, decorated with equal extravagance, this time with hunting scenes painted on the walls and plush drapes at the windows. Viscount Viktor Petrovitch was lounging somewhat indolently in a chair beside an elaborately carved desk, on which rested his booted feet, a ceremonial sword and a pair of gloves. After a brief hesitation, he got up as Murad Amrad entered and nodded to the servant, who withdrew and closed the door behind him.

Viscount Viktor Petrovitch was considerably taller than Murad Amrad, but the latter was immediately aware that the younger man was either unwell or very nervous. The skin on his clean-shaven face had a pasty appearance, his forehead damp and shiny. His brown curly hair was stuck to his head and his jacket, with its high collar and ornate lapels and braiding, was undone at the top. His general appearance was unkempt and slightly dirty.

Formal greetings were briefly but correctly exchanged, during which the Viscount appeared to look down on Murad Amrad with distaste. He fidgeted with a lace handkerchief and repeatedly put it up to his face.

"I wish to borrow a sum of money, Jew," Viktor Petrovitch said, in heavily accented Polish. "I believe you are a moneylender of some repute?"

"You have chosen the right person, sir," Murad Amrad replied. "And may I enquire as to the amount you wish to borrow?"

Much to Murad Amrad's surprise, the Viscount then named a fairly modest sum, certainly not an amount Murad Amrad needed to have any concerns about providing. He nodded in agreement and gave his rates of interest, at which it was Viktor Petrovitch's turn to look momentarily shocked. He was beginning to sweat profusely, but he recovered his composure and assured Murad Amrad of his intention to repay the sum within a month to avoid the greater amount of interest.

"I will have the money ready for your collection from my workshop tomorrow," Murad Amrad told him. "All I require from you is a promissory note as confirmation of your intention to repay the total amount, together with any interest incurred."

The Viscount nodded, then abruptly waved his handkerchief in the air with a flourish, indicating that the interview was at an end, and giving the impression that what they had agreed was of no consequence. He barked out another one worded command and the same servant re-entered the room. It was clear that Murad Amrad had been dismissed. He inclined his head obediently and was escorted out of the room and the palace. The whole interview had barely taken ten minutes.

Back in the market square, with the bustle of normality going on around him, Murad Amrad took a deep breath. He felt mildly tarnished and somewhat insulted by what he took to be the Viscount's distaste at conducting business with a Jew. It also seemed strange to him that Viktor Petrovitch had requested such a small amount of money. Was it the sum of a single debt he wondered? Or perhaps all he knew he could afford to borrow? Despite the obvious wealth of the household, if his father kept him as short of funds as was rumoured, then either could be a likely explanation. Murad Amrad gave a little shrug. It was not of much consequence to him either way, although he looked forward to telling Tamara all about his meeting. He knew she would be longing to know what the inside of the palace was like. But by the time he had walked across the square and into the market hall to open up his store for the day, he had already ceased to give the matter any further thought.

Several hours later Murad Amrad was summoned from his shop by a messenger boy and instructed to return home immediately. This he did, and as he ran up the stairs two at a time to get to the room where he and Tamara slept, it was the smell that hit him first.

Fishy and sour, it was the smell of cholera and of fear. He stood at the open door and his senses reeled in horror and revulsion at the scene before him. Tamara lay on the bed, soiled linen heaped up around her, the physician crouching at her side. He had cut the inside of her forearm and was catching her blood in a small bowl, the bright red trickle stark against her white skin. Further gashes on her arms and neck exposed his earlier attempts at alleviating her symptoms. Dinah was lying in her cot at the edge of the room and Murad Amrad could see her chest heaving up and down as she drew in tiny shuddering breaths. He was struggling to take in all that he saw as he walked over to the bed and sat gently down beside his wife. She was deathly pale, her eyes were closed and her face was distorted with pain. She rolled her head from side to side and tried feebly to fight off the physician.

"I am here, Tamara," he said, and took her hand. She opened her eyes then, and Murad Amrad saw they were sunken deep into her head. She appeared to relax a little when she saw him and tried to talk, but her mouth was parched, her tongue swollen and the effort was too much.

"Dinah?" was all she managed to gasp.

"Hush, *Bubbala*," Murad Amrad said, and pushed her damp hair from her face. Her skin felt clammy and looked strangely wrinkled. "Do not try to speak. She is in good hands."

He glanced desperately across the bed at the physician as he said this. The man looked grey and exhausted and as their eyes met he gave a barely perceptible shake of his head. He had not had time to see to both victims, and as he believed the mother to have a greater chance of recovery than the daughter, he had concentrated all his efforts on her. His services were now required next door where Murad Amrad's cousin Isaac had also succumbed to the cholera and was in a bad way, and there were a dozen more cases in the town for him to visit. He sighed and stood up. There was little more he could do here except leave a phial of his herbal potion to be administered by the family, and encourage them to pray. Cholera was a killer and only the very strong survived, if it was God's will.

Murad Amrad released Tamara's hand and went over to where their daughter was lying. Her bedding was badly soiled and there was dried matter around her mouth. Her eyes were drawn up into her head and she appeared to be barely conscious. Only the day before she had been robust and happy. Now her young body seemed too small and frail to cope with such an illness, and a sob caught in his throat. He covered it with a cough and turned back to the physician to ask what there was to be done.

Throughout the afternoon, Murad Amrad divided his attentions between his wife and his daughter, doing what he could to make them comfortable and willing them to get better. He became immune to the putrid smell filling the room. He wiped their faces and wetted their cracked lips, but they turned away from him. He spooned the physician's potion into their mouths, but they were not able to swallow it. As the hours dragged by he became more and more desperate. He held Tamara's hands and called out to her to live. He stroked his daughter's forehead and tried to sing the songs her mother had sung to help her sleep. He became increasingly tormented by his inability to make a difference, feeling his helplessness as a physical pain. As they became weaker and quieter, he alternated between pacing up and down the room and crouching in a corner with his hands over his face. He prayed to God, and then raged against Him. But in the end he knew there was nothing more he could do.

Much earlier, Szejna had taken Hanna and Elzbietta into her own house to protect them from having to witness the full horror of cholera, and throughout the day she had done her best to keep them busy. But by the time Tomas and Utah returned home from their studies for the evening meal, their mother and little sister had lost their struggle to hang on to life. The girls were inconsolable, but the boys refused to believe that their mother and baby sister were dead. Szejna knew that they needed to see their bodies so that they could reconcile themselves to the harsh reality. But it was not to be until Murad Amrad and Abram had cleaned Tamara and Dinah as best they could; not until they had wrapped them in lengths of cloth and placed them on the floor; not until they had surrounded them with candles. Only then could Szejna bring the children in to say their farewells.

They found their father standing beside the two wrapped bodies that lay side by side, the one small shrouded shape tucked in close up against the larger. Murad Amrad's face was grim and ashen in the flickering candlelight and for a second none of the children recognised him. But he turned as they entered and held out his arms. They ran to him then, sobbing and shaking with shock, calling over and over for '*Mammeh*'. Murad Amrad held them close for a long, long time, and all the while his own tears rolled unchecked down his cheeks. When finally the children's crying ceased, the only sound in the room was of their combined jagged breathing and the spitting of a myriad of candles.

Murad Amrad and Abram stayed as chief mourners next to their loved one's bodies all night, while Szejna comforted the children. The rabbi had arranged the burials for the following day in the new Bema cemetery, where victims of the cholera epidemic were all being interred together. As well as Tamara and Dinah, there had been thirty other deaths from cholera in the town on that day alone, including that of Isaac, who had died during the night. There was much discontent in the town among the Jewish community over the concept of mass graves. But the physicians and the rabbis had insisted that because of the sheer numbers of dead from cholera who needed burial each day, mass graves provided the only solution at the current time. Murad Amrad hadn't become involved in the issue previously. Now that it affected him personally however, the thought that he was to lay his wife and child, unnamed, into a mass grave, was almost more than he could bear. But he, like everyone else, had no choice. They would at least be among friends.

In the days that followed the funeral, Murad Amrad fell into deep despair. As friends and relations came to the house to bring food and offer condolences, he greeted them all unseeingly and forgot they had been when they departed. Left on his own, he just sat in a chair or stood in one place, staring out at nothing. The children too were deeply shocked and grieving and although Szejna did her best to help them cope with the loss of their mother and sister, as the days grew into weeks and the harsh winter weather set in, she believed they needed their father to show them that the life of the living needed to continue. So when she found Murad Amrad sitting alone at the kitchen table one day, she went to him and made him look at her as she spoke.

"My son. You have grieved in public enough. Now you must grieve in private. The passing of Tamara and Dinah, of Isaac, and of all the others in the town, are part of God's plan for us all. But you have a duty to continue to live and work for your family in the way Tamara would have wanted you to. Your children need you, your father needs you and your business needs you."

As Murad Amrad looked up at Szejna, she took in his hollow eyes and his unkempt appearance. She held his head to her breast and they remained like that for some time. Then, pulling away gently and drawing himself upright, Murad Amrad wiped his eyes and said, "You are right, Mammeh. I know you are right. I will do as you ask and endeavour to fulfill God's plan."

The following day, as the family sat for their midday meal, Murad Amrad made a conscious effort to look around the table at them all. To his shame, he noticed for the first time how pale Hanna and Elzbietta were. Hanna, the eldest, had always been a quiet and shy child who had been especially dependent upon her mother. Now she had dark circles under her eyes and he saw that she didn't eat much. Elzbietta, the more outgoing and independent of the two, was markedly quieter than usual, although thankfully she ate with a good enough appetite. He noticed that Tomas and Utah kept shooting quick uncertain glances at him, as if trying to assess his mood. Utah occasionally dug Tomas in the ribs with his elbow, causing Tomas to hiss at his brother angrily. Murad Amrad felt a sudden surge of anguish, not only for his recent absence in all but body, but also for their loss. To lose your mother so young was a terrible thing. He looked across at his own mother and realised they would all have been lost without her. She was serving out ladles of food and had a kind word for each of them as she handed out the full plates. He had to admit that what she had cooked smelled very good, and for the first time in a long while he found himself feeling hungry.

His father, in a valiant effort to distract the two boys from an escalating, albeit silent quarrel, was asking them about their lessons that day. Isaac's wife, Sonja, and their little girl, Fanny, were also seated at the table. They too were in mourning of course, and yet his mother had told him how Sonja had quietly stepped in and started to help with the cooking, shopping and household chores. He watched Sonja tending to his children's needs at the table and felt tremendous gratitude. He remembered that she had no family in the town, so of course she and Fanny were now his responsibility. But more than that, he could see that the children were responding to her warmth and affection. She and Fanny couldn't fill the void left by their mother and sister, but they were nevertheless a valuable alternative. Fanny was the same age as Utah and seemed a quiet, serious little girl. He was sure she would be no trouble to have around and he was content to offer Sonja and the child his financial and personal protection out of gratitude as much as duty.

"I must thank you, Sonja. Mammch tells me that you've been a great help to her and a comfort to the children. I would not like you to think I don't appreciate what you have been doing for us."

"The past weeks have been a difficult time for us all, Murad Amrad," Sonja replied quietly. "It's given me pleasure to assist your mother where I've been able."

Sonja was a strong, capable woman, who was happiest when she was busy. Although she was grieving for her husband, she had understood that her cousin's children, like Fanny, were in need of comfort and support at this time. She had also seen how hard Szejna was working, having to cope single-handedly with the children's grief as well as running the house. Helping Murad Amrad's family overcome their grief over the past weeks had helped her to cope better with her own, and Fanny too had found comfort from being with her cousins. They had all lost parents.

Slowly Murad Amrad began to take notice of his surroundings once again. He made a conscious effort to play his part in the family and was quickly rewarded by the benefits of his involvement. The children began to find reasons to smile, colour returned to their cheeks and the atmosphere in the home slowly relaxed, as if the family had breathed a communal sigh of relief at his return to the land of the living. He also started going back into the town to work, to pray at the synagogue and to attend meetings at the *Batei Madras*. The town at this time was full of Russian soldiers and the talk at the *Batei Madras* was of nothing but unfolding events in Poland.

"They say Polish troops from the garrison in Warsaw have launched a rebellion against the Russian authorities."

"That is brave."

"Or stupid. I presume all the Russian soldiers who have passed through the town recently have been on their way to Warsaw. There have been thousands of them. The rebels will never defeat the Russians. They are a mighty force."

"It's worth a try though isn't it? And who knows where it might lead. The Polish people have no rights under Russian rule and life is hard. We are lucky here in Bialystok. Away from here, the peasants, both Jews and Poles alike, are treated like cattle. No, worse!" This was from Eliezer Perlis, whose face flushed with emotion as he continued. "The Russians want all the agricultural land in Poland for themselves. All the refugees in the ghettos at the edge of our town once earned a decent livelihood from the land before the Russians drove them out with their rules on who can or can't do what. The rebels speak with the voice of many. Their actions are those of desperate people who are prepared and brave enough to take the risk."

There were cautious murmurs of agreement from around the hall as one voiced what many were thinking.

"I think most of us would agree with that. But if we are overheard expressing such opinions we could be imprisoned for treason and we will lose our livelihoods. We must be careful what we say."

But Eleizer was not to be silenced. "Well I tell you now that I for one will not be able sit here quietly if this rebellion continues. If it means I lose my business here in Bialystok, then so be it. To join the rebels and do my bit to support the rebellion would at least mean I would be doing something that my heart believes to be right."

Several of the other younger men nodded their heads and began to voice their support.

"And I. And I."

The elders looked around the room and at each other in concern, casting nervous glances towards the door. The noise inside the hall was escalating.

"Gentlemen!" The rabbi called out. "Gentlemen."

The voices fell to a murmur and he was able to continue. "I believe we should keep our voices down."

Murad Amrad then spoke quietly. "We would not want to see you go, Eliezer. It's a very big decision to make. But if it's something you have to do, then I'm sure we can make a plan to take care of your business for you until you return."

"Thank you, Murad Amrad," Eleizer Perlis said gravely. "That's good to know. I'll not make my decision lightly I promise you. But the Polish army is going to need as much help as it can get and every man who joins forces with them could make a difference."

Someone then voiced what perhaps many were thinking.

"If you leave to join the rebels, you would be putting the security of every one of us at risk, as well as that of our families and businesses. We would be accused of collaboration."

"The authorities would certainly enjoy making our lives very difficult in retaliation," said another. And everyone began to grumble among themselves.

"I don't believe the authorities would want to imprison us all," the rabbi said gently with a wry smile. "They would have the sense to realise that if they did, commerce in the town would come to a halt. But we would have to claim no knowledge of Eleizer's decision to join the rebels, and deny our support, whatever else we feel in our hearts."

"That I would understand," said Eleizer. "And that's just the way it will have to be."

From its beginning in November 1830, the rebellion spread rapidly and soon developed into a bloody war between the Polish and Russian armies. Bialystok, situated as it was between the borders of Poland and Russia, became a base for the Russian army as it attempted to suppress the uprising. But that didn't prevent Eleizer Perlis and some of the other younger men leaving the town under the cover of darkness to join the rebels. Frequent partisan skirmishes took place in the surrounding heavily wooded countryside after that, and the citizens of Bialystok found themselves subjected to constant surveillance over any suspected allegiance to the Polish cause. The atmosphere in the town became very tense, and Murad Amrad and men like him who had families to support and businesses to run and who might have had much to say in support of the rebels, whispered their opinions furtively to one another in the *Batei Madras* or exchanged them behind the closed doors of their homes. At other times it was safer to keep a low profile, not to trust anyone and make every effort to continue with business as usual. This suited Murad Amrad. He was more than happy to work hard and say little at this time.

But the rebellion was badly managed and the Polish army, although swelled by Jewish and other partisan militia groups, was nevertheless no match for the superior fighting force of the Russians. In October 1831, a year after the rebellion had begun, the Russian Army eventually captured Warsaw and crushed the rebellion. Over 20,000 resistance fighters and their families fled across the border into Prussia and moved into exile in Germany and France, Eliezer and those of his comrades still alive among them. Although Murad Amrad was sad to see his young friend's business premises finally forced to close, he prayed that Eleizer might one day be able to return and start again. Eliezer Perliz was a man Bialystok should be proud of.

After the uprising, the Russian authorities retained Bialystok as the centre of their administrative power in the area, and from there began to implement a series of harsh repressive measures throughout Poland in retaliation. They introduced heavy taxes on trade between Poland and the rest of the Russian Empire. And they created further discriminatory legislation against both Jews and Polish peasants.

This resulted in a new wave of destitute families making their way over the border to Bialystok in search of work and charity. Like most better off Jews in town, Murad Amrad continued to give considerable sums to Bialystok's struggling welfare organisations. But these were already severely over-stretched and were barely able to cope with the volume of people seeking aid. Conditions in the town's slums became untenable and poverty and starvation was a huge problem. During the winter of 1831/2 alone, many of the poor and homeless died on the streets or in the freezing mud of their ghettos.

Meanwhile, with the added intention of reducing any

dependency on Poland, the Russian Government continued to support all industrial activity in Bialystok, and the town soon benefited from a massive surge in commercial growth. Among Bialystok's most successful business concerns, none expanded more quickly than the town's textile industry, and the many cloth factories in the town soon began to make their Christian and Jewish owners extremely wealthy. Other businesses developed and flourished as a result; a Hebrew printing press, timber merchants, artisan centres and traders of all commodities. All benefited from Bialystok's low taxes, and the town was on its way to becoming the thriving centre of industry, learning and philanthropy that, albeit for a short period in history, it would later become.

To take advantage of the town's growing prosperity, Abram started creating a number of jewellery pieces specifically aimed at the non-Jewish population. For these he was able to be more flamboyant, using gold instead of silver, and designing each piece around gemstones or pearls to create exquisite necklaces, earrings, hair combs and bracelets. He made no two pieces the same, and each was worked with Abram's unique artistic talent. Word spread fast among the Christian community and interest in Abram's new line of jewellery grew daily. Eventually, even the Russian Army Officers and government officials visited the Galperin's shop in the market hall to buy pieces for their wives, mistresses and mothers.

Murad Amrad now found that to be busy was the only way he could deaden the pain he felt over his loss. There wasn't a day that passed when he didn't want to talk to Tamara about something that had happened, and each time he forgot for a few seconds that he couldn't. When he remembered, he felt his grief renewed. So he buried himself in his work. He was most gratified to see that his money lending business was not greatly affected by the presence of the Russian troops, or by the poverty on the streets around him. It had, in fact, never been in greater demand. Every business in town wanted to expand, and in order to do so they all needed financial assistance. In addition, his father's work was selling well and he felt confident that Galperin Silverware and his own business affairs would continue to flourish as the town grew.

In the months after his meeting with Viscount Viktor Petrovitch,

Murad Amrad continued to receive further requests for reasonably modest amounts of money, and before long a monthly pattern was established. The Viscount would send his servant, always the same one, with a sealed letter containing another request for money. On the following day the same man would arrive to collect the money as arranged and to bring a renewed promissory note from the Viscount. However, Murad Amrad was becoming increasingly concerned that contrary to his initial assurances, the Viscount had not repaid any of the monies he owed. Although each of the amounts he borrowed were reasonably small, by the time the Polish Russian war came to an end, and a year had passed since their first agreement, Viktor Petrovitch owed him a considerable amount of money. And taking into account the accruing interest, it was a sum that increased each week that passed. With this in mind, he decided that it was time to demand some collateral. He was determined to make no further funds available to the Viscount until he had, in his possession, some form of insurance against the escalating debt.

When Viscount Viktor Petrovitch received a letter from Murad Amrad the following day, he paled. He sat down heavily on the chair behind his desk and tried to think calmly. The Jew had written demanding an immediate repayment, either complete or in part or, at the very least, something to be held as collateral. Murad Amrad had stated that if none of these were forthcoming within the week, he would be requesting an audience with the Viscount's father, Count Alexei Petrovitch. The Count had joined his regiment in St Petersburg a year earlier and marched into Poland as part of the force attempting to quell the rebellion. He hadn't been back to Bialystok for over a year, but it was general knowledge that he was expected home within the month. Murad Amrad had written that he would show the Count the promissory notes as signed by his son and demand repayment. This was just one more reason among many why the knowledge of his father's return filled Viktor with dread, but it was one that he knew he had to redress.

Viktor was not a well man. Although still young, excessive alcohol consumption and lack of exercise had dulled and bloated his appearance. He sweated a great deal, especially in the mornings when his eyes were bloodshot and his skin yellow. He blamed his condition on his inability to afford enough of the best food, and for this he blamed his father, as he did most things. His father, for example, had no idea how impossible it was for him to live on the meager allowance he was given. But when he had introduced the subject of increasing it the year before, he was told in no uncertain terms, that his choice was between living within his means in Bialystok or joining his father's regiment in the Russian Army. Viktor was rather taken with a young woman from the town at the time, and had avoided compulsory military service due to weak lungs as a child. He certainly had no desire to join the army now. So he'd acquiesced and the subject wasn't brought up again. But then his father left town and Viktor had found it almost impossible to make his monthly income last, especially with all the troops garrisoned here over the past year and all the entertaining he had been forced to do.

So it seemed an answer to his prayers when, one evening, while drinking at the inn he most frequented, he had befriended a thickset man with a bald head and bad teeth named Igor Sikorski. As the evening wore on, and Viktor became more intoxicated, he had started to talk openly to Igor Sikorski about his financial difficulties. He had spoken of them initially with some humour, and then with barely disguised distress. Igor Sikorski proved to be a good listener. If Viktor had been more himself he might have wondered how his new friend, while appearing to match him drink for drink, had remained sober, his eyes hard and clear. But as it was, towards the end of the evening Igor Sikorski had said he would like to help. He was the frontman of a syndicate of Russian officials who had started selling the new lottery tickets from Europe, he told him in hushed tones. Then lowering his voice even further so that Viktor had to lean in to hear him, he intimated there might be an opportunity for Viktor to buy his way into the syndicate. All he would need to do, he said, was to prove himself a viable partner in the scheme by providing a regular sum of money as a deposit.

Viktor had not been able to stop grinning. He had heard of people who were making considerable amounts of money in this way and he welcomed the chance to join them. There were families in the town so desperate to win the lottery that they were pawning their valuables in order to buy tickets. Selling them seemed to Viktor a failsafe way to make money and he had accepted the offer as graciously as he could, given his excitement and intoxicated state. Igor had then made him promise that all their financial dealings were to be kept a secret. Through his drunkenness, Viktor had sensed something vaguely threatening about Igor Sikorski. But he knew that to sell lottery tickets was forbidden by the authorities, and assuming this to be the cause he had pushed any other misgivings he may have felt to one side.

It had been arranged that Viktor would pay Igor Sikorski in monthly installments, on the understanding that when a sufficient amount had been laid down, his investment would start to earn him money. By regularly borrowing from Murad Amrad, Viktor had found he was easily able to pay the agreed monthly sum. But each time he asked Igor when it might be that he would start receiving money as opposed to paying it out, he was told that the price of the tickets had increased or that he hadn't yet paid a sufficient amount. More recently, after enquiring yet again, Igor Sikorski had made a few unsettling comments about the possibility of counting him out of the scheme after all. So Viktor had not pursued the subject. Igor had assured him that he would eventually make enough money to repay all his debts, and while ardently hoping it would happen before his father's return, Viktor had no choice but to believe him. The promise of eventual reimbursement meant that Murad Amrad was still an essential part of Viktor's hopes for the future, and he knew it was vitally important for him to keep the Jew on his side.

What he could offer as collateral was now of some concern however. His parents owned a great many artifacts and other items of value and his mother, he knew, had some priceless jewellery. Viktor wondered if any of it had been left in her chambers here at the palace. Perhaps he could lay his hands on something that would placate the Jew. He was sure it wouldn't be missed until his mother's return, which wasn't imminent. She preferred to stay in their mansion near St Petersburg and rarely came to Bialystok. Once he began to receive sufficient income to repay his debt to Murad Amrad, he could then retrieve the item and return it to his mother's chambers. Viktor smiled. He began to think this was an excellent plan and one his father and mother need never know anything about.

Throughout their marriage, Count Alexei Petrovitch had regularly presented his wife Sophia with gifts of jewellery; a tradition long upheld by members of Russian nobility. Emperor Peter I of Russia had begun the trend a century earlier by accumulating a magnificent royal collection of jewels, which he decreed were to be preserved for the glory of the Russian Empire and could never be sold. Stored at the Winter Palace in St Petersburg, he had called the collection his Diamond Fund, and instructed that subsequent emperors and empresses should add further jewels to the collection for their continued insurance. In much the same spirit of familial glory and material preservation, Count Alexei Petrovitch regarded the precious gifts he bestowed on his wife as a valuable asset to future generations of his family. Sophia loved her jewellery and, much like the current Empress Alexandra Feodorovna, took great pleasure in the pieces she was given. But she also accepted that the majority of her jewellery collection ultimately belonged to her husband's estate and as such should remain in their family vaults. So whether it was for reasons of absent mindedness, or a concern for travelling with valuable jewellery on her person, the Countess Sophia had left a number of her more recent gifts in a large chest in her chambers at the Branicki Palace. She would have had no cause to doubt the safety of her jewellery. The palace was well guarded and her son was in residence.

It was for this reason that when Viscount Viktor Petrovitch visited the premises of Galperin Silverware later that same evening, he was holding a package in his hand. He arrived alone and unannounced, shrouded in a long, velvet, fur-lined coat and covered with a dusting of snow. On seeing who the visitor was at that late hour, Murad Amrad led him in quickly and closed the door behind him. He lit a lamp and the young Viscount placed his package on the large table in the centre of the workshop and pushed it towards him. He grunted, but no other words passed between them as Murad Amrad began to unwrap the soft leather around the package.

As its contents were revealed, Murad Amrad caught his breath, unable to control his reaction. In his hands was a gold circular jewel box. Around its circumference, triangles of brightly coloured enameling were set in a geometric pattern. The removable lid was bound by the finest embossed silver and intricately covered with rows of triangular cut gemstones, arranged in such a way as to echo the pattern on the box itself. And in the centre of the lid, probably the largest diamond he had ever seen was set into a ring of gold. As the two men looked down at the box, one in considerable shock and the other with some shame, the multifaceted edges of the cut amethysts, topazes and white diamonds caught the lamplight and threw a million tiny reflections around the room and onto their faces, while the central diamond seemed alive with colours. Murad Amrad didn't need to hear any words to tell him that this was something of enormous value.

"It is my mother's," Viktor mumbled. He looked shiftily around the room. "You must keep it safe until I can repay you what I owe. And now I must go."

After the Viscount left, Murad Amrad knocked on his father's door. Abram had approved of Murad Amrad's demand for collateral, and on inspecting the box knew enough about jewellery to appreciate that the workmanship and styling warranted his homage. Almost lovingly he touched the stones, turned the box over and held it near the light. This was indeed an exquisite piece of work and an overly extravagant piece to have offered as insurance. He was silent for some time, after which he began to frown.

"This box is of unimaginable value, Murad," he said. "The diamond on its own is worth a hundred times more than the debt. And the other jewels the same again. This box would be highly prized by collectors of such pieces and is therefore of no value to us. If we were unable to call in the debt, where would we sell it? Any legitimate local dealer would instantly recognise an item of such unique style and workmanship. I believe Viscount Viktor has offered us something to which he has no right and this must be kept in secret merely as a means of placing pressure on the Count should the need arise." Almost reverently and with obvious regret, he handed the box back to Murad Amrad.

"You are right, Father, and we will keep it safe. We would certainly have to travel far before this could be sold." Murad Amrad then rewrapped the fine leather around the jewel box and placed it into their strong box at the back of the workshop.

As it happened, given the early onset of winter following the crushing of the Polish rebellion, Count Alexei Petrovitch decided to travel straight to St Petersburg to join his wife and spend the winter there. Viktor was much relieved and was consequently able to do as he pleased. And although the severe weather did much to minimise his hunting, riding out and entertaining, the money saved that he would otherwise have spent on these pastimes meant that he was still able to visit the drinking houses in the town and continue his modest payments into the lottery syndicate without any further borrowing from Murad Amrad. By the middle of March however, the promised income to repay his debts was still not forthcoming, and with the snow soon to melt and his father's return more likely, Viktor made the decision to place pressure on the syndicate by threatening them with exposure. It was time he reaped the rewards of his long investment, he decided. He would speak with Igor Sikorski.

Meanwhile, with the jewel box in his possession, Murad Amrad had been content to push the problem of the young Viscount's outstanding debt to the back of his mind, at least until Count Alexei Petrovitch and his wife returned in the spring, as no doubt they would. But in late March, he once again received an unannounced evening visit from the Viscount.

Murad Amrad was somewhat taken aback by the young man's appearance. He was very thin, with dark shadows under his eyes and visibly shaking hands. Murad Amrad showed him into the workshop. Viktor slurred his words and smelled strongly of liquor.

"I need a further loan, Jew. And I can give you my word that this will be the last time. As you know my father returns next month…" Viktor didn't finish his sentence.

The Viscount seemed genuinely, if uncharacteristically, humble and there was no doubt that Murad Amrad felt enormous relief that this situation might soon be rectified. It had been a hard winter for them all and Viktor Petrovitch's debt was now sufficiently great that repayment of the money would be much appreciated by the business in the year ahead. So once again, and on condition it was for the last time, Murad Amrad agreed to the amount requested, although it was a considerably greater amount than usual. He wrote out a promissory note and handed it to the Viscount to sign, wondering as he did so whether the Viscount was capable of writing. But although it was shaky, the signature was recognisable. Murad Amrad counted out the money and Viktor Petrovitch placed it in a leather pouch that hung from a belt around his middle. He then took his leave and Murad Amrad quickly shut the door behind him. Although winter had loosened its grip somewhat, the air outside remained many degrees below freezing at night.

As he left the Jew's house, Viktor felt a wave of excitement, something he hadn't felt for a long time. When he had spoken with Igor Sikorski a few days before, Igor had told him that if he could contribute one final payment of a greater value into the lottery fund, his reimbursements could begin. At last, Viktor thought, he would be able to start repaying his debts, and he had arranged to meet Igor that night to hand over the agreed sum of money. But the trouble was that he suddenly couldn't remember where. He found this incredibly funny and laughed out loud as he made his way unsteadily through the dark streets, where the snow was still banked up against the buildings and the cold made his head ache. He decided to head towards the furthest of the inns, the one to which he owed the least amount of money. Once he'd got warm and had another drink, he was sure he would remember. Having waited so long, a few more minutes wouldn't make any difference. He stopped at this thought and laughed again, so he didn't hear the sound of light footsteps behind him, and never knew who or what it was that jumped at him from behind. It happened so quickly that there was no time to call out. Just a brief, heart-lurching moment as a weight fell onto his shoulders and a cold knife sliced across his throat. Then nothing. As his body slumped to the ground, a dark figure behind him stooped to pull at his belt and release the leather pouch. The coins inside jingled as the figure straightened, looked down at Viktor for a few seconds and then ran away, quickly disappearing into the darkness, while the life of Viscount Viktor Petrovitch bled out onto the frozen streets of Bialystok.

Over the next few days the conversation in the *Batei Midras* was only about the murder. It was said that a messenger had been sent to recall the Viscount's father. Also that Russian officials had started to conduct a murder hunt, going from door to door and asking questions. But this Murad Amrad already knew. Accompanied by another official, an officer named Igor Sikorski had already visited him at the workshop and had been somewhat aggressive in his line of questioning.

"We have been talking with a servant of Viscount Viktor Petrovitch, Murad Amrad. He has told us that the Viscount came to visit you on the night he was murdered. It would appear therefore that you were the last person to see him alive. At what time did he leave? Did he tell you where he was going? Do you know if he was meeting anyone? He wasn't far from your house when he was attacked. Did you go out again after he left?"

The questioning had gone on for some time and Murad Amrad had made a conscious effort to answer in a calm voice, although he was able to tell them very little other than that the Viscount had been to borrow a sum of money and had left with the coins in a pouch on his belt.

"Do you have proof of this?" Igor had asked.

Murad Amrad had then felt it necessary to show Igor Sikorski the last promissory note the Viscount had signed. Afterwards he wished he hadn't. The Russian's expression had almost been one of triumph when he saw it. After the two men had left he had felt unsettled and disturbed. And the fact that the murder had been committed so near to his home was not something Murad Amrad liked to dwell on as he sat in the *Batei Midras* listening to the talk around him.

"Viktor owed a lot of people a great deal of money."

"He had many enemies."

"We all know what we have heard – he hated Jews."

"Was he robbed as well? He had just left Murad Amrad's house and had many rubles in his pouch."

"No-one seems to know."

"There are many strangers in the town. And many are very poor. It could have been any one of them."

"Well whoever it was will most likely be far away by now."

And so it went on. Murad Amrad kept his thoughts to himself, but later he spoke alone with the rabbi and told him the whole story of his involvement with Viktor Petrovitch and his concerns with Igor Sikorski's line of questioning.

"I fear that my family and I may be in danger, Rabbi. Count Alexei will be looking to avenge his son's death and will want the authorities to find the killer as soon as possible. I believe I could be an easy suspect if they don't find anyone else. Viscount Viktor owed me a great deal of money it is true, but holding this priceless jewel box does not make me feel any better. I am honour bound not to sell it under the agreement I made with the Viscount. But if I take it to the Count, will he in turn honour his son's debt? Or will he merely reclaim something his son had no right to give me and renounce any responsibility? If Viktor Petrovitch's debt is not paid off, I have to tell you that we will have lost a considerable amount of money and that is not something I wish to contemplate." Murad Amrad realised he had been talking too fast, but the rabbi appeared to be listening attentively. He then nodded slowly and thought for a few moments before replying.

"If you have promissory notes from the Viscount, then you must show these to Count Alexei. You need not tell him about the jewel box to begin with. If he fails to honour his son's debt then you are within your rights to keep it. If he repays you, then you will earn his respect by returning the jewel box before he even knows you have it. But as for being blamed for the Viscount's death, it seems unlikely, unless you have made an enemy among the officials? We all know that they need very little excuse to condemn us."

"I do indeed have many promissory notes from Viktor Petrovitch and it is clearly documented that he hadn't repaid any of them," Murad Amrad replied. "But if the Count refuses to repay Viscount Viktor's debt, and I omit to tell him about the jewel box, I believe I will be at even greater risk of being considered the prime suspect. If it were ever to become known that the box was in my possession, it would be perceived as reason enough for me to have murdered the Viscount. The box is of far greater value than Viktor Petrovitch's debt."

An uncharacteristic feeling of panic was threatening to

overwhelm Murad Amrad and he placed the palm of his hand onto his forehead and closed his eyes for a few seconds. Then he took a deep breath and carried on, trying to present his concerns more calmly.

"We are all in agreement that many of the Russian officials are known to be extremely corrupt. It will be of prime importance for them to find the young Viscount's killer. In fact, they may be in a great deal of trouble if they do not. And if the Countess's jewel box is discovered missing and they were to search my premises and find it, not only would I be accused of the murder, but they would be more than capable of keeping the jewel box for themselves and then denying all knowledge of it."

Murad Amrad and the rabbi continued to toss the problem backwards and forwards but came to no conclusions. On his return home that evening, Murad Amrad was quiet throughout the meal, but once the children had gone to bed, he, Abram, Sonja and Szejna continued the same conversation around the table. Late into the night, after many candles had burned down, they were still no nearer a decision on how to solve the problem of Count Viktor Petrovitch's debt without also being accused of his murder.

The following evening, as the family were preparing for bed, Murad Amrad was surprised to hear a knock on the workshop door. It was the rabbi, who had a grim expression on his face and seemed especially anxious to get into the house. He waited until Murad Amrad had shut the door behind him before speaking, and the news he brought could not have been more devastating.

"Igor Sikorski has been overheard discussing the murder case with other officials," he said quickly. "It seems very clear that they suspect you of murdering Count Viktor Petrovitch and there is to be a warrant out for your arrest in the morning. I have called an urgent meeting of the *Batei Midras* tonight and urge you to come with me immediately. There may not be much time."

Sonja and Abram had come into the workshop in time to hear what the rabbi had said, and they now stood in stunned silence. Abram was in his nightshirt and Sonja without her bonnet or apron; immodest dress that no one noticed nor at that moment cared about. Murad Amrad felt as if the bottom of his world had dropped out and he began to walk up and down, trying to calm himself and think of what to do. How could this have happened? What was it that Igor Sikorski had against him to be so ready to accuse him of Viktor's murder? As he paced, his initial surge of adrenalin and fear abated slightly and his thoughts became more rational. He knew that he was not prepared to jeopardise his own safety or that of his family and he needed to formulate a plan. He continued pacing for several minutes and none of them said a word. Then he came to a halt in front of the rabbi, threw back his shoulders, took a deep breath and gave a short decisive nod. The time for thinking was over. Now was the time to take action and a clear course had presented itself to him. While fleeing may imply guilt, staying would be the greater folly.

"I will come," was all he said to the rabbi. He then turned to his family and shrugged his shoulders, turning up his hands in resignation. "So. It has come to this. If they are to play dirty tricks, then so will I. They will not take away my life or that of my family. We will not be here when they come for us in the morning. Please dress yourselves and the children in many layers. We will all need warm clothes. Pack only our most valuable possessions. Also cooking utensils, provisions, rugs and furs. Place everything in sacks and baskets, one or two for each of us who can carry them. But load everything into the handcart for now. I will return as soon as I have finished consulting with the rabbi and the elders. Do everything in silence and alert no one of our intentions. I believe we will have to leave town before daybreak and I need you all to be ready. Once we, and the jewel box, are safely away from Bialystok we will have time to think."

His mother had entered the room, also dressed in her nightwear with a shawl wrapped around her shoulders for warmth. As Murad Amrad spoke she went over to Abram and they clung to each other in shock, the white knuckles of their intertwined hands betraying their emotions as they stared at their son, eyes wide in disbelief. They were short people, he especially so for a man, and as Murad Amrad looked at them in the dim light of the workshop with their greying hair uncovered, he was suddenly aware of their age and vulnerability. He was going to be asking much of them. To leave everything they held dear; their home, their friends, other family members and their town – was going to be an almost unthinkable wrench for them. He gave his head a miniscule shake. He must harden himself against pity and be strong enough for all of them. Hastily pulling on his coat, he addressed his father.

"Father, I would like you to pack as much of our silverware and tools as possible into the strong box. We must take what we can of our business with us. And all our money must be divided. It cannot all be in one pouch."

In a gentler voice he addressed his mother.

"We have no choice, Mammeh. And by staying together we will give each other strength to do God's will. I will need your help with the children. And they need you."

Szejna pulled herself upright, away from Abram, and nodded.

To Sonja he said: "Please take the jewel box from the strong box, Sonja. Wrap it well and conceal it in your clothing. There must be a way to ensure it cannot be seen."

Sonja had been hugging her arms around her ample middle in a rather childlike pose until this moment. Now with something to do, she let out an audible breath, pulled herself upright and immediately put her mind to what Murad Amrad had asked of her. She was an accomplished seamstress and she would get Hanna and Elzbietta to help.

Murad Amrad then turned to the rabbi and placed his hat on his head. "I am ready," he said.

There were only a dozen or so men at the *Betei Midras* at that late hour, all dressed in the same long black-belted coats and felt hats, knee length trousers, stockings and leather shoes. But it was obvious from their disheveled state that most of them had dressed hurriedly to attend this emergency session of the *Betei Midras*. These were all men well known to Murad Amrad. They had played together as children, attended school together, grown up together and were now close friends and business associates. But there wasn't time for pleasantries and it was fairly quickly agreed that the family had no option at the present time other than to flee. The words of his friends reverberated around Murad Amrad's head and he found it hard to believe all that was taking place.

"This Igor Sikorski seems to have decided you are to blame for the younger Count's death, Murad Amrad. You are better off leaving town for a while. Who knows what the Count will do when persuaded by his officials. You and your family are no longer safe."

"We will send a delegation to the Count and put your case to clear your name."

"We will look after your house and workshop until you return."

"Or you could go far away, sell the jewel box and find a new home."

"My son," said the rabbi, after this last suggestion. "It may indeed be God's plan for you to leave and make a new life. But even if you were to travel as far as the land of Israel, He would show you the way to be among friends."

Nochem Minc touched Murad Amrad on the arm. Nochem owned one of the largest textile factories in Bialystok. He was a man with a large and ready smile for whom no task was too great.

"Murad, I have a consignment of cloth waiting to be taken to Warsaw. My carriers are Shaul and Moshe Yaglom who I've known for a long time. In fact, I would trust them and the drivers who work for them with my own life. Their wagons are already loaded and they were due to leave any day now, or as soon as the snows had melted sufficiently and the road passable. But I believe it will be safe enough to travel now. I'll speak to them tonight and ask them to leave tomorrow morning at first light. I will tell them of your predicament and I know they'll do this for us. They will have room in the wagons to take you as far as Brisk."

As Nochem Minc continued, Murad Amrad felt his heart begin to lighten.

"There are six wagons and we can reload them in such a way as to conceal your family. The distance to Brisk is about eighty-five miles and the journey will take maybe a week, maybe two, depending on the conditions of the trail. You'll be following the old trade route that goes all the way to Odessa so there could be other travellers on the roads. But you can remain hidden during the day to avoid being stopped and questioned. The nights are still very cold, but each day the snows melt a little more. And by the time you arrive in Brisk, the weather may be gentler and travelling more comfortable. In Brisk it should be easy enough to find transport to take you further away, maybe to Kiev. There are many Jewish settlements along the route and many people who will help you. And the further you are away from Bialystok, the safer you will be."

Another man, Eliezer Halbern, suddenly produced a piece of paper and started writing furiously. He regularly traded broadcloth with Turkish merchants and knew the route well.

"From Brisk you can travel on the river, maybe through the Kanał Królewski (The Royal Canal) to Pinsk. I will give you a note for my good friend Amos Weiner. He is in Brisk. He will help you get a boat, and the journey will be easier for your mother, father and the young ones. After Pinsk, the rivers carry you to Kiev on the River Dnieper. Kiev is a very large city with many Jewish people. You could settle there, at least for a while."

One by one his friends offered help and encouragement and Murad Amrad was profoundly moved by their generosity. Having decided to flee, the whole undertaking was beginning to sound considerably easier thanks to their efforts and suggestions. His eyes filled as he bade hasty and fond farewells to the men he had known all his life, men to whom he now owed his life it would seem, and he could find no words to convey his feelings. The rabbi was last to say goodbye.

"Murad. Take the jewel box as a gift from God. Consider it now yours, to sell when you need to. I believe this to be part of God's plan for you." He then placed his hand lightly on Murad Amrad's forehead and gave a short blessing. "May the Lord bless you and protect you, Murad Amrad."

After he had left the house with the rabbi, Sonja woke the children and explained the situation to them. Keeping the element of danger to a minimum for the sake of the younger ones, the need for speed and silence was nevertheless made clear. They asked if they could say goodbye to their friends, but Sonja explained that it wouldn't be possible. It was vitally important that their leaving was a secret, she told them. In any event, they would be gone long before dawn the next day, and there was a lot to be done before then to prepare for their departure. For the children, the whole of their world had, until now, been contained in Bialystok, and the concept of travelling away from the town had never occurred to them. But for Tomas, Utah and Fanny, it very quickly became a great adventure as they went about dressing themselves in the many layers of clothes that Sonja put out for them. Hanna and Elzbietta, being older, were more aware of the potential for danger in their imminent departure and began to ask numerous questions.

"How are we to travel? Where are we to go? Where will we live?"

But Sonja had no answers to give them. Instead she kept the two girls fully occupied in order to keep their minds from worry. She took a bag of rubles from the strong box and showed them how to sew some of the coins into the hems of their coats, and others into the linings of the broadcloth sacks into which their possessions were to be packed. She also instructed them to make several money pouches in which to put the residue of the coins. She meanwhile made a larger pouch out of padded broadcloth to hold the jewel box. When this was completed, she hung it around her middle underneath her skirts and was happy with her efforts. She then packed a set of her own and the children's finest clothes. For her and the girls, black silk dresses, and for the boys, silk kaftans. She also packed her pearls. She then packed clothing for Murad Amrad. Finally she gently picked up the family *Torah* from which Abram or Murad Amrad read out loud on the *Shabbat* (Jewish Sabbath), and placed it in the sack with everything else.

Abram and Szejna were only too aware of the uncertain times ahead. They remembered the journey to Bialystok in the early days of their marriage. The heartbreak of leaving loved ones in Lithuania, the weeks of arduous travelling to get to their new home, and the hardship of building a new life, were times they would never forget. Suddenly it looked as if it had all been in vain and the heartbreak was to begin all over again. They had three grown up daughters in Bialystok, each with husbands and children of their own. Not only were they unable to say goodbye but Szejna also feared she may never see them again.

"We may be back before too long, *Bubbala*." Abram briefly tried to console Szejna. "Or if we are forced to settle somewhere else, perhaps we can encourage the others to join us. In time they too may want a change." He patted her on the shoulder before moving away. He needed to begin the task of packing a stock of silverware and jewellery into a wooden crate, together with the tools that he and Murad Amrad used everyday and a supply of silver, gold and precious stones.

Szejna sighed and went into the kitchen. Abram and Murad Amrad shared the family business and she knew that Murad Amrad was as essential to their livelihood as Abram himself. It was more than just their duty to travel with their son and his children. She placed two large baskets on the kitchen floor and methodically began to fill the first with small sacks of grain, salt, herbs, spices, lentils, onions and dried fruit. She wedged a flagon of wine among the sacks, some cabbages and a pot of honey. On the top of those she placed loaves of dark rye bread and many biscuits wrapped in a large cloth. She and Sonja had been baking that morning. From a chest in the corner of the room she then took out some of the best embroidered household linen, their silver candlestick and wine goblet and some essential crockery. These went into the second basket, along with a large cooking pot, tinderbox, kettle and a few knives.

She then went outside and deftly caught six of her hens. The birds voiced their protests loudly and she worked quickly to put them into the small wooden crate in which she normally transported them to and from the market. Once they were all inside she covered the crate with a sack and they immediately quietened down. She stopped to listen and was thankful when some seconds passed and it was apparent none of her neighbours had heard the commotion. She knew it would be safer for them all if no-one knew they were leaving, but having to be so secretive made her feel very uncomfortable. She took the crate inside and placed it beside the other provisions before going into her own house to begin packing everything she and Abram would need for the journey.

Dressed in a multitude of layers, Tomas, Utah and Fanny had been told to lie down on the furs they were to take with them and to try and get some sleep before they left. As the oldest, Tomas had been given instruction to make sure they remained silent, but all three children were in a contained but still evident state of excitement. They found it most amusing to be dressed in such a way and, despite much shushing from their elders, their suppressed giggles were contagious and did much to help lighten the atmosphere in the house.

When Murad Amrad returned home he looked grey and exhausted. But he was resolute as he told them of Nochem Minc's offer and of their immediate departure. By now the family was more or less ready to leave, but before they did so, they all wrote short letters to friends and family. These they were to give to Nochem Minc, who had promised to be at the factory yard to see them off. Finally it was time, and with a last look around their home, the family quietly let themselves out of the door. Murad Amrad looked resolutely ahead, his mouth set in a grim line as he led his family into the dark street. Szejna, however, looked back into their home, and when she turned to follow the others, her lined cheeks were wet with tears.

It was bitterly cold outside and their breath streamed from their faces in clouds of vapour as they walked. But it was a clear night with a bright moon, and once their eyes had become accustomed to the darkness it was comparatively easy to see where they were going. Abram had loaded much of their luggage onto the handcart, but although they needed only to travel a few streets, they still struggled. Murad Amrad could see that walking any distance on this journey was not going to be at all possible or advisable. He gave thanks again for Nochem Minc, but he was convinced that their departure would be spotted or heard by someone. The snow had been cleared from the centre of many of the streets and the wheels of the handcart rumbled over the rough surfaces. The covered chickens kept emitting quiet clucks of alarm and everything they were carrying seemed to be rattling as they walked. By the time they arrived at Nochem Minc's factory yard Murad Amrad was sweating with fear and tension and it seemed nothing short of a miracle to him that they had arrived there undetected.

Lit by a collection of lanterns, the yard was bright and welcoming. The air was filled with the sweet smell of horses and felt warmer for their presence. Murad Amrad allowed himself to relax a little as his friend came forward to greet them. Nochem Minc welcomed them kindly and, with one of his huge smiles, introduced them to the six men who were to accompany them to Brisk. One by one the drivers came forward and quietly greeted the family. They too were warmly dressed in thick quilted coats, long boots and padded flat hats. Some of them wore leather aprons that appeared heavily ingrained with grease. But their greetings were short. There was still plenty to be done to prepare both wagons and horses for departure and the yard was a hive of muted activity.

The six wagons were all constructed from traditional wooden carts with simple flat bases and strutted sides. They had been modified by the addition of curved wooden frames, over which cloth had been stretched to form a canopy, ensuring that the loads inside remained protected from the weather. Nochem Minc and the drivers had redistributed the rolls of cloth in three of the wagons to make more than enough room for the family's luggage in one wagon, and for four or five people to sit in each of the other two. Not only would they be sheltered, but they would also be hidden from sight.

The horses were already harnessed up, one to each wagon and Murad Amrad noticed two more tied alongside. All were eating from sackcloth nosebags suspended from their bridles. Occasionally one or other of them would snort into its bag or shake its head, causing its complex trappings of harness to jangle. But the huge animals gave out an aura of calm rather than expectation. When everything and everybody was eventually loaded however, and their nosebags had been removed, the horses began to fret, and the drivers jumped up to take their seats on the wagons behind them. Murad Amrad whispered a final heartfelt farewell to Nochem Minc.

"My home is your home," he told him and he pressed the keys of his house and workshop into Nochem's hands, along with their letters. He then heaved himself up into the back of one of the wagons and as the horses finally pulled out of Bialystok, the sky was beginning to lighten in the East.

THE JOURNEY: 1832

The long line of horses and wagons rolled through the bleak snow covered landscape, each horse closely following the wagon in front, its breath streaming from dilated nostrils in clouds of vapour as it pushed its shoulders against the huge leather collar around its neck. The Galperin family rode in the third and fourth wagons; the men and boys in one, the women and girls in another – an arrangement the drivers considered the safest distribution of their load. The spare horses were tied onto the back of the first and second wagons, and the sixth and final wagon was loaded with fodder for the horses and provisions for the men.

Murad Amrad was impatient to get far away from the town as quickly as possible. He wondered how long it would be before Igor Sikorski and his men discovered they were missing. He presumed they'd search the town first. Hopefully, it would be a day or two before they suspected the family had fled. But how long would it take the Russians to catch them up? It had quickly become apparent that the horses rarely moved beyond a walk, and the pace felt agonizingly slow. The terrain around them was for the most part flat and heavily wooded, and the same journey done later in the year would have been a much faster one. But although the snow had thawed sufficiently in places to reveal occasional patches of blanched earth, it still lay in deep drifts at the edges of the road, and often the way was deeply rutted and icy where melted snow had frozen overnight.

Given the difficult conditions on the road, Murad Amrad was surprised at the number of heavily laden traders who were travelling on foot towards Bialystok and he constantly feared discovery each time the drivers called out a greeting or exchanged words with passers-by. But Shaul and Moshe Yaglom were well known in the area and it would have been more suspicious if they had neglected to do so. They and the men with them had been transporting goods for many years, regularly travelling along the well-worn routes between Moscow, Warsaw and Western Europe. As well as cloth for Nochem Minc, they transported grain, furs, leather and even horses for other merchants. They spoke fluent Russian and, as respected holders of a special license to trade in Russia itself, they were considered to be tradesmen of the highest caliber by the Russian Government.

"As soon as the snows begin to thaw, everyone is anxious to trade in the town again," Shaul Yaglom later told Murad Amrad. "It's good for you that there are other traders on the road. We'll not be as conspicuous and there'll be less reason for us to be stopped or questioned. But you must all remain hidden to prevent your presence being reported to the authorities."

So every day, as on that first morning out of Bialystok, the family crouched among the hard rolls of fabric and kept well out of sight. Despite the slight rise in daytime temperatures, it still felt bitterly cold and they were glad of the layers they all wore and of the furs they had brought with them. Apart from times when calls of nature had to be answered, the wagons kept moving. But it was not comfortable. The jolting movement meant they were constantly being thrown against each other, and by the end of the day each of them was aching and stiff. Abram and Szejna suffered the most. They were older and prone to aches and pains at the best of times. But neither of them complained.

Sometimes one or other of the wagons became stuck and a spare horse was needed to help pull it out. This task was made more difficult if the wagon concerned had the weight of the family inside it, in which case Murad Amrad longed to get out and help. At these times, it seemed as if fate was doing all it could to prevent their progress and he feared they would never get to Brisk. He expressed his concerns to the drivers the first time they came to a halt. But they had done the same journey many times before and were able to reassure him that the roads would be passable enough provided they proceeded with care. The wellbeing of their horses and the safety of their wagons were of paramount importance, they told him, and they had no option but to take the horses slowly. It would be all too easy for the animals or the wagons to get damaged if they went any faster.

They crossed a number of rivers, the horses struggling through fording places where melting snow and ice had swollen the water course to many times its normal depth and speed. To the family cocooned inside the wagons, the increased discomfort of the crossings was nothing compared to the added element of fear as they were dragged jerkily through the rushing water and over hidden boulders that threw them from side to side and threatened to overturn them. But they were still on the main route from Bialystok and each day that passed saw more vehicles and travellers on the road. The Galperin's whereabouts, if known, could still be reported, if only by accident. So they were forced to remain hidden, to hold on and listen helplessly as the drivers shouted and cracked their whips at the frightened horses, driving them on to keep their momentum and to prevent the carts from becoming stuck.

After a few days, the initial novelty of the journey wore off and what had started by being merely uncomfortable began to feel like torture as they found themselves unable to stretch or move freely for hour after hour. To make matters worse, boredom began to be a major problem for the children and they frequently squabbled and fought. Sonja sought to remedy this by arranging for the young to travel in the wagon with her, where she began to talk to them in Hebrew and Russian to keep them occupied, devising simple games and tests to broaden their knowledge of both languages. She was a well-educated woman whose own father had made sure she spoke other languages apart from the Yiddish they all used on a daily basis. She was well aware that among the Russians and the wealthier Jewish middle classes, Yiddish was beginning to be frowned upon and could well stigmatize them in their new town, wherever that may be. She knew that the boys would be missing out on their religious studies during this journey, but at least she could make sure that all the children were being schooled in other ways. She worked them hard but the children enjoyed the challenge of learning something new and their lessons did much to keep them busy for some hours each day. And when other travellers appeared on the road, the drivers gave a loud whistle, a pre-determined sign to alert the family to remain silent.

One afternoon, when the roads were empty and their wagons appeared to be the only vehicles for miles around, Sonja though it would be good for the children to be allowed to sing. She was a great believer in the power of music and felt singing to be the best way to alleviate boredom or distress in both children and adults. Released from the constraints of their usual need for silence, the children proceeded to sing loudly and with great enthusiasm, and it was for this reason that they were not able to hear the sudden piercing whistle given by their driver.

Murad Amrad heard it, however. He was reclining alongside Abram and Szejna in their wagon up ahead, and he tensed in disbelief as he heard the children continuing to sing, oblivious to the danger signal. He opened the canopy a fraction and peered out. At first he saw nothing. Then to his horror he noticed a group of horsemen approaching them from behind. They were moving at a brisk trot and were gaining on them rapidly. He heard the driver of Sonja's wagon give another whistle, but still to no avail. Sonja and the children were making too much noise.

The driver then turned around and gave a loud shout directly into the wagon behind him. There was a second or two when Murad Amrad thought even that hadn't worked, but suddenly all went quiet. By now however, the horsemen weren't far behind the last wagon and it seemed impossible to believe that they hadn't heard the shout, if not the singing. Murad Amrad's mouth went dry and his heart thumped loudly in his ears as he withdrew from the canopy and crouched down again beside his parents. All at once, they heard the same driver begin to sing loudly and tunelessly, shouting some of the words to disguise his previous call of alarm, and giving an excellent impression of having had too much wine. Amazingly, they heard one of the horsemen laugh and shout something to the driver, who obligingly lowered the volume of his singing as the horsemen rode past. Through the tiny gaps between the planks forming the sides of their wagon, and the slits in the canvas covering it, Murad Amrad, Abram and Szejna caught glimpses of metal, leather and hooves as the riders passed by, only a short distance from their faces. The horsemen then slowed to keep pace with the lead wagon driven by Shaul Yaglom, and Murad Amrad heard voices apparently engaged in conversation and bursts of intermittent laughter. The voices were too muffled to hear what words were being said, but the guttural sounds were easy enough to recognise. The horsemen were Russian. For a split second he wondered if they were being betrayed, and then felt shame for having done so. Instead he held his breath and prayed that the others were doing the same.

The Russians rode alongside them for what seemed an interminable length of time, and the sounds of human voices were interspersed with those of horses blowing and harnesses jingling. But at no time did their drivers pull up. Eventually the tone of the conversation changed, an indication that farewells were being said, and at last they heard the horses ride on, the sound of hooves growing fainter on the frozen track ahead. They breathed a communal sigh of relief. The wagons kept going however, long after the Russians had gone, and it was only later when they stopped for the night that the family was able to learn what the Russians had been speaking about.

"They asked us to look out for a fugitive family who might be travelling out of Bialystok on this road," Shaul said. "I told them they wouldn't get far without freezing to death."

"That caused them to laugh," said Elad, one of the drivers, with a chuckle.

But Murad Amrad was deeply shocked. Their lucky escape was a cause for relief of course, but the fact that they were already missed from Bialystok was of great concern. It was something he had hoped they would avoid for a slightly longer time than this. He was also fearful for Shaul and Moshe Yaglom. Being holders of a Russian trading license was no doubt a contributing factor to their being beyond suspicion by the Russian horsemen. But they had a great deal to lose if their current human cargo was discovered and his admiration for their courage and kindness knew no bounds.

Over the following days they occasionally passed through small settlements where the drivers would stop to trade with locals for meat, bread, vegetables and tobacco. Szejna found it immensely frustrating that she couldn't just get out herself and buy the provisions they needed, but she had to be content with giving the drivers a list. More often than not however, she was disappointed in what they brought back. Supplies in most places were limited after the long winter.

By nightfall, with other travellers off the road, their caravan pulled up to set camp and they could all climb down from the wagons. The relief at being able to stretch, walk, cook and eat after the day's discomfort was immeasurable and after a few days they settled into an evening routine. Everyone was given a task. A fire had to be laid and lit, water collected if there was any. If not they used water the drivers had collected in gourds during the day. Hanna and Elzbietta, as the oldest girls, were expected to help Szejna and Sonja to prepare the meal. Tomas, Utah and Fanny were permitted to help the drivers unhitch the horses and settle them for the night. These were the times the younger children enjoyed the most. Having never had anything to do with horses before, they were now keen to know all about them. Shaul liked to tease his brother that he preferred horses to humans, but while Moshe did indeed have a great affinity with the animals, he was more than happy to answer all the children's questions about them. They learned that unless one of the horses had an injury, they took turns in hauling. By swapping the horses around, each animal had about one day in four of comparative rest when they'd be tied to the back of the wagons instead of between the shafts. Moshe told the children that the spare horses often had to carry loads on their backs, or extra passengers. Sometimes they had to be hitched up to help pull a particularly heavily laden wagon. But whether they'd been hauling one of the wagons all day, or just walking along behind them, the horses seemed pleased to stop and rest each evening. Moshe's normal reserve dropped away when he showed the children how to check the tired animals over for cuts, pick the stones from their hooves and fix a rug over them for the night. He spoke to the horses in the same way as he spoke to the children. He chatted away as he tethered them loosely to a tree or stake, or while he gave them hay and water, and he bade them goodnight when he left them to rest. Tomas, Utah and Fanny were enchanted. Before long the children had gained a great deal of confidence around the horses and, to the delight of the normally reticent Moshe, had begun talking to them in the same way.

"They understand you know," he told them with a gentle smile. "And they work better if you talk to them."

Szejna slaughtered two chickens each evening, and she and Sonja boiled the meat in a pan over the fire with onions, lentils, handfuls of grain, spices and chopped cabbage. They served the resulting stew with bread and wine, the family sharing everything with the drivers. After they had all eaten, and despite the plummeting temperatures, the children were permitted to run around and play. They had a great deal of excess energy to burn off after their sedentary day. They were forbidden to go beyond the light cast by the fire, but that area still left plenty of scope for exploration and amusement. Sonja excelled at making up games for them all, sending them on treasure hunts or showing them how to play counting and jumping games using little stones as markers. Tomas was always the loudest, taking the lead in all the games, while Utah and Fanny were content to follow. And with their womanly chores completed, Hanna and Elzbietta joined in and remembered they too were still only children after all.

The drivers left the fireside early to bed down for the night in the hay wagon. They had discovered after the first evening that if they wanted to be able to sleep, it was better to park the hay wagon at the furthest point from where the children played. Later, the family would settle around the fire for the night. But while the children played, the adults did their best to come to terms with all aspects of their current situation. The abruptness of their departure had shaken them, and as they sat by the fire in the evenings or walked up and down to loosen their stiff limbs, they talked of little else. As each day led slowly into the next however, they started to think ahead and make plans for the future. One evening Abram surprised Murad Amrad by suggesting they remove the diamond from the middle of the jewel box, replacing it with something else.

"The box is of such value," he said, "that even without the diamond, we should make a great deal from its sale. We will have more wealth than we could ever have imagined. We can buy

46

ourselves land and a new life, maybe in Kiev or even Odessa. But if we could withhold the diamond, it will provide a separate fund for us to use if and when it is most needed." He chuckled then. "Our own Diamond Fund, Murad."

Murad Amrad smiled and didn't have to think about this idea for long. He was impressed at his father's resourcefulness.

"You are right, Father. And if the diamond is replaced, the box will look different. I have had a fear that because it is so distinctive, it could easily be recognised. We must think what to place in the centre of the lid to make it less so. We will of course, have to hide the diamond well. But that is what we will do".

Just over two weeks after leaving Bialystok they finally arrived at Brisk, the Yiddish name for Brest, a small town in which Jews had been predominant residents since the 16th Century. The roads by that time had become so crowded with fellow travellers that Murad Amrad believed they were less conspicuous as a result. Somewhat against the advice of the drivers, he permitted the children to ride with them on the seat behind the horses as they drove into the town. The adults too jumped down from the wagons and took some much-needed exercise by walking alongside. The family suddenly felt less like fugitives and more like travellers with somewhere to go.

Along the bustling main street men, women and children moved aside to let them pass, Poles and Jews distinguishable from each other by their dress. Smaller horsedrawn carts trotted past, vendors pushed handcarts on their way to the market square, and the little wooden shops on either side of the street reminded them of their home. But Brisk was a much smaller town than Bialystok, with no budding industry to provide employment, and it was very evident that many of the tradesmen were struggling to make a living. Their stock was low and their clothing in rags. There were also a number of families who appeared to be living on the streets, adults and children with sunken cheeks and hollow eyes huddled together under blankets. As they passed by, many held out their hands for food or money, while others seemed to have given up hope and merely sat doing nothing. But it was something else that sent the Galperin family rapidly back to their wagons and into hiding. The street was full of Russian soldiers.

Unknown to them, following the 1830/31 Polish uprising, Nicholas I of Russia was beginning to build a series of fortresses in the area to suppress the chances of further rebellion. The first of these was already completed in Warsaw, and the second was to be built in Brisk. Construction wasn't due to begin for a few more years, but the Russian general in charge of the project was at that time billeted in Brisk and was busy making plans to demolish the whole town, including what had been the Polish Royal Castle, and move it to a new position a few miles away. Having decided that the town's location was the ideal site for their fortress, at the junction of two rivers and on high ground above the marshes, the Russian Government was going to let nothing prevent it from being built on that spot, not even the existence of a town. This move subsequently happened between 1836 and 1842, long after the Galperins had passed through, but as they drove into the town on that April evening in 1832, all they saw was the evidence of Russian occupation.

The drivers kept the horses going however, urging them on through the streets of the town, shouting out to anyone in their way, calling out an occasional greeting and giving every indication that all was as it should be. When the drivers eventually pulled up, Murad Amrad peeped through the canopy and saw they were in a large yard edged with rough wooden barns, some of which were obviously for animals, and others stacked high with firewood. Poking his head out further, he saw that the yard was behind a two story wooden building. Shaul then came round to the back of the wagons where the family still crouched and opened the canopies to let them out.

"Amos Weiner owns this inn," he said. "He is a Jewish man well known to us and you will be safe here for a while."

Murad Amrad remembered the name. He was the good friend of Eliezer Halbern who had written the note for him to deliver. He felt a rush of relief.

Amos Weiner turned out to be a larger-than-life character, florid of complexion and extremely plump and jovial, in complete contrast to the majority of Jewish men who tended towards the pale, lean and serious. He welcomed them heartily and told them that any friend of Eliezer Halbern was a friend of his. The Galperins were shown into a spacious room at the back of the building. There were pallets to sleep on along three walls, each one separated by a curtain, and they rejoiced in the room's warmth and space. And there was a well for their use in the yard outside; the opportunity to wash themselves and their clothes a welcome treat.

The day was Friday, the eve of *Shabbat*, and Amos Weiner insisted that they join his family for the customary celebratory meal that evening. Before entering the Weiner's home, they dressed in their finest clothes and felt much restored for doing so. A long table in the kitchen had been prepared for the meal and they were invited to sit, the men on one side and the women on the other. Amos Weiner sat at the head with his wife Ada beside him. Ada lit the candles and said prayers in Hebrew, moving her arms over the candles as she did so. Amos then chanted the *Kiddush* (blessing) over the silver goblet full of wine and broke the *Hallah* bread, giving them all a small piece to dip into a bowl of salt. Amos and his family were perpetuating the Jewish lore of welcoming everyone to their table; salt being the biblical offering to God and bread the symbol of hospitality. And none were more grateful for this than the Galperin family that evening.

The ensuing meal was long with many courses, eaten slowly in order to appreciate them more. There was chopped liver and fish, chicken broth with noodles, and boiled goose served with sweet carrots. Szejna and Sonja frequently shed tears of relief and joy as they marvelled over every dish and remembered similar meals on Friday evenings in Bialystok, when they too had entertained guests. After they had eaten the sugar rich dessert of '*kugel*', made from noodles baked with raisins and cinnamon, Ada was lavished with praise for her cooking and they all joined in the singing. And when everyone eventually went to bed, their cheeks were glowing, their stomachs were full and Murad Amrad felt even more optimistic for their future. Knowing that men like Amos Weiner would open their home to them wherever they were in the time honoured custom of Jewish hospitality and charity, was something to be celebrated after all, and he felt proud to be Jewish.

The following day was *Shabbat*, the day of rest, when the men traditionally attended the synagogue to pray. But Murad Amrad, Abram, Tomas and Utah could not risk being seen in the town and had to be content to stay in their room with the rest of the family, where their prayers were short. They were anxious for the next leg of their journey to begin and there was much to talk about. They shared the Saturday midday meal with the Weiner family, but returned to their room later in the day when neighbours and friends called, as was the custom, for tea. But by the evening, when Amos Weiner brought out his silver box filled with aromatic spices and said final prayers over the wine-filled silver goblet, the *Shabbat* was over and plans to move on could be made.

The next morning, Amos came to their room, his face beaming with satisfaction.

"Listen," he said. "It's all arranged. My friend Label Zemmol is a waterman on the Kanał Królewski. He has just finished loading his timber and the ice is melting on the canal. He and his oldest son, Lazlo, can leave Brisk at first light tomorrow. He has space to carry your family on his barge all the way to Kiev, although he says it will be cramped. But he wants to get back to work after the long winter. I told him you would pay him well and that I would get the money from you today, and he was pleased. He will give the money to his wife before leaving. She has a small shop in the market square and the money will help her feed the children. It has been a hard winter here, as indeed it has been for Jews everywhere I imagine. There have been so many laws introduced since the war. Here in Brisk, hundreds of refugees arrive daily, all driven from their homes for one reason or another. But it is difficult to feed them all."

"It is the same in Bialystok," Murad Amrad said.

"Ah! Bialystok," Amos replied, as if suddenly remembering something, and his face became more serious. He lowered his voice so that only Murad Amrad and Abram could hear. "I made a few enquiries in the town and there is someone asking about you. A man named Igor Sigorski. Does that mean anything to you? I'm sure there is no need for you to worry as you are safe here, but you are wise not to show your face in case you are stopped and questioned. There will be many in town anxious to help this man. He seems to be someone in authority."

Abram struck his knee with his hand in frustration and muttered something inaudible. Murad Amrad felt incapable of speech. Was he ever going to be free of this nightmare? He sat down heavily on a wooden chair and there was silence between the three men for a few long seconds.

"Will Label Zemmol keep quiet?" he asked eventually.

"He will." Amos replied quietly. "And you can trust him completely."

There was nothing more to be said then. To take Murad Amrad and Abram's minds from their troubles, Amos began to tell the family about Label Zemmol and the life of the watermen of Brisk.

The Kanal Królewski was so called after the King of Poland, he told them, in whose reign two hundred years earlier the canal had been built to connect the River Bug at Brisk to the River Pripyat at Pinsk. It had been and still was a vital extension of a network of ancient water routes connecting the Baltic Sea in the North to the Black Sea in the South. Now the Russians were building ships and much of the timber required for their Black Sea fleet came from the dense forests around Brisk, from where it was transported by water all the way to the Crimean shipyards in the Black Sea.

The watermen working the canals were usually Jewish and Label Zemmol's vessel was one of many shallow barges that left the town each spring loaded with timber for transport to Pinsk. From there they continued down the Pripyat River and then out into the wider Dnieper River, both waterways by that time of year full and fast flowing with the spring floods which made managing the boats hard work. When the barges docked at Kiev on the banks of the Dnieper, the watermen would have been travelling for two to three weeks. In Kiev they sold their cargo to timber merchants and brokers who operated along the banks of the river. From here the timber was sold on again and this time loaded onto larger sailing barges that carried impressive quantities of cargo down the Dnieper River to the Black Sea. When these barges needed to return to Kiev, a distance of over six hundred miles, they were pulled back by gangs of barge-haulers, sometimes numbering as many as forty, usually poor and destitute peasants who, for pitiful payment, would work during the summer months hauling barges back up the fast flowing river.

Meanwhile Label Zemmol, like the other watermen of Brisk, spent the summer trading between points on the river. In the autumn they would reload with food items and other essential commodities to take back home. Although the rivers were slower moving by then, the bargemen had to haul their boats against the flow on the return journey, and it could take them well over a month to get back. By this time they would have been away from their home for anything between six to eight months, and they needed to complete the return journey before the winter set in. The Jewish watermen provided many of the provisions the town depended upon during the winter months, a trade that in turn brought men like Label Zemmol and his family a valuable income. If the watermen timed it wrongly or if winter came early, they were forced to spend the winter wherever they were stranded, unable to get home to provide for their families.

Despite his predicament, Murad Amrad had been pleased to know more about the man in whose hands he was next to place the safety of his family, and he was grateful to Amos for the distraction. He counted out a generous sum of money for the waterman and Amos then left, acknowledging Murad Amrad's effusive thanks with a cheery wave and leaving the family to pack. Apart from the obvious threat of being discovered by Igor Sikorski, he had made the next leg of their journey sound very simple.

Later, the family came out into the yard to say farewell to Shaul and Moshe Yaglom and their drivers, whose wagons were still in the yard. They and their horses had shared Amos Weiner's stables, taking a well-deserved rest and celebrating *Shabbat* with friends. But they too were leaving the next day and were now busy loading the wagons with a newly delivered consignment of leather and food products for transportation to Warsaw. Murad Amrad knew that Shaul, Moshe and the others had probably saved his life and those of his family as well, but he had no way of repaying them except with money. It didn't seem enough of a gift, but they were pleased with what he gave them. The youngest children were particularly sad to be leaving Moshe and the horses.

"We will never forget you," said Fanny, who was near to tears.

Tomas tried to cover his emotion with light heartedness. "But at least you won't have to sleep in the hay wagon any longer," he pointed out. "We won't be there to keep you awake and you can sleep around the fire at night."

The drivers laughed. It was true, but they would miss the family and the meals the women had cooked, they told him.

Long before daybreak the next morning Amos took them through the dark and deserted streets of Brisk. He was carrying an oil lamp that lit up his face and the cobbles at their feet but little else as they shuffled along in silence behind him. Their bags, boxes and baskets were loaded onto a handcart and its rumbling wheels echoed around the silent buildings whose occupants still slept. Ada had been able to provide them with everything they needed for the next few days, including another clutch of live chickens that now clucked softly to each other at every jolt of the cart. Murad Amrad was reminded of their flight through the streets of Bialystok. But the streets of Brisk were much narrower, and the upper floors of the houses above them sometimes seemed almost to touch those on the opposite side. Then they became narrower still, until they were little more than alleyways through which the cart only just fitted. To be safe, Amos was leading them on a circuitous back route.

They came upon the canal quite suddenly, when the path they were on ended at right angles to the waterway. In front of them a long line of vessels were moored bow to stern, suspended on black water where a skin of ice moved and shimmered on the surface with an eerie iridescence. Amos led them along the canal for a short distance until they arrived at what was obviously a loading wharf. The shapes of davits and wooden warehouses were silhouetted against the paler dark of the sky. A complication of ropes, planks and chains under their unsuspecting feet suddenly hampered their progress and they stopped. Lit by the glow from three burning braziers, groups of men were occupied in the business of loading piles of stacked shapes onto their barges. They were talking quietly among themselves as they did so, occasionally cursing or chuckling. Dogs lurked in the shadows, pacing expectantly, sometimes leaping sure-footedly between the wharf and the barges and back again, as if wanting to hasten the proceedings. But none of them barked at the family's approach. On board the vessels, smoke drifted out from tented shapes.

Amos called out softly and a man approached. This was Label Zemmol. Introductions were brief and quietly spoken and he wasted no time in leading them straight to his barge. Like all the others, it was long and narrow, the central part heavily loaded with lengths of timber. The boat appeared to be sitting very low in the water as a result. A long pole, supported by frames at each end, was suspended along the whole length of the barge above the timber. On a flat platform at the bow, a length of sailcloth was slung over the pole to create a covered area. A narrow walkway or 'deck' all around the boat was the only way to reach the stern, where a thin black chimney protruding from a raised roof indicated the comforting presence of a cabin with a stove inside. Aided by another lantern, a slight lightening of the sky and a second man who they correctly assumed to be Lazlo, their baggage and the crate of chickens were loaded onto the barge. Amos then departed, taking with him their eternal gratitude, blessings and promises to keep in touch. He left the family standing together in the small area between the door of the cabin and the stacked timber.

Dawn was beginning to break in streaks of red and mauve in front of them when Label gave a sharp whistle and a pale-coloured shaggy dog jumped onto the barge to join him. Lazlo untied the mooring ropes and tossed them onto the barge. Then, picking up a long rope that was coiled neatly on the wharf, he draped it over his back and shoulders and began to walk down the narrow pathway that ran beside the canal and away from the town. The rope was attached to the bow of the barge, and as Lazlo took the strain to pull the boat from its berth, Label sank a long wooden pole into the water at the stern and pushed. After an initial jerk that sent the family on board staggering and clinging onto one another, the vessel slowly began to move, the thin ice cracking against its hull.

A group of children suddenly appeared on the bank and skipped along beside Lazlo, chattering and laughing. Label smiled and waved at them for a while. Finally he called out to them.

"Go home to your mother now, children. Be good for her."

They stopped then, dejected, and stood on the bank waving as the boat slid away.

"Farewell, Father. Farewell," they called out. But Label looked resolutely ahead as he pushed the boat from the stern. Lazlo turned occasionally to wave until they were out of sight, but the dog kept his gaze fixed on where they had been for a long time after that.

As they became acquainted with their new home, the cabin – although it was never discussed – was quickly designated to the women. Szejna was to sleep in one of the two bunk beds, Sonja and Fanny in the other, while Hanna and Elzbietta would sleep on rugs on the floor. The men and boys, meanwhile, were to sleep under the canopy at the front of the barge, with furs and rugs to keep them warm. With the temperature at night still falling to well below freezing, Sonja and Szejna were concerned that the boys especially would not be warm enough. Label assured them that with the sheets of sailcloth lowered around them, the temperature inside their tented area would be quite warm. And when they found out that he and Lazlo intended to sleep along the narrow side decks of the barge, it seemed inappropriate to take the discussion any further. The watermen had turned their barge over to the family without question and there was, after all, nowhere else for them to sleep.

It became apparent from the outset that Label and Lazlo were silent men, well used to keeping their own council. Often, in their identical knee length coats tied at the waist by a belt, and the same soft woollen hats on their heads, Murad Amrad found it hard to tell them apart. He assumed that to have so many extra people on board was something of a challenge. The boat sat more heavily in the water for a start. But they were always pleasant and courteous. They were extremely nimble on their feet and, despite the many obstacles, managed to move about the barge at great speed. And he marvelled at their strength. On most mornings they had to free their boat from the ice that formed over the canal at night, then take turns throughout the day to haul the barge along the canal with the rope or push it from behind with the pole. He was glad that the family could at least assist the two men in some small way by providing all their meals. From the small stove in the cabin, Szejna and Sonja produced sufficient quantities of stew each day to feed everyone, including the dog, which, to Szejna's unvoiced horror, fed from Labels plate. But Murad Amrad gave thanks to God every day for men like Label and Lazlo Zemmol.

During the first few days of their journey, the barge rarely moved much faster than walking pace, and taking advantage of a milder turn to the weather, the family was able to walk alongside the canal. After the enforced secrecy of their stay in Brisk, and before that the constant fear of discovery in Nochem Mincs' wagons, moving freely in the open daylight seemed unreal and somewhat disturbing. But after a few days they settled into this new and gentle mode of transport and all began to benefit from the exercise and fresh air. The children had faired the worst during their three weeks of confinement, and they now revelled in their newly found freedom. Sonja had been growing increasingly concerned about Fanny who, since leaving Bialystok, had become more and more withdrawn. Hanna and Elzbietta too had started to look pale and tired. And the boys, who were competitive at the best of times, had been quarrelling more than usual. But as she sat on the deck of the barge one day, mending some of the children's clothes, she was overjoyed to see all five of them laughing together as they played with the dog in the snow. Sonja believed play to be every bit as vital to a child's development as learning, and although she didn't know much about dogs, this one seemed equally happy to have young company. She wondered if it missed Label's children. She was in no doubt that Label missed them. She noticed that he seemed happiest when showing the boys how to do things like tying the boat up, fending it off the bank or lighting the fire at night. He often gave Tomas and Utah tasks that made them feel useful and the boys soon became his constant companions. Sonja frequently feared that one of the younger children might fall off the barge and drown, but she trusted Label's commonsense and tried her best not to let her vivid imagination spoil the children's fun.

She also continued to instigate a time each day during which she instructed the children in Russian and Hebrew. She had added arithmetic to their daily curriculum now. But as the days passed, she and Szejna began to have another concern, this time over the children's spiritual welfare. As devout Jewish women, they believed the family should at least celebrate *Shabbat* each week. However, it was evident that Label and Lazlo had no intention of taking a day of rest, and Murad Amrad and Abram were both keen to keep going, so they kept their own council. But each evening, one or other of the women took the *Torah* from their cabin and asked Abram or Murad Amrad to read a passage out loud to them all, as had been the way at home in Bialystok.

In later years, they came to think of the time they spent on the barge as one of reflection; a time during which they were all, each in their own way, given the opportunity to adjust to their altered position in life. For apart from the knowledge of their hidden wealth, as homeless Jews they differed little from thousands of others like them who were being forced by circumstance, repression or economy to travel and find a new life.

When the canal ran through the centre of the small town of Kobrin, they halted briefly to purchase what they needed from traders whose stalls were set up beside the waterway. A week later, and further along the waterway, the next town was Pinsk, where once again they moored up. This time it was among a number of other barges, some whose crew were trading in the town and others who were preparing to leave. The family was thrilled to be able to walk around Jewish markets and shops again, and they felt in a celebratory mood. Believing they were now safe from Igor Sikorski, Szejna, Sonja and the children went shopping for provisions while Murad Amrad and Abram visited a café; a modest but popular Jewish owned establishment recommended to them by Label and Lazlo. Taking their orders for drinks, the landlord was a talkative man who welcomed them with questions. They had been hoping to hear the gossip of the town without having to give too much about themselves away. But there seemed no harm in the bare facts so Murad Amrad responded fairly openly to the landlord's initial line of questioning.

"We're with the rivermen," he said. "We've come from Brisk."

"How far will you go?" asked the landlord, waving and smiling at a group of men entering the café.

"Maybe Kiev? Maybe Odessa?" Murad Amrad hesitated. "My father and I are silversmiths and we are looking for a new place to set up our business."

"But you don't want to go to Kiev now." The landlord gave them his full attention and looked surprised. "Didn't you hear? They were driving Jews out of the city last year. Before the winter set in there were many Jewish families travelling through here. Some had been forced from their homes in Kiev and some from the surrounding villages. Most of them stayed here for a while to rest, and some remain here still. But it is difficult for us to feed them all. They tell us that Jews are forbidden to live in and around Kiev anymore. And now here you are, heading straight for it! Your bargemen will be safe enough. They're bringing trade and passing through. But as you are not trading, you'd be better off avoiding Kiev. I wish you luck my friend."

Murad Amrad and Abram were shocked into silence as the men in the café around them took up the conversation. And as details of recent events in Kiev began to emerge, they could only listen in horror, finding it hard to believe that until that moment they had been travelling towards the city in total ignorance of what might await them as visiting Jews. There had been every reason for them to believe they would be among friends in Kiev, other Jews who might be able to help them start a new life. Kiev was a town where Jews had been living and prospering for centuries and where Jewish merchants, businessmen and professionals alike had all contributed greatly to the city's growth. With a new university in the city and many business opportunities available, Kiev was known to be a thriving and culture-rich city with a vibrant social life, where Jewish professionals rubbed shoulders with members of the Polish and Russian nobility. But Murad Amrad and Abram now learned that with a new Russian fortress dominating the city and the Russian military very much in evidence, all was not as they had thought for the Jews of Kiev.

It had all changed two years earlier, when the influx of Jews from the countryside looking for work had swelled the Jewish population of Kiev to such an extent that the Russian Government had decided on a series of plans to drastically reduce their number. The tzar had proposed that they alter the boundaries of the Pale of Settlement once again, this time to exclude Kiev and a portion of the Ukraine immediately to the South of the city. With the new legislation duly put in place, hundreds of Jews from the newly forbidden territories were forced to leave their homes immediately. Those Jews who had been born in Kiev, or who owned property or businesses in the Kiev area, were allowed two years to leave. From then on, they would only be permitted entry to trade in the city for short periods at a time. Failure of any Jew to adhere to these instructions would result in deportation to Siberia or conscription into the Russian Army.

Since the Polish uprising however, the Russian military commanders had advised the government to call a temporary halt to the Jewish eviction from Kiev, in the fear that Jews might emulate the Poles and implement a new rebellion. Although the remaining Jewish citizens of Kiev had been given a brief reprieve however, the movement of Jewish traders being allowed entry to the city was being strictly monitored.

Living and working in Bialystok, Murad Amrad and his family had escaped persecution by the Russian authorities. Although they had witnessed the plight of the hundreds of refugees pouring into their town each day, the problem hadn't directly involved them, other than the need for charity. Now it was being brought home to them that perhaps nowhere was safe. It seemed that everywhere they went Jewish people were on the move, displaced for one reason or another by the Russian authorities, evicted first from the countryside and now from a major city like Kiev. But with no time to think about an alternative plan, the family could only return to the barge, where they were quickly on the move again, Lazlo maneuvering them under a complexity of bridges to accommodate the meeting of waterways and their transfer onto the River Pripyat.

Leaving Pinsk behind them, the River Pripyat was much wider than the canal had been. The course of the river twisted and turned to such an extent that it sometimes seemed almost to double back on itself as it flowed through level marshlands edged with thick forests where wolves howled at night. Each day, as the snow continued its rapid thaw and the river gathered speed, more of the land on either side of the river became flooded. The barge was now propelled for the most part by the force of the water, Label and Lazlo only guiding and turning it with their poles. Other barges began to join them from different points along the river, creating the need for greater vigilance. As the barges passed one another or jostled for position, both crews averted collision with great skill, at the same time as shouting out greetings and swapping pleasantries.

With no obvious walkway alongside the swollen river, they were now all forced to stay on the barge. But although the children were once again confined, this time there was plenty for them to look at. To their never-ending fascination, they found Label and Lazlo could name every one of the abundant variety of waterfowl and bird life around them. As it became a little warmer each day, frogs began to croak in tentative competition and Label could even distinguish the different species by their sound. He showed them the new green shoots of vegetation on the edges of the river. And he pointed out the geese that began to make a regular appearance overhead, flying in their distinctive formations, their haunting call heralding the arrival of spring. But for Murad Amrad, the scenery offered no distraction from the problem of where they were ultimately headed or what they would do when the barge arrived in Kiev.

When they came to the next town of Mozyr, they found it to be situated high up on a sharp rise of ground above one side of the river. To reach it, a narrow street sloped and zigzagged steeply upwards. Like Bialystok, the town was predominantly Jewish, and although the temptation to visit the markets, shops and cafés was great, Sonja decided to stay on board the boat. She had sewing to do and suddenly craved some solitude. So while the rest of the family left to buy provisions, and Label and Laslo went to talk with other river men whose boats were moored, like theirs, at the base of the rock face, Sonja sat with her mending, the dog beside her, and allowed her mind to drift. The sudden silence was at first unnerving, then deeply relaxing. The sun had some warmth in it that day, and her head began to grow heavy.

She was awoken by a voice calling for her attention, and she opened her eyes to see two Russian Army Officers standing beside the boat. She felt her heart miss a beat, and then begin to pound heavily in fright, but she did her best to remain calm on the outside. The dog was growling with its every outbreath, and the two men kept looking at it nervously. Although Sonja normally had little time for the animal, she now felt comforted by its presence. The men were speaking to her in Russian and she shook her head, pretending to understand less that she actually did.

"How many of you on this boat?" one of the men then repeated, speaking very slowly. "Where are you from and what is your business? What is your name?"

There were so many questions, and Sonja had to think quickly. She had no way of knowing whether these men were looking for them, or whether they were merely doing routine checks. But she dared not take any risks.

"My name is Ada Zemmol," she replied, making her Russian heavily accented and grammatically poor. "I am travel with my husband and brother. We have gone from Pinsk and we take timber to Kiev. We are three. And dog," she added as an afterthought.

One of the men made as if to step on board and Sonja's horror was eclipsed by the dog, which suddenly increased the volume of its growls and lurched forward. The Russian staggered back onto the shore and narrowly missed falling through the gap between it and the barge. Sonja called the dog to her, and to her surprise it came.

"My apologies, sir," she said. "Our dog is not friendly."

The officers exchanged a few words in Russian. From what she could hear, it seemed they were certainly looking for someone, and she prayed they would lose interest in her. But then she saw Label walking briskly towards them. He had seen the Russians standing beside his boat. As soon as he was within earshot, Sonja raised her voice to him.

"Husband!" she called out in Russian. "You are back." Then in Yiddish she said: "These men are asking many questions."

To her immense relief, Label understood at once. He gave a rough greeting to the men and jumped on board to come and stand beside her. The two Russians began to look slightly embarrassed. There was a short silence, then they each gave a curt nod and left, walking away along the line of moored barges.

"We must warn the others," Sonja whispered, reluctant to believe their good fortune.

"I will go," Label said shortly. "Lazlo will return to be with you." And with that he bounded up the hill at great speed, leaving Sonja feeling very shaky.

By the time Label brought the family cautiously back to the boat, the Russians had disappeared and Sonja had regained her composure. But the whole incident served to highlight the fact that they had to remain vigilant. It was not safe to relax their guard for one minute.

The River Pripyat widened as it neared the Dnieper, and at the point where the two waterways eventually merged, their combined flow created a vast lake where currents swirled and heaved as if in combat. As they turned into the larger river, Lazlo and Label each worked feverishly to keep the barge as close to the right hand bank as they could. Here the movement of the water was slower and it was easier to maneuver. The family could do nothing to help except try and ensure they were safely out of the two men's way.

They were little prepared for the sheer magnitude of the Dnieper River and gazed in amazement. Never had they seen such a huge expanse of water, one that seemed to stretch as far as they could see in both directions. To the North, Label had told them that the river started in the swamplands of central Russia. To the South it flowed past Kiev and on for six hundred miles to the Black Sea. It was so wide that people waiting for a ferry on the far bank were only visible as tiny dots in the distance.

By this time, at the end of April, the ice that held the river in its grip all winter had virtually melted and dispersed, although large floating lumps of it still provided a frequent hazard for the watermen. But Lazlo could once again get onto the riverbank to help control the barge with ropes, so their progress was considerably easier. There was now a steady stream of barges making their way down the river towards Kiev. They had all nearly completed their first journey of the season and would be celebrating together once they reached their destination. Large wooden warehouses and other industrial buildings began to appear. They were nearing the outskirts of the town. Eventually a timber yard came into sight with a wide quay in front of it, where barges of all sizes were moored end to end. As they drew nearer Label called out. A man on the quayside lifted his arm in acknowledgement and pointed to an available mooring place. Label and Lazlo pushed their poles deep into the river and manoeuvred their barge into place. Lazlo then jumped up onto the quay, pulled them in close and secured the ropes. They had arrived.

Here Label and Lazlo had the task of negotiating a good price for their load, while Murad Amrad had to somehow arrange immediate transport for his family for the next leg of their journey away from Kiev. The time had come for them to leave the security of the barge and bid farewell to the watermen of Brisk.

After the slow pace and comparative silence of the past three weeks, the family found it difficult to absorb the turmoil of activity and noise on the quay. Workers moved huge lengths of timber onto and off the barges with the aid of ropes and hoists. Other men stood in groups, instructing or bartering, hands gesticulating and eyes wary. Horses struggled to pull heavily laden carts and everyone seemed in a hurry to get a job done. Murad Amrad knew the family must be very much in the way as they stood huddled together, a disparate collection of people surrounded by all their belongings. Within minutes a man came purposefully towards them, walking with a slight stoop as if he'd been carrying heavy loads all his life. He rubbed his hands together as he approached them and had the air of someone in authority. Sure enough, he introduced himself as David Bragman, the owner of the timber yard, and although he was courteous enough he was distinctly guarded as he asked them how he could help.

Murad Amrad was surprised at how easily everything fell into place after that. Perhaps the rabbi in Bialystok had been right after all and they were indeed following God's will. Since Tamara's death, he had been of a mind that God was not on his side. Being accused of a murder he didn't commit as well as having to leave everything that he and his father had worked so hard to build up had not convinced him otherwise. But he had to admit that the assistance and kindness given by all those who had so far aided their flight from Bialystok was gratifying and somewhat humbling. It was perhaps an indication that God had better things in mind for them. David Bragman proved to be no exception.

When Murad Amrad told him how they'd got to Kiev from Bialystok, and explained that they needed to get on the road away from the city as quickly as possible, possibly to Odessa, he didn't have to say any more. That they needed to avoid discovery in Kiev was something David Bragman immediately understood. He too was Jewish, and it was only because his timber yard was a sufficient distance from Kiev that he had so far managed to evade the evacuation laws. And he was able to give Murad Amrad good news.

"You coming at this time is extremely fortuitous," he said. "My sister and her family are about to make the same journey. Her husband is from Odessa and they have decided to live there. There are others in their party I believe, and they are taking several wagons. If you wish, I could speak with them and request that you go with them?"

Murad Amrad could not have been more delighted, or astonished, at their good fortune. "We are blessed in having met you, David Bragman. If they will have us, we would be honoured to accompany them. But we will need a wagon and a good horse. Do you think it safe for me to go into Kiev to secure my transport?"

"I think not!" David Bragman was very definite. "But if you're content to wait here, I will see what I can do to help you. I can probably get you a decent enough animal and I have a large wagon you can have."

Murad Amrad couldn't think how to thank him enough, but David Bragman had moved away and was leading the family from the timber yard. They walked some distance down the river before coming to an old warehouse. Showing them inside he invited them to make themselves as comfortable as possible while he made arrangements for their departure. He also advised them against going back to the docks for any reason.

"You will be safe enough here, but it may be better for you if your presence is not too well known."

Outside the warehouse, David Bragman and Murad Amrad discussed the financial side of the arrangements and Murad Amrad paid the agreed amount. David Bragman then departed, leaving Murad Amrad feeling distinctly uneasy at the amount of trust and money he had just parted with. But the timber merchant seemed a good man and Murad Amrad tried to put doubt to the back of his mind. He looked around. The warehouse was set some way back from the river and was surrounded by trees, which although not in leaf, would afford them some privacy from passing boats and the bargemen walking alongside. Behind it a muddy track led towards the docks and presumably to the town beyond.

Going back inside, his eyes took a little while to adjust to the comparative dark. The air was filled with the strong smell of wood shavings, and particles of dust hung in the shafts of light beaming through the gaps in the wooden walls. He looked around at his family. The children were silent and morose. He'd been amazed at how they'd expressed more sadness at saying goodbye to Label, Lazlo and the dog than they had been at leaving their home. Utah and Fanny had sobbed out loud, and Tomas had gone pale and silent, refusing to talk. Hanna and Elzbietta were now sitting beside each other on the wooden crate that contained the whole of the Galperin Silverware business. Hanna was staring down at her hands and Murad Amrad wondered what she was thinking. He saw Elzbietta reach out to Fanny, pull her onto her knee and hug her. Fanny was looking very glum. But there again, Murad Amrad thought, she often did. He checked himself and looked across at Sonja. Despite their situation and some culinary deprivations, she was still a comely woman whose round face glowed with health and good cheer. The jewel box must still be hanging around her middle he presumed, and although it must have been very uncomfortable at times, she never mentioned it. He knew he was hugely indebted to her. Managing without her didn't bare thinking about and he knew the children would be lost without her. She was sitting on a pile of timber talking to Tomas, trying, he imagined, to get him to say something in return. He snorted to himself. Once Tomas had decided on something there was no changing him, whether it was a course of action or a mood. It was a characteristic that annoyed him intensely. He caught Sonja's eye then and she smiled. She knew Tomas as well as he did. And always ready with a practical solution to most problems, she would probably have started them all singing if there hadn't been necessity to keep quiet.

He went over to where Abram and Szejna sat with Utah, all three looking very comfortable among the piles of rugs, furs and the large sacks containing their belongings. He noticed how tired his parents looked. Despite the ongoing stress of their situation, Szejna had been consistently cooking and helping to care for the children, much as she would have been doing at home. While he imagined this gave her great comfort, he knew she was fearful for their future and it had obviously taken its toll on her. Abram seemed to have shrunk in stature. Never a very communicative man, he had been noticeably more silent since leaving Bialystok and now appeared rather lost and withdrawn. Murad Amrad wanted to lift their spirits.

"When we get to Odessa, Father, we will rent an apartment and you and I must look for somewhere to set up our business. But the first thing we must do is to find a replacement for the diamond in the lid of the jewel box. Have you had any more thoughts about what to put in its place?"

The two men discussed options for a while and Murad Amrad was relieved to see a spark of interest in his father's eye. He was sure Abram would be fine once he was back working at what he loved.

They stayed in the warehouse for the rest of that day, their belongings stacked around them, feeling powerless to do anything about whatever was going to happen next. As the day drew in, Sonja and Szejna prepared a meal of salt beef, bread and wine, after which they had no choice but to settle themselves as comfortably as possible for the night.

Early the next morning Murad Amrad's faith in David Bragman was rewarded. Hearing a sound from behind the warehouse, he went out and saw the timber merchant walking down the track towards them leading a large rust-coloured horse, harnessed between the shafts of a deep-sided wooden cart. With cries of delight, the family came out of the warehouse. David Bragman handed the reigns of the horse to Murad Amrad and began to give him directions to the place where his sister and her husband would be waiting.

"We are so very grateful to you, David Bragman," Murad Amrad said. "I thank you."

David Bragman smiled and inclined his head. "I wish you all a safe journey. Now I must return to work." And with a brief wave of his hand he strode off through the trees towards the wharf.

Murad Amrad smiled at his family. The arrival of the horse had re-energised them. The children were petting the animal, and the adults were laughing with relief. The final leg of their journey could now begin.

Whether through stubborn determination or an equine sense of humour, the horse at first seemed intent on going its own way and at its own pace. Murad Amrad had no experience with horses. They had not owned one in Bialystok and he had never needed to know anything about them. Abram, however, had regularly driven his father's horse and cart while growing up in Marijampole, although that had been over forty years ago. But as the only one of them who had any experience at all, he was given the task of driving. Tomas and Utah volunteered to help their grandfather, reminding him that they had helped Moshe Yaglom with the horses every day. They were duly given the task of walking along beside the horse until Abram regained his confidence and the horse began to pay heed to his directions, which eventually it did. Over the following weeks, Tomas and Utah proved themselves invaluable at the task of caring for the animal. They named him Koenig, meaning 'King', and not only were they able to make sense of the multitude of chains and ropes that attached it to the cart, but they remembered how to groom and care for a horse, how to pick stones from its hooves to prevent it becoming lame and how to tether it at night. Murad Amrad felt great pride in his two boys and the way in which they took on this new responsibility. And when he saw his father sitting in the driver's seat behind the horse, with one of his grandsons on each side of him, he was gladdened to see how much happier he looked with something worthwhile to do.

According to David Bragman, who had made the journey through the Ukraine many times, the distance between Kiev and Odessa was some three hundred miles. The trail was reasonably level and the route well worn, he told them, and could be completed in about three weeks if horses were driven hard. But Murad Amrad knew that this was not going to be possible. Their horse was big boned and strong enough, but their cart was of a particularly heavy construction. Loaded as it was with all their belongings, he imagined it must weigh a great deal even before any of them took a ride. If something happened to their horse, they would be stranded. Instigating a rota whereby, with the exception of Abram and Szejna, they did not all ride in the cart at the same time, he acknowledged to himself, in some desperation, that their journey would have to be completed at a walking pace. Therefore, they would be lucky to cover as much as six or seven miles each day. Notwithstanding that, there were four other heavily laden carts in their party. They too would only want to walk their horses. Murad Amrad had no choice but to resign himself to the fact that it would possibly be the beginning of June before they arrived at Odessa.

David Bragman's sister and her husband, Razel and Valvel Levinson, proved to be unlike anyone the Galperin's had ever met before. They had no children and it quickly became obvious that Valvel and Razel were equal partners in their business. Valvel had grown up in Odessa where he had worked in the cloth trade with his father and brother. Seeking to expand the family business, he had moved to Kiev ten years earlier where he had met and married Razel.

"It is because of Razel that my business grew so quickly," he said, looking at his wife with pride. Razel was a good-looking woman, it had to be said, and Murad Amrad was embarrassed to look at her. Her head was barely covered. But Valvel appeared unfazed and continued.

"She is so good with the customers, and her head for figures is excellent. I always left our affairs in her hands when I had to travel back to Odessa to collect further stock."

This immodest display of flattery made Murad Amrad even more uncomfortable. It was not usual behaviour between husband and wife. But when Razel and Valvel smiled at each other, a fresh stab of grief suddenly caught him by surprise. Tamara might have enjoyed meeting Razel. He clenched his hands in his lap and looked away.

Valvel's passion for his trade was evident as he told Murad Amrad about the agents they employed to find the finest fabrics from around the world. He talked about the excitement he and his father always felt each time they took delivery of a new consignment from the docks in Odessa, the beauty of which was only revealed once it had been unloaded in their warehouses. Silks and brocades from the Orient, gossamer fine cotton spun with gold from Turkey and intricate lace from Malta. Back in Kiev, the Polish and Russian noblemen and women who flocked to the city every year for the winter's social season had sought out Valvel and Razel's fabrics above all others for their elaborate gowns, coats, shawls and headdresses. And with each year that passed, the reputation and popularity of Valvel and Razel's business had grown. But their success had not been welcomed by everyone, as Razel explained.

"Our regular customers always came back year after year. They knew our cloth was of the finest quality and that we would provide them with the best price." She spoke of their business with great pride, but as she continued her eyes welled up with tears. "But the Christian merchants in the town couldn't stand to see a Jewish trader become so successful. They were jealous of our success and had been making life very hard for us long before this latest eviction order; spreading slanderous stories about us, undercutting our prices, daubing paint on our doors. I really believe it was they who did much to influence the Tzar's latest legislation to evict Jews from the city."

"My dear." Valvel put a hand on her arm. "You must remember that they had to pay dearly to get their hands on our business."

"But they couldn't wait, could they!" Razel said bitterly.

Valvel turned to Murad Amrad. "That is how it was. Even knowing we would be forced to leave in two years, they couldn't wait. One of our Christian competitors offered us a very good price for our business premises and our home. We'd have been fools not to accept it. We have been very blessed to come away with much of what our business was worth. So many of our friends won't be so fortunate."

Murad Amrad had already observed that the cart Razel drove was loaded with shapes reminiscent of the rolls of cloth among which they had hidden some weeks before. On hearing this story, he presumed that Valvel and Razel had withheld some of their stock to take back to Odessa. He hoped so anyway.

The other couple travelling with them were Levi and Anna Rosen, a grim faced couple who also each drove a cart. But apart from an occasional call to the horses, they remained silent and withdrawn, merely nodding in greeting or response and barely talking, even to each other. One evening, Murad Amrad was forced to enquire about them and Valvel told him that Levi had worked as a delivery driver for them in Kiev.

"But that was before their two sons were both conscripted into the Russian Army," Valvel said. "There is little chance they will ever see them again and something died in them when the boys left. Levi hasn't worked since. The community has provided for them as best they can."

Valvel explained that a few years before the legislation to remove Jews from Kiev came into effect, the Russian authorities had started conscripting young Jewish boys into the army, forcing them to sign up for twenty-five years, to renounce their Jewish faith and to become Christian. A certain quota of boys was expected from each Jewish community, and if an insufficient number was obtained, the authorities merely kidnapped boys off the streets.

"Levi and Anna tried to hide their sons, but one night there was a terrible scene when soldiers pounded on their door and hauled the boys out onto the streets. Levi tried to reason with them that his boys were being educated, and Anna screamed and tore her clothes, but to no avail. They have sent food and letters but haven't seen or heard from their sons since. And now they too must leave. There is nothing for them in Kiev."

Murad Amrad glanced across at Levi and Anna who were sitting silently beside the fire. He couldn't imagine the pain of losing his two sons to the army.

"Were they not blessed with other children?" he asked.

"There was a daughter, Ella. But they disowned her and cast her out of their house."

Murad Amrad looked shocked.

"Ella fell in love with a Christian boy and when she told them they wanted to marry, they told her she was no longer their daughter and threw her out of their home. That was an evil day. Their friends in the community ran the girl out of town and they have no idea what happened to her after that. They have no daughter." Valvel spat on the floor in distaste, though whether for Ella's actions or those of her parents, Murad Amrad couldn't be sure. He remembered the comparative comradeship between the Christian and Jewish traders of Bialystok and said nothing.

Two weeks into their journey Szejna began to cough. At first it was a small, irritating noise that interrupted their sleep around the fire at night. But within a few days it was thick and bronchial and she began to struggle for breath. It was evident to them all that she was becoming increasingly ill and they knew they must find a village in which to shelter until she was better.

They had previously passed a number of small farms and from each one they had been able to secure some produce, though not very much. Scratching a living from the flat lands around them was hard and the Russian peasants did not have much to sell. Nor were they very friendly. But they were usually happy enough to take money from Jewish travellers in exchange for a chicken or two, a few handfuls of grain or some pickled cabbage. However, now that refuge was needed, the land around them seemed empty of human habitation.

By the third day of Szejna's illness, they finally approached a small *shtetle* and Murad Amrad gave thanks to God. Here would be Jewish people to offer them accommodation and hospitality and help them nurse Szejna back to good health. The warmth of a house and nourishing food would do her so much good. But as they entered the village and drove past the rows of wooden houses, there seemed no sign of life other than the tail end of a few rats that scuttled out of their way. They pulled up their horses in the central market square. Somewhere a shutter banged repeatedly to and fro in the wind and a crow called plaintively from among the wooden roofs, but apart from that, the silence was total. The whole village was completely deserted and every home empty.

"The villagers have left here!" Valvel voiced the obvious conclusion out loud as Murad Amrad and Abram jumped down and pushed at the door to one of the houses. It opened into a large whitewashed kitchen with an earth floor. An empty cage for chickens and geese hung open, chairs were pulled up to a rough wooden table on which a lamp had been knocked over, dried herbs were strung up above the stove and sleeping pallets were set against the far side of the room. It had once been a home, had smelt of cooking and had welcomed visitors from the street. It had been some time since this room had been occupied, however. The grate was cold and the room was filled with dust. But it would have to suffice.

Sonja and the girls immediately went to work. They lit the fire, swept the floors and did their best to clear away some of the dust. They then spread their rugs and furs over the pallets and helped Szejna to lie down. They unloaded wine and food from the carts outside and before too long the room was warm, the lamp was lit and a pot of stew was cooking on the stove. Later, with the horses bedded down in a barn and their travelling companions ensconced in a neighbouring property, the family was able to sit down at the table and eat a meal together in warmth and comfort for the first time in weeks. From her bed, in between bouts of deep chesty coughs, Szejna smiled as she watched them. She did her best to eat a little stew and sip some wine, but she wasn't very hungry. She just wanted to go to sleep, she said. She closed her eyes and listened to the fire crackling in the grate and the girls talking quietly to each other. Abram was sitting beside her bed holding onto her hand and chanting quietly. She had always loved to hear him sing. Szejna squeezed his hand. She felt weighed down by a weariness she had never known before and longed to succumb to it, but she was content. They were in a Jewish home and were spending the evening together as generations of others like them had done before and that was how it was meant to be.

After the meal Murad Amrad, Tomas and Utah sat at the table reading the *Torah* while Sonja and the girls kept busy by attending to some sewing. The sound of Szejna's laboured breathing filled the room and, as the night wore on, it became worse. The younger children lay on a single pallet staring out with frightened eyes and listening to their grandmother's frantic gasps, while the adults did what they could to try to aid her breathing. Sonja put water on to boil to fill the room with steam, they sat her upright, they gave her sips of water and they rubbed her back, but all to no avail. Szejna had pneumonia and there was nothing they could do to help her other than wait and pray. The hours dragged on and, despite their best intentions, they intermittently dozed as exhaustion overtook them. Only Abram stayed vigil, his gentle melodic chanting providing some comfort for them all.

In the early hours of the morning Szejna was suddenly quiet, her laboured breathing stilled and her features finally at peace. It was over.

There was an overgrown cemetery just outside the shtetle, where the tombstones sat at awkward angles, their Hebrew inscriptions mostly worn away and illegible. Newer graves provided evidence that the village was inhabited until quite recently, the last one being for a young girl who had died the winter before. Cutting a new gash in the long grass the following day, the men began to dig a grave for Szejna. While they dug, Abram remained by Szejna's side and declined all food or water. In the evening, they brought her wrapped body to the cemetery and placed it in the grave. Each of them then threw in a handful of earth and Abram began to speak. He talked of his love for Szejna, of her devotion to him and their family, of her love of God and of her good character. He spoke the words of his eulogy hesitantly and quietly but it was the more powerful in sentiment for his doing so. Afterwards, as the men filled in the grave, Murad Amrad recited prayers and psalms.

They had no headstone to place on the mound of fresh earth. But each of them had collected stones and, so that she would be known, they crouched around Szejna's grave and pressed the stones into the earth to form her name.

"One day soon we will come back and bring her a headstone, Father." Murad Amrad wiped his eyes. But Abram was looking up at the evening sky. Awkwardly, and with their legs hanging down, the first of the migratory storks were flying in after the winter, and he smiled sadly.

"Szejna loved to see the storks arriving," he said. "She used to say that they brought spring on their wings. She would laugh at the way the males arrived first, always going year after year to their old nests and getting them ready for their mates to join them. And they come today of all days. It is surely a sign from God that he welcomes her to his side."

ODESSA: 1832

They drove into Odessa on the 13th June 1832. To the passer-by who dodged the horses, crossed the cobbled street in front of them and stepped onto the wide pavements, they appeared shabby and under nourished, inappropriately dressed for the early summer heat, their eyes dulled by exhaustion. But the stranger on the street would not have given them much thought. They were just another group of people arriving in the city to make their fortune, and he and they soon disappeared among the diverse population thronging its streets.

Founded in 1794 by Empress Catherine II of Russia on the site of an ancient Greek fortress, Odessa had made full use of its strong position as a warm water port on the Black Sea. The city had grown extremely prosperous, most especially through the export of grain, grown in the fertile lands of the Ukraine to the north, and shipped from Odessa to other countries around the world. After Odessa was granted the status of a free port in 1819, trade among all nations was conducted with minimum taxation and the city became the commercial gateway to the Russian Empire. Since then, it had become a popular resort among members of the Russian nobility, who flocked there to enjoy its sunny climate. They had built fabulous palaces and *dachas* (summerhouses) along the shoreline. Opulent hotels, theatres and churches followed, then a library, an opera house and a botanical garden. By 1832, when the Galperin family arrived, Odessa was fast becoming one of the largest cities in the Russian Empire and notably the most cosmopolitan. Reflecting the many different nationalities of both the people who lived in Odessa and those who had designed it, the extravagant architecture combined European, Classical and Moorish influences; French and Italian were widely spoken, European papers and magazines were on sale, and Odessa had more the outward appearance of a European city than a Russian one. Because the taxes were so low, the standard of living in the city was universally good. The citizens of Odessa also enjoyed considerably more political and religious freedom than in the rest of the Russian Empire. This benefited the Jewish residents of Odessa especially. Unfettered by the more orthodox dictates of Jewish behaviour or by the restrictions and anti-Semitism of Russian domination, Jews enjoyed countless economic opportunities not to be found elsewhere.

All this Valvel had spoken of during the days since Szejna's death, when the last leg of the journey had seemed interminable and the Galperin family were lost in a dense tangle of grief. He was intensely proud of his native town and wanted to try and inject some hope back into Murad Amrad with his words. Murad Amrad had never felt so despondent, and much of Valvel's enthusiastic chatter about the city they were approaching was lost to him. But he heard enough to know that Odessa was obviously a place where it would be good to settle. The gruelling, sheer physicality of the journey, compounded by their devastating loss, meant that now more than ever before they needed to find a permanent home. He was greatly concerned about his father, who had barely spoken since his mother's death, although he knew only too well how he felt. They needed somewhere to rest, somewhere to grieve, and somewhere to begin to make sense of their lives again.

The nearer they had got to Odessa, the more animated and excited both Valvel and Razel had become. When they finally drove into the city, and Murad Amrad saw for himself the gracious buildings, the elegant cobbled streets and the wide-open spaces embellished with statues and green foliage, he began to feel his spirits lift. Valvel called out that he had a surprise for them. Levi and Anna Rosen had taken their leave soon after entering the city, and Valvel now led the three remaining carts onto a wide street lined with newly planted Acacia trees. Running along one side of the street were the most extravagantly designed houses Murad Amrad had ever seen, and opposite them, through ornate iron railings, they could see the vast expanse of the Black Sea. The houses had been built to take full advantage of the view, but as none of the Galperin's had ever seen the ocean before, they didn't immediately realise what it was they were looking at. Slowly the children's faces lit up, and while Murad Amrad was equally awe-struck by the sparkling expanse of water, he felt the most joy just to see his family smile again. They sat for a while in their carts, looking down at the harbour where sailing ships larger than any they could have imagined were anchored within the harbour walls. Murad Amrad noticed that one of the ships moored against the docks below them had what appeared to be a long black chimney rising from the middle of it, out of which black smoke belched. He pointed down to it.

"Is that ship not on fire, Valvel?" he asked in some concern.

Valvel burst out laughing. "That is a Steam Ship, Murad," he replied. "There are two of them; the 'Yalta' and the 'Odessa'. They carry mail, goods and passengers across the sea. A steam-powered propeller helps them sail faster, even with no wind. There are many who believe steam to be the future of transport and who knows, one day it may even take over from horses! This is a city where anything is possible."

Valvel grinned and Murad Amrad shook his head in disbelief and gave an amused snort. But all at once he was surprised to feel optimism surging through him. Igor Sikorski could not find them now. They had arrived at the end of their journey and here, in this magnificent and thoroughly modern city, they were about to forge a new life for themselves. They had completed their journey at a vast cost, but Murad Amrad vowed to himself there and then that he would make that cost count for something. Together he and his father would rebuild their business and create a good life for their family. This he promised to God and to himself as he looked down at his first steam ship.

To help them find an apartment, Valvel and Razel introduced them to an acquaintance of theirs named Sholom Babel, a Jewish man who owned many such properties in the city. They were duly shown a three story building on a predominantly Jewish street, and straight away secured a three-month lease by giving Sholom Babel the full payment. As they all explored their new home, and the children ran up and down the stone stairs, Sonja was overjoyed at what she called the refinement of their accommodation and announced that she would feel like an empress living here.

An airy ground floor stable gave Koenig plenty of room to rest after his weeks of hard work. There was also space for the cart. Behind the stable, a room with a stove and a central table would suffice as a workshop and forge for the present, and beyond that was a small courtyard containing an underground water tank, of which Sholom Babel had been very proud when showing them around. The tank collected rainwater to supply the many apartments in the block, although he had been insistent on the amount of water they were allowed. Once they'd used up their allocated amount, he said, they should buy water from the water carriers who came around the streets with a cart and sold it by the barrel. On the first floor, a large living room and kitchen provided more living area than they had ever been used to and, on the second floor, three bedrooms gave them all ample sleeping space. At long last they had a home again.

Their first task after unpacking was to collect all their money into one place. That which they'd put in pouches before their flight from Bialystok had all but gone, but they still had all the coins they'd sewn into the hems of their coats and into the linings of the sacks in which they'd kept their clothes. And by the time Sonja and the girls had unpicked their handwork, even after they'd made allowances for the new clothes and personal items they all badly needed, they found they still had more than enough money left to last for many months. Finally, from among her clothing, Sonja removed the pouch she had so carefully kept throughout all the weeks of travelling and presented it to Murad Amrad.

"I am happy to hand this over to you, Murad. I imagine you will want to sell it as soon as possible. I feel it is an ill omen to have in our possession and I for one will be glad to see it go."

As Murad Amrad unwrapped the jewel box from the bag, the diamond caught the light and dazzled him for a few seconds. He gazed down on the exquisite workmanship dispassionately. Like Sonja, its presence made him uncharacteristically nervous, reminding him of all the reasons they'd had to flee from their home. He took it straightaway to Abram, who was setting up the workshop. Murad Amrad smiled to see his father among his tools again. He hoped fervently that Abram would find some solace in the work they must do to build up their new business.

"Father, the time has come. I must ask you to do your best to remove this diamond and replace it with another precious stone or an alternative decoration. We will keep the diamond against future need as you suggested. Our own Diamond Fund! But we must sell the box as soon as possible."

Abram nodded. He would work on it immediately.

Unpacking the tools of his trade and inspecting all the stock they had bought with them had indeed given Abram the comfort of being reacquainted with old friends. Now, as he sifted through his collection of precious stones and small trinkets, he knew what he was looking for and gave a grunt of relief when he pulled it from the chest. It was a silver disc, delicately embossed with a floral motif. He had no idea what its history was, but he'd taken it as part payment from a young man in exchange for a fairly modest piece of jewellery for his wife. The man had been new to Bialystok and rather short of funds. Abram had taken pity on him, taking the silver disc more for its worth in silver than for its style. Now, however, the disc was the perfect size to place in the gap the diamond would leave, and he was pleased to have remembered it so well. He would light a fire immediately and get to work. Far from detracting from the glory of the jewel box, it would compliment the fine embossed silver around the edge of the lid and the box would look quite complete.

A few days later, Murad Amrad and Abram left their house and walked to Greek Street, the main trading area for Jewish merchants. Here, Sholom Babel had told them, you could buy 'twenty thousand different things'. Certainly the street seemed overflowing with merchandise of all kinds that spilled out from the open doorways of shops or around the tented stalls. And the noise was excessive. A vibrant mix of bartering, of money exchanging hands, of laughing and joking, all a far cry from the rather sombre Jewish markets they were more acquainted with, where the traders always had one eye on the look out for a Russian official who might make trouble for them.

Faced with the confusion of the crowds, Murad Amrad and Abram were extremely relieved that they had thought to ask Valvel where they should go to sell a particularly valuable piece of jewellery. Valvel had unhesitatingly directed them to the door of a man named

Isaac Rosenthal, a jewellery dealer known to Valvel and his family, and not for the first time they acknowledged the huge debt they owed Valvel. Without his recommendation they would have had no idea of the best place to find a buyer for the jewel box. Isaac Rosenthal dealt with private collectors of valuable pieces of jewellery, Valvel had assured them, and he was definitely the right man to speak to.

They found the house easily enough and, as friends of Valvel Levinson, Isaac Rosenthal welcomed them heartily. They were shown into a windowless room brightly lit with countless decorative lamps. Vibrant hangings adorned the walls and richly embroidered cushions were set on the floor around a brass table, at which they were invited to sit. Abram and Murad Amrad did so, but were so overawed by the appearance of their host that they could initially say very little. Dressed in an extraordinary combination of vibrantly coloured clothing, his head wrapped around with a length of cloth, Isaac Rosenthal certainly blended well with his décor. But there was nothing about his person that indicated he was a Jew. He was clean-shaven, his voice was excessively loud and his mannerisms wildly exaggerated. His demeanour was as unfamiliar to Murad Amrad and Abram as the room in which they sat and they found themselves feeling somewhat uncomfortable in his presence. But they were here to do business and he had been recommended to them, so Abram took out the jewel box and placed it on the table.

Isaac Rosenthal whistled through his teeth and was then quiet as he inspected the quality of workmanship on the box. Murad Amrad was pleased to observe that the silver disc looked quite at home in place of the diamond.

"I may indeed have a buyer for such a piece," Isaac Rosenthal said finally. "Many Russians arriving in Odessa for the summer seek valuable trinkets for their wives. They come to me regularly and I will take much delight in showing them this piece. Because you are a friend of the Levinson family, I will not request my usual commission but I hope we can come to an agreement that suits us both?" He looked at Murad Amrad expectantly.

"I hope so too," Murad Amrad replied, and the three men began to haggle. That the jewel box was worth a small fortune was without doubt, and Isaac Rosenthal finally displayed all the shrewd and quick-witted characteristics of any normal Jewish trader in his desire for a portion of its value. In the end they settled on a satisfactory arrangement, but Murad Amrad and Abram insisted on taking the box home with them. Any viewing or sale was to be done in their presence they said, a small detail to which Isaac Rosenthal eventually agreed.

Over the following few weeks, the family wrote letters to friends and relations in Bialystok, telling them only that they were well and informing them, as gently as they could, of Szejna's death. There was no way of knowing whether their letters would reach their destination for they dared not tell anyone where they were for now. But they felt better for having written them, even though they longed to hear news from their home. In the meantime, they began to integrate with the Jewish community and, as their lives took on a new routine, they gained some much-needed semblance of normality.

Sonja got to know the markets and quickly discovered where best to purchase the things she needed. Apart from the classes the boys were now attending in the Jewish study halls, the children were doing so well under her tuition that Murad Amrad had suggested she continue to teach them at home, at least for the time being. This was something she and the girls could fit around running the home. But after their months of freedom, both boys found the renewed focus on learning somewhat hard to get used to again.

Meanwhile, Murad Amrad and Abram secured a stall on Greek Street where they could display their silverware each morning. The unusual pieces immediately attracted considerable interest and requests for individual items were soon in the order books. From then on, while Murad Amrad continued to man the stall and generate business, Abram began to work in their new workshop. And he was pleased to have a reason to do so. It was the nights he dreaded the most, when his hands were idle and his mind filled with sadness.

Nearly a month passed before they heard from Isaac Rosenthal again, but early one morning he came to Murad Amrad's stall, dressed as before in vivid colours and flowing robes. Murad Amrad could not help but notice that the jewellery dealer attracted little undue attention from passers by in the street. He had occasionally observed other similar instances of unconventional dress or behaviour among the citizens of the city, and had come to the conclusion that the scope for individuality, perhaps part of the attraction of living in Odessa, did not in the end merit much attention. Nevertheless, as Isaac Rosenthal came towards him and leaned in close to speak in a hoarse whisper, Murad Amrad could not help but feel a certain level of distaste and checked a natural reaction to pull away.

"I have someone interested in taking a look at your specialist piece," Isaac Rosenthal rasped, looking from side-to-side as he did so. "Perhaps you would like to bring it to my premises this evening?"

Murad Amrad nodded, and while doing his best to remain upright, assured him that he would. Isaac then took his leave, with a final flourish of his curious garments, and Murad Amrad was able to relax his posture.

Later that evening they sat as before, upon cushions on the floor of Isaac Rosenthal's colourful room. Murad Amrad and Abram sat on one side of the brass table and Isaac Rosenthal and a Russian man on the other. As an older man of some evident authority, the Russian had been introduced merely as Count Andrei Shuvalov, but no other details had been provided or were needed. The fact that he was a Russian Count made Murad Amrad distinctly nervous, but he comforted himself in the knowledge that there were many members of the Russian aristocracy in Odessa for the summer months and they could not possibly all know one another. For much the same purpose as the previous owner of the jewel box, Count Andrei Shuvalov now wanted something valuable to present to his wife, and Murad Amrad duly placed Countess Sophia Petrovitch's erstwhile gift on the table for him to look at.

The Count picked it up and Murad Amrad waited for the usual sounds or expressions of appreciation. This time, however, there were none. The curious silence that followed seemed to last for a long time. Eventually the Count put the box down and asked its value. When Abram told him he finally expressed some emotion in the form of genuine or contrived disbelief, Murad Amrad was suddenly unsure which. They then began to negotiate; Isaac Rosenthal literally rubbing his hands together in excitement as the acceptable price rose, and Murad Amrad discarded his misgivings as inconsequential.

The purchase value they finally agreed upon was a considerable amount of money and every bit as much as Murad Amrad and Abram had hoped for, despite the missing diamond. They insisted on being paid in solid coinage however, rather than the new paper money issued by the Russian banks, and the Count obviously found this request rather distasteful. He informed them that it would take a few days to gather that number of rubles, and that they would have to be placed in a strong box and would weigh a great deal. But Murad Amrad was determined it should be so and finally all arrangements for the sale were completed. Murad Amrad and Abram were to return to Isaac Rosenthal's establishment with the jewel box when the Count sent word, and upon their payment Isaac Rosenthal would receive his commission.

That evening the family celebrated. They were going to be wealthier than they could ever possibly have imagined and they ate their meal in high spirits. It did concern Abram that he wouldn't really know what to do if he didn't have to make his silverware pieces, and Murad Amrad had similar thoughts. He could not envisage a life without the necessity of work. But neither man voiced their fears. There would be plenty of time in the future to adjust to their new position in life and now was not the time for making concrete plans. Tonight was a time to rejoice and they both took great joy in seeing the family so full of excitement. Sonja led them all in song and they drank wine and gave thanks to God that their flight from Bialystok had brought its just reward.

But very early the next morning, Murad Amrad was woken up by a frenzy of muffled knocking on the door to the apartment. Wrapping a robe around himself, he went down the stairs to find Isaac Rosenthal standing in the street in some disarray, his clothing barely covering his undergarments. Murad Amrad was shocked to see him and brought him into the kitchen, where Sonja joined them. She too had been woken by the noise from the street.

"Sit, Isaac. Take your breath. What has happened to bring you here so early?"

Isaac wrung his hands together as he sat at the kitchen table. Then he began to talk, barely drawing breath, his words spilling out so fast that it took Murad Amrad some time to take in what he was saying.

"Late last night I had a caller, Murad Amrad. It was Count Andrei Shuvalov. I was surprised I can tell you. I invited him in and offered him refreshment, but he said he had something to ask me. He was troubled, he said. He thought he had recognised the jewel box, he said. He was quite sure it was the same as a box that belonged to his cousin in St Petersburg. I didn't catch the name. But Count Andrei Shuvalov said he could remember this box as he and his cousin were together in Paris when he had bought the box for his wife. It was the work of an eminent jeweller, he said. A man who had assured them there was no other like it. Although his cousin's jewel box had a large diamond set into the top, your box was a replica in every other way. In this he was quite certain."

Murad Amrad felt as if he'd been kicked in the stomach. Sonja too had paled and sat down heavily on a chair. The shock and disbelief of what he was hearing descended on Murad Amrad like a tangible weight, and he had to fight to catch his breath as Isaac Rosenthal continued.

"He told me that before he purchased the box, he wanted to know how it had come to be in your possession. He said he wished he'd asked you more about its origins. Could it be a fake, he asked? I assured him that it wasn't. Then he said he was reluctant to hand over so much money to a man who may be a fraud or a thief. He asked me about you and how you came to have the box. I didn't tell him you had newly arrived and that I didn't actually know you, Murad Amrad. As you are a friend of Valvel Levinson, I wanted to speak with you first. Then he told me that he was expecting his cousin and his wife to arrive in Odessa any day now. He would wait for their arrival, he said. His cousin had recently suffered bereavement, he said, and his wife was unwell. They were coming to Odessa to regain their health. And he wanted his cousin to see the box before proceeding with the deal."

Isaac Rosenthal took a cloth from within his garments and wiped his mouth before continuing. He was so distressed that thankfully he failed to notice the effect his words were having on both Murad Amrad and Sonja.

"I… we don't want to lose this sale, Murad Amrad. Count Andrei Shuvalov is a man everyone takes notice of. If he doesn't buy the box, he'll make sure no one else does. And he could ruin my reputation. I've been awake all night and I couldn't wait any longer to speak with you. What can I tell Count Andrew Shuvalov to put his mind at rest and encourage him to make an immediate purchase? Is this box a fake?"

Murad Amrad had his head in his hands, his elbows leaning on the table. His thoughts were jumbled. Would he ever be able to get rid of this box? Surely the chances of events unfurling like this were almost nonexistent? Was Sonja right and the box an ill omen? And how could he prove his innocence to this man, or to Count Andrei Shuvalov? Maybe he should face Count Alexei Petrovitch with the truth, if indeed it was he who was heading for the city. But wasn't it too late? His flight from Bialystok spoke of guilt. He couldn't think straight but knew it was important to do so. He stood up.

"No, Isaac Rosenthal. The box is not a fake. And I am not a dishonest man. This I want you to believe, and I ask you to trust that it is so. In good faith I will let you take the box to show Count Andrei Shuvalov and his cousin when he arrives, and I am happy for you to negotiate with the Count yourself. Let me know once the sale of the jewel box is completed, but all I ask of you in the meantime is to keep my address from the Count until I have found a way to prove my right of possession."

He hoped his apparent clarity of thought and generosity of spirit was enough to lay any doubts in Isaac Rosenthal's mind. All at once he wanted more than anything to be rid of the jewel box. The trinket seemed increasingly to be a harbinger of ill. Everything that had happened to them in the past months was because of the jewel box.

When Isaac Rosenthal left a short time later with the jewel box wrapped in his cloak, he seemed altogether calmer. But Murad Amrad was considerably less so. He looked at Sonja and shrugged. He felt incredibly afraid and had an overriding desire once again to protect his family. After a while he spoke.

"Sonja, I need to go out to think. Please make sure none of you leave the house until I return. The boys can remain with you today."

And with the remainder of the household still asleep, he dressed and slipped out.

The sky was only just beginning to lighten as he left, but the day was going to be hot, that much he could tell. It was now the end of August and the temperatures in the day were considerably higher than those they had been used to in Bialystok. They all wore lighter clothing now, of course. Valvel Levinson had taken them to his own family's tailor and dressmaker soon after their arrival in Odessa. But Murad Amrad still found it hard to acclimatise himself to the heat. He knew there was always a breeze from the sea however, and although he had no plan, it was towards the sea that he now walked.

He came down to the docks and sat on a pile of ropes, the activity on the dockside holding his attention and allowing his mind to remain empty for a while. Dockworkers yawned and stretched in the early morning sunshine. He heard them greet one another and laugh once or twice at a shared joke. Others consulted paperwork and began to give instructions. The harbour was coming to life. After a while he got up and walked further along the dock until he found himself standing beside the Steam Ship Yalta.

He looked at the vessel in awe for some time. There had been no chance to get close to the ship before and he hadn't appreciated how much larger it was than most of the other ships in the harbour. He assumed extra space was required to house the machinations of steam propulsion. The vessel had three masts and all her sails were furled. The chimney he had noticed from a distance rising up through the rigging looked vaguely incongruous at close proximity. Several horse-drawn trailers had arrived to stand beside the ship. They were heavily laden with large sacks. Then a group of men began to spring nimbly up and down the gangplank, transferring the loads from the trailers to the ship. They were obviously taking on provisions and cargo and Murad Amrad wondered if it was due to sail soon. He was beginning to feel very much in the way among the increasing activity however, and turned to leave. As he did so, he nearly collided with a man standing behind him on the dockside who, like him, appeared to be watching the proceedings. The man was in the uniform of a high-ranking sailor and Murad Amrad tilted his hat in greeting.

"Is this ship sailing soon?" Murad Amrad asked, as much to make conversation as in genuine interest.

"Indeed she is," replied the sailor, giving Murad Amrad a salute. "And I am her captain! We sail again at six this evening, bound for the Bosphorus."

"What is your cargo?" Murad Amrad asked, intrigued now despite himself.

The captain called out a series of instructions to the men on the deck before replying.

"Well, we are primarily a mail vessel, but we also take on passengers and cargo as and when we can. We arrived from Sebastopol on the Crimean Peninsular two days ago with a full cargo of passengers bound for Odessa. Now we have reloaded with grain."

The driver of one of the horse carts came up to him then and requested he sign a receipt for what Murad Amrad presumed was the delivered grain. The captain obliged before turning back to Murad Amrad.

"Once through the Bosphorus, we will sail through the Sea of Marmara then out through the Turkish Straights into the Aegean. There are many ports on the route and much mail to deliver and take on board. But the grain is bound for Jaffa. That is our final destination. Once there, we will take on a consignment of oranges, among other things, to bring back to Odessa."

"All the way to Jaffa!" Murad Amrad said in wonderment. He was surprised at the proposed length of the voyage.

"Indeed!" The captain looked amused. "Jaffa is the main trading port in Palestine. And now I must get back to work. I wish you good day." He gave another half salute and turned to go.

Murad Amrad felt as if everything was suddenly moving in slow motion. Renewed waves of panic washed over him as the captain walked away and he remembered why he was here. But the words the man had spoken had triggered a memory in his head. All at once the parting words of the rabbi in Bialystok had come back to him as clearly as if he was being told them once again:

"Even if you were to travel as far as the land of Israel, God would show you the way to be among friends," he had said. Murad

Amrad's mind was suddenly working very fast. He knew what to do, and he called out.

"Wait. Please wait a moment, sir. Do you have room for any more passengers on this trip?"

When Murad Amrad knocked at the door of the Levinson household on his way home, he was enormously relieved to find Valvel at home. His friend was surprised by his early visit, and even more so when Murad Amrad asked if they could talk. They walked to a café nearby and he listened as Murad Amrad told him the whole story of his flight from Bialystok and his reasons for now fleeing once again.

"The jewel box is ill fated, Valvel. I believe we will be better off without the wealth it might bring us. Let Isaac Rosenthal get what he can from its return to Count Alexei Petrovitch. I am done with it. We will go to Palestine and be free of this Russian curse once and for all. I will leave you to tell Isaac Rosenthal what you will. All I ask of you is to give us your blessing and your promise to see to the welfare of our horse. The children have become very fond of it." Murad Amrad suddenly felt choked and rose abruptly. "I have kept you too long," he said.

Valvel stood as well and the two men grasped hands. "I am forever indebted to you and to Razel," Murad Amrad said finally. "You have been good friends to us all. The best."

"You have my blessings, Murad," Valvel too was visibly moved. "This is a sad day for you but most definitely the most advisable course of action. There is too much at stake for you to stay."

Murad Amrad turned to leave, and Valvel watched as his friend marched with purpose along the street in the direction of his home.

From the minute he arrived back and told them all where they were going, Sonja was ecstatic. To go to Palestine, the land of Israel in her prayers, was beyond her wildest dreams. They would leave their troubles behind with the jewel box, she said, and she was glad they were not to benefit from it after all. Murad Amrad was inclined to agree with her. Abram merely sighed as he began to pack up his tools and silverware once again. Another country, another continent! There would never now be a headstone to mark Szejna's grave. But he knew it was marked forever in his heart, and she would have been so proud to know he would be producing his sacred silverware pieces in Palestine. To the children, it was another great adventure, and apart from the regret at having to say goodbye to Koenig, they had no qualms about leaving. Tomas especially felt a huge sense of relief at being spared the new religious school his father had found for him and his brother. He wasn't at all sure that God listened much and he would be quite happy never to have to read the *Torah* or speak Hebrew again. But he knew well enough to keep those thoughts to himself.

Later that evening, as the setting sun cast an orange wash over the sea, the Galperin family stood on the deck of the SS Yalta as it began to power west through the Black Sea, and watched the city of Odessa disappear. Once again they were on the run, but this time there would be no going back. This time they were going to the land of Israel, the birthplace of the Jews. Murad Amrad hadn't given much thought to this concept before, other than to pay it lip service in prayer, but now that they were on their way it felt the correct course of action. He felt they were headed in some way towards a spiritual home and he felt calm for the first time in many months. He shut his eyes and took in a deep breath of sea sprayed air. Then, putting one of his hands into the deep pocket of his coat, he closed it tightly around the leather pouch containing the diamond, and smiled.

JAFFA – PALESTINE: 1832 – 1834

The Steam Ship Yalta dropped anchor outside the ancient port of Jaffa in late September, the incessant throbbing of its engines finally stilled. There was no harbour for the town. Cargo and passengers from visiting ships were transferred the considerable distance to the shore in large rowing boats, each one manned by four oarsmen. Between the ship and the land, waves broke repeatedly over jagged rocks jutting out from the sea.

While waiting for the boats to reach them, the Galperin family stood along the deck of the ship and gazed in silence towards their new homeland. The wind in their faces was hot and carried unfamiliar scents and after the long summer the land appeared dusty and colourless. Jaffa itself was built high up on a protruding piece of coastline overlooking the open sea. They could see houses, minarets and a citadel, all contained within a castellated city wall. Below it waves lapped onto a white beach, on which they could just make out some horses and carts waiting for the cargo and mail from their ship.

Murad Amrad was impatient to begin his new life on that September day in 1832 and, if asked, would no doubt have been unaware of Jaffa's long and bloody past. But as the gateway to Palestine and Jerusalem, and the historical entrance to the Holy Land for Jewish and Christian pilgrims, Jaffa had long been a pivotal town in a part of the world destined to be a melting pot of political and strategic importance.

Jaffa had existed as a port for many centuries. The fortunes of the town had waxed and waned from biblical times; through Egyptian, Greek, Roman and Arabian rule, to occupation by the European Crusaders, and subsequently to its inclusion into the vast Turkish Ottoman Empire. Here the town had remained for the past three hundred years. But throughout its long history, Jaffa had been repeatedly destroyed and its inhabitants massacred in countless battles for its domination.

Under Turkish rule, the most recent destruction of Jaffa had taken place in 1799, when Napoleon had bombarded the port as he unsuccessfully tried to conquer Syria. After his withdrawal, Jaffa had remained in ruins for nearly ten years before being reconstructed by a new Turkish governor of the town, Muhammad Abu-Nabbut. He rebuilt the old city walls, redesigned the market squares, installed wells and built a new mosque. He became most known for the large water fountain he had built outside the town for the use of travellers on the road to Jerusalem. In the years since then, Jaffa had continued to develop its export trade and the town had become famous for its soap industry and its 'Jaffa' oranges. But the Ottoman government had actively discouraged all foreign and non-Muslim visitors to the area, more often than not forbidding them from landing at Jaffa or any of the other ports along the coast.

Shortly before the Galperin family's arrival however, the fortunes of the town changed once more, this time to their advantage. In November 1831, the governor of Egypt, Muhammad Ali, decided to invade Syria. This was an act of rebellion against Turkish Ottoman rule in Egypt. He sent the Egyptian fleet to Jaffa and his army, commanded by his son Ibrahim Pasha, duly occupied the town. A year later, Ibrahim Pasha had taken much of greater Syria from the Ottoman army, including the area within Greater Syria known as Palestine. By the time Murad Amrad and his family arrived in Jaffa, the city and the surrounding country was under Egyptian rule, with Ibrahim Pasha as its governor.

Had he but known it, the ease with which Murad Amrad and his family were able to enter Palestine via the port of Jaffa owed much to the new Egyptian government. Finding the area underdeveloped and the people very poor, Ibrahim Pasha had recognised the importance of modernising the country. Keen to open it up to Western influences and trade, he had immediately instigated new legislation that made it easier and safer for non-Muslims to visit. As a result, Christian pilgrims and foreign visitors like the Galperins were now beginning to arrive in increasing numbers, both to work and travel in Palestine.

But as Murad Amrad helped his family down the gangway into one of the rowing boats, together with the many boxes, sacks and the trusty handcart that constituted all they owned, his thoughts, like those of any traveller arriving in a foreign land, were merely full of the pressing problem of finding somewhere they could stay. He was unaware that the city was in the process of a major change of government. But it was a development that would inevitably affect his future, as well as that of the whole of Palestine.

When their boat finally ran onto the beach below the city, Abram climbed out first and fell to his knees to kiss the sacred ground. Murad Amrad nodded and grunted in approval as he helped Sonja and the children out of the boat, unloaded the luggage and paid the boatmen. But he didn't make the same act of homage as his father. There was much to keep him occupied and the moment passed. Sonja meanwhile appeared to be in a daze and the children almost beside themselves with excitement. He prayed they would find lodgings soon.

The captain of the Steam Ship Yalta had told them to go to Dar al-Yehud, an area in Jaffa where, ten years earlier, the Jewish community had built a synagogue and hostel for Jews on their way to visit the holy cities of Jerusalem, Hebron, Tiberias and Safed. Translated from Arabic the name meant 'The House of the Jews' and the area was the centre of the Jewish community in the city. But despite the captain's directions, navigating their way through the busy streets of Jaffa proved to be more difficult than they had imagined. Their progress was repeatedly hampered by the sheer volume of people and animals; a noisy heaving sea of life whose current was persistently contrary to theirs. Hanna and Elzbietta clung onto Fanny between them to prevent her from being swept away, Tomas and Utah held onto each other's coats and Sonja and Abram did their best to protect their possessions in the handcart as they all tried to keep Murad Amrad within sight.

After Murad Amrad thought he recognised a street for the second time, he called to his family to stop. The crowd behind them halted briefly then divided and jostled for the space they'd vacated. A donkey hesitated and staggered under the weight of its load as its rider whipped it on, steering it around them. They flattened themselves against the wall of the street and Murad Amrad tried to take stock of where they were. He had looked in vain for a fellow Jew to ask the way, but all around them voices spoke only in Arabic. The stench from open sewers, unwashed bodies, cooking food and animal dung was overpowering and he unconsciously placed his sleeve over his face as he looked around, but each narrow unpaved street looked very much like the next and the few shops they had passed were small, dark and uninviting. He had no doubt that they were completely lost. But he needed to put the safety of his family first, and from newly acquired habit he assumed it best to keep as low a profile as possible among strangers. Trying to remain positive, he beckoned the family on and they all had little choice then but to be swept along in the same direction as the majority of people, donkeys and camels around them.

Eventually, they were deposited into a market square, where the light and comparative freedom to move was a welcome relief. But the space was a whirl of alien sounds, smells and spectacles and offered no solution to their predicament. Around the edges of the square, shop fronts were dark and windowless. Over their gaping entrances, roughly constructed canopies were strung up offering shade from the heat of the sun, still intense enough to be uncomfortable despite the time of year. Under one of these, a group of men sat cross-legged on the ground. They were passing the mouthpiece of a Nargile pipe between them. This was something Murad Amrad and Abram were unfamiliar with and they covertly watched the process of sucking smoke through a long tube attached to a lamp like instrument, apparently filled with water. The smell of wood-smoke carried with it that of cooking meat mingled with a sweeter smell of spices and incense.

At one end of the square a group of women and children gathered water from a well. Some of the women filled clay pots that they then placed on their heads. Others loaded them onto each side of a donkey. They were laughing and talking in shrill voices. A number of the women had veils over the lower part of their faces and all had shawls over their heads. Around their feet a pack of mange-ridden wild dogs quarrelled over a discarded scrap of food and the children ran around unchecked.

In the centre of the square craftsmen and traders crouched on the rough dirt beside their merchandise, their camels hobbled behind them occasionally emitting loud gargling noises of complaint. These haughty looking creatures were as strange to the Galperins as the baskets of brightly coloured fruits, vegetables, dried spices and beans offered for sale. There were also clay pots and plates stacked in piles and gloriously coloured rugs and carpets heaped upon the ground, all with very little effort at display. Abram was immediately drawn towards a large collection of silver jewellery, quite different in style to that which he made.

Watching the people in the market square, Murad Amrad was of course aware that the majority of them were Arabs. Their robes and headdresses made them easily distinguishable as such, although the nuances of dress that identified members of a specific Palestinian or Egyptian tribe escaped him. There were a certain number of other men and women in the market who he could not immediately identify however. Their clothing was oriental in style and they were, for the most part, poorly dressed. Murad Amrad noticed that they seemed to be regarded with disdain by the Arabs in the market, who very pointedly turned away if any of them passed by. He observed one of these people, an old man, being spat upon by an Arab trader who then proceeded to shout what appeared to be abuse. The man seemed well used to such behavior, and merely turned and walked away. Murad Amrad was later to learn that these were Palestinian Jews.

In contrast to the Jews of the Russian Empire, who were Ashkenazi with probable German origins, the majority of Jews in Palestine in 1832 were Sephardic; descendants of a race of people who had originally come from Spain and Portugal. While both were alike in their religious interpretation of Talmudic Law and their modes of prayer, each spoke a different language and had a distinctly different way of life. They were, in effect, a different nationality of people. Sephardic Jews had lived in Palestine among the Arabs for many generations and had long been accepted as Ottoman subjects. But as non-Muslim inhabitants of a Muslim country they had no official rights and were regarded as 'rayah', a term used to refer to someone of inferior status. As such, they were often subject to maltreatment and injustice at the hands of the Arab population.

Ibrahim Pasha had recently introduced legislation to outlaw official discrimination against non-Muslims, but these were the early days of his rule and the new policy of tolerance towards Jews and other minority religions was not always enforced.

But Murad Amrad was still unaware of these facts, and he was pulled from his observations to see Abram having little success at communicating with the Arab Jewellers in the market square. There seemed no common language between them. Indeed his attempts were merely drawing attention to the family from other traders, whose faces were growing increasingly hostile and suspicious. In their distinctive dark clothes and with their strange speech, the Galperin's may not have been instantly recognised as Jews – Ashkenazi Jews were still a comparative rarity in the country at that time. But the Arab traders suspected them of being rayah nevertheless. They talked among themselves and many spat onto the ground in front of them before Murad Amrad took his father's arm and quickly led his family away.

It was then that he noticed a small group of European men and women conspicuous among the crowds of Arabs and Jews. The women carried parasols and were wandering among the goods on display rather aimlessly, while a young bearded man among them appeared to be engaging the men in animated conversation. Murad Amrad instinctively turned to avoid them.

But all at once the young man broke away from the group and walked briskly towards them, dodging through the traders and leaping over the baskets of produce with great confidence. On reaching them, he lifted his hat to Murad Amrad and Abram and introduced himself in Yiddish.

"My name is David Darmon," he said. "I could not help but notice that you seem lost and ill at ease. I am the Acting Consular Agent for America in Jaffa and I am happy to be at your service."

For a few seconds Murad Amrad didn't know what to say. He was deeply shocked to hear a stranger in European clothes addressing them in Yiddish. Then he remembered his manners and introduced himself, his father and his family. It occurred to him that they must look a ragged little group, and therefore little wonder that this stranger had noticed them among the crowds.

"We're most grateful to you," he said. "We are, however, not from America but from Russia."

"That's of no consequence," David Darmon smiled and waved his hand dismissively in the air. "I'm very happy to offer my protection and assistance to all travellers visiting Palestine, whatever their nationality or religion. Were I not, visitors such as you would be defenceless against the whims of the local authorities. I can at the very least help you find somewhere to stay."

"Then we'd be most grateful to accept your help, sir," Murad Amrad replied. There was no denying that he felt vastly relieved to have someone with whom to share the immediate responsibility of keeping his family safe. The Acting Consular Agent for America seemed a genial fellow and one who was obviously very eager to help.

"I'm afraid we are indeed lost!" he went on. "Until we can find more permanent accommodation, we had intended to find temporary lodgings at the Dar al-Yehud hostel."

David Darmon nodded in approval. "Then I'd be very happy to lead you to it."

"Thank you," Murad Amrad said. "And I must compliment you on your Yiddish!"

David Darmon chuckled. "Well I, like you, am an Ashkenazi Jew. I am from France, and Yiddish is the language of my childhood. Now come, I will show you the way to the hostel where you will be comfortable enough until we can find you more permanent accommodation." He turned away and indicated they were to follow him. Murad Amrad caught Abram's eye and his father smiled.

"This is a good omen, my son," Abram said quietly, as they left the market square. "A very good omen."

Murad Amrad was later to learn that the Acting Consular Agent spoke fluent Arabic as well as the Yiddish, Hebrew and French of his homeland. He also spoke enough of the strange Ladino language of the Sephardic Jews to get by. Strangely for an American Consular Agent, his weakest language was English. However, he had lived in Palestine for many years and his knowledge of the country was considerable. He was generally accepted and well thought of by the Arab population among who, because of his preference for

European dress, it was not commonly known that he was Jewish. It was a fact about which he preferred to keep quiet, remaining instead apparently impartial to any religious group.

When the American government had become concerned that the increasing number of their countrymen travelling in the area had no diplomatic protection, they had duly requested and been granted permission from Muhammad Ali to install an agent in Jaffa. They wanted someone to protect the needs and rights of their visiting nationals, and David Darmon had been highly recommended for the post. He was subsequently appointed, and was now in possession of his exalted status, with the protection of the American flag at his disposal. In addition, he was now absolved from any risk of being regarded as a rayah by the authorities.

David Darmon was to prove an invaluable asset to the Galperin family over the coming months. He began by finding them a small house to rent in the centre of Jaffa. As a matter of good manners he introduced Abram and Murad Amrad to the Sephardic Jewish elders and the local rabbi who, despite language barriers, welcomed the family cautiously. But the ways of the Sephardic Jews were very different, and Murad Amrad felt reluctant to join the Sephardim community. Instead, he was impatient to establish his business in Jaffa. To do this he needed to set up a line of trade with fellow jewellers and most of these were Arabs. David Darmon told him that there was one man whose approval they needed before they began to trade in the town. The man was a wealthy Arab merchant named Sheikh Abu al Khayr, and David Darmon told them he would be happy to arrange a meeting and act as interpreter. He suggested that a payment might speed things up, and having provided the suggested sum, Murad Amrad was now forced to wait patiently until word came from the Sheikh that their meeting could take place. But it was hard to be patient when they had no new income.

In the meantime, Sonja and the children did their best to acquaint themselves with their new town. Sonja was reluctant to let any of the children stray far from her side; it would be some time before she felt it was safe enough to allow any of them to run errands for her, a far cry from Bialystok where the children had complete freedom within the constraints of family rules. Instead, they explored Jaffa as a group. At first they were always getting lost down the myriad of shadowy alleyways, where figures ahead of them would disappear through doorways that were quickly shut as they approached. As they began to find their way about, they learnt where the best markets were and who were the more friendly traders. They even managed to pick up a few Arabic words to make shopping a little easier. And through trial and error in the kitchen on Sonja's part, they learnt about the strange new vegetables, fruits and spices for sale. But their favourite place was the beach. They would go down to the seashore in the early morning and watch, while the vast flocks of gulls hovered and swooped over the fishermen bringing in their catch. Sonja purchased the fish straight off the boats and cooked them the same day with salt and lemon juice. Sometimes, horsedrawn carts brought crates of oranges and lemons onto the beach, the delicate smell of the fruit doing much to temper the pungent and all pervading smell of fish. They would watch the crates being loaded onto waiting boats which were then rowed out to the ships at anchor way out from the shore. The seas were often quite rough and the oarsmen did not have an easy task. But they managed to manoeuvre their crafts through the reefs with great skill. They often returned with passengers, and Sonja would watch these people come ashore and feel all over again the miracle of stepping for the first time onto the shores of the land of Israel. She never lost an opportunity to remind the children how hugely privileged they were to be living here. This was where they belonged, she repeatedly told them; this was where God wanted the Jews to live.

The only shadow passing daily over Sonja's joy was that she found it hard to reconcile herself to the house they were in. It was dark, airless and cramped, and however much she scrubbed the floors and walls she never felt it was clean. She couldn't get rid of the putrid smell coming from the open sewers outside, into which they were expected to throw their slops. She felt hemmed in by the narrowness of the streets around her and frequently found herself thinking longingly of the wide-open spaces in Bialystok or of the luxurious apartment in Odessa. She was sufficiently pragmatic to understand that this was only the beginning of their new life however, and was determined to put on a brave face for the family. They should all be able to cope with a few deprivations until they got themselves established, she thought. But sometimes she would climb the outside stairs of their house onto the flat roof, where the air was cooler and fresher and she could see a small portion of the sea beyond the flat rooftops of the surrounding houses, and she would dream of living somewhere where she could see the ocean every day. It was this dream that comforted her.

Occasionally Sonja and the children encountered hostility. An Arab trader in the market would turn his back and refuse to serve them. Women at the well would jostle them and push them aside. Or people around them in the street would talk openly amongst themselves whilst looking at them, making it obvious through hand and facial movements that their presence was not welcome. These were small, infrequent events, but they were frightening nevertheless. Sonja realised that their inability to speak Arabic was a considerable barrier, but she also wondered if relations with the Arabs of Jaffa were made more difficult by the distinctive and unique way in which the family was dressed. Among the predominantly Arab population and the relatively small number of Sephardic Jews in the town, she had assumed they would not be recognised as Jews at all, but this did not seem to be the case. One day she decided to ask David Darmon if he thought they should dress in a different way when they went out, much as he himself did.

"Well, you wouldn't be the first Ashkenazi Jew in Palestine to use disguise to avoid persecution," David Darmon said, and then paused for maximum effect. He was a man who liked to be taken notice of and when Sonja looked suitably interested, he continued.

"One hundred years ago a group of Ashkenazi Jews came from Poland and settled in Jerusalem among the resident Sephardic Jews, much as you're doing here. They were very poor, but they wanted to build a synagogue, so they borrowed money from the local Arabs to do so. The synagogue was built but, as time went on, they were never able to repay their debt. The Arabs eventually became very angry and one day decided to set fire to the synagogue and attack the homes of the Ashkenazi Jews."

Sonja gasped at hearing this and David Darmon continued, pleased that his story was having the right effect.

"The Ashkenazi's were forced to flee from the city, and many disguised themselves by dressing as Sephardic Jews. For a long time afterwards, if any Jew was spotted in Jerusalem wearing Ashkenazi clothing, he was immediately set upon by the Arabs of the town."

"But that was a long time ago!" Sonja exclaimed.

"Many of the traders in Jaffa may remember the story from their parents and grandparents. Old wounds are easily reopened among these people. But you're right." David Darmon now smiled reassuringly. "This is indeed a story from long ago. And if the hostility you talk about is not for this reason, then it's merely because you're a recognised rayah. As a non-Muslim, they believe you have no rights and as such do not command their respect. There's nothing you can do."

Sonja thought for a while, and then she asked, "And what of the Ashkenazi Synagogue in Jerusalem?"

"Oh, that's become known as the *Hurva*, the 'Ruin'," David Darmon told her. "Maybe one day it'll be rebuilt by the few Ashkenazi Jews who have settled in Jerusalem since then. But for now, they too probably experience problems with the Arab residents."

"So there are still other Ashkenazi's in Jerusalem?" Sonja enquired.

"There aren't many living in Jerusalem at the present time," David Darmon answered. "But there are a growing number of Ashkenazi communities in Palestine and Syria. Many come from Europe and Russia much as you have done. A few come with their families, but others come to end their days here. They devote themselves to prayer and rely on *Halukka* (charity) to survive. Most for now have settled in the other holy cities of Safed, Hebron or Tiberias. But under Ibrahim Pasha's new regime of toleration, I imagine more will eventually make Jerusalem their home. The Sephardic Jews on the other hand have lived in Palestine for many generations and work where they can find it."

Much to Tomas and Utah's delight, the absence of an Ashkenazi community in Jaffa meant there were no study halls for Jewish boys in Jaffa. The male members of each Sephardic household were expected to school their sons in the scriptures at home. This Murad Amrad did too, but only once a week during *Shabbat*. For the rest of the time Sonja taught all the children together at home as before.

In exchange for a small fee David Darmon began to teach Murad Amrad and Abram the language and ways of the Arabs. Matters of etiquette and manners were of vital importance throughout Syria, he told them. Knowing the right way to behave could make all the difference between successful relations and hostile ones. He was a good teacher and although the language was difficult, he devised a way for them to learn which was, he told them, quick and easy. He wrote words in Arabic on small pieces of paper, with the same word in Yiddish on the other side. As the weeks went by, Murad Amrad found the Arabic gradually began to make sense, meanings suddenly appearing out of what had previously been a senseless arrangement of lines and squiggles. In the evenings, Murad Amrad passed the words on to Tomas and Utah and was fascinated by the comparative speed with which they picked the language up. It was important that they should learn Arabic too and he was glad to see they were so quick to do so.

A few days after his conversation with Sonja, David Darmon told Murad Amrad and Abram that he had been giving the subject of the family's safety and protection much thought.

"I am anxious to help you avoid trouble from the authorities," he told them. "As non-Muslim residents of Jaffa, you have no rights. With no documentation, you could easily find yourself held over any number of seemingly minor trading offences. I would like to offer you the protection of the American flag."

Murad Amrad looked slightly shocked. "But we are not American," he replied. "How can we receive their protection?"

"That need not be a problem," David Darmon replied. "I believe I could easily remove any legal obstacles, such as they may be. If you didn't mind paying me a small fee, just to pay for any expenses you understand, I'd be very happy to provide you with letters of protection."

"Can these letters really give us all security?" Murad Amrad sounded as doubtful as he felt.

"Indeed they can," David Darmon assured him. "The new Syrian Government has been ordered to protect and guard anyone seeking shelter with the American Consul. I am that person. A letter with my seal and name on it giving my protection is everything you will need." As he made this pronouncement, his smile grew even wider.

Murad Amrad exchanged a look with his father but learned nothing from it as to what Abram thought. His own opinion was that something didn't feel quite right. He looked back at David Darmon, whose open face appeared to give out nothing but well meaning. Murad Amrad suspected that the Acting Consular Agent for America was keen to make use of his new position of authority. There was no doubt that he was very proud of it. But what of it! If all it took to be able to trade with safety was to part with a small payment, then it was money well spent.

"Then I would be pleased to accept your offer," he finally said.

Sheikh Abu al Khayr (whose name meant 'one who does good') had all the bearing one would expect of an Arab leader. His movements were measured and graceful and he wore his clothes with a natural elegance. Under his turban, the tanned skin of his face was somewhat wrinkled from long exposure to the sun, but his black eyes were youthful and steady and his beard was neatly trimmed. In his mid-forties, Abu al Khayr was still considered young to hold the title of Sheikh. But since his father's premature death ten years earlier, his large and extended family had depended on him as its head. As a man of commonsense and learning he was much respected among the Arabs in Jaffa and he held considerable influence. It could be said that very little went on in the town without his notice.

Although Abu al Khayr hadn't been present in the market square when the Galperins had first arrived, he had nevertheless discovered much about the new visitors since. He had learned that they were Jews from Russia, and that although they spoke a different language they were educated men. He had also learned that they were jewellers and for this reason alone he was curious to meet them. He knew David Darmon as well as he knew anyone in the town and had duly responded to his request for an audience by giving him permission to bring the two Russians to his house. He never missed an opportunity to trade with other merchants and to build on the considerable collection of jewels and artefacts in his possession, but he had another reason to see the work of the Jewish jewellers.

The Sheikh and his family lived on a hillside behind the town. What had originally been a modest square stone house had continually been added to over the years to accommodate his growing family and give the women separate quarters. The resulting property appeared on the outside to be many houses attached to each other, rather than the single house of considerable size that it was.

On the ground floor, all the rooms opened out under stone arches into a series of interior courtyards separated by high walls. All the courtyards had their own well and shared between them a collection of mature trees that provided shade and privacy. Open stone steps led up the sides of the buildings to the upper rooms and onto the flat roofs. From here, access to each of the houses could be gained, and the many children of the family climbed between the properties like monkeys.

Sheikh Abu al Khayr was sitting in the courtyard of the largest house when David Darmon bought Abram and Murad Amrad to meet him. He had been thinking about his youngest wife, Fatima. He had two other wives and a great many children, but Fatima was most often in his thoughts. She was a Bedouin woman whose beauty had been much praised by her father and whose dowry had been considerable. Their engagement had taken a long time to arrange and all he had seen of her before their marriage was her extraordinary green eyes above her veil, eyes that often held his for a split second too long. He now knew Fatima's considerable beauty to be fact and the thought of it made him sigh. She was soon to be delivered of her first child and was therefore not available for his attentions. He hoped his mother and the other women were making her comfortable. Putting his mind resolutely away from her, he was glad to learn that his visitors had arrived.

David Darmon had suggested to Abram and Murad Amrad that they take some of their work to show the Sheikh, and they had thought long and hard about which pieces to take. They had already decided they would not be displaying their ceremonial Judacai silverware in Jaffa. These were sacred pieces and would mean nothing to Arabs, however impressive the craftsmanship. But they had been told that Sheikh Abu al Khayr bestowed a great deal of jewellery on his wives and that he had a considerable collection himself. They had noticed that the Arab jewellery for sale in the market was extravagantly decorated with chains, beads and even bells and they wondered how their more delicate work would compare in the Sheikh's eyes. Did he want to see their jewellery with the objective of buying or did he just want to assure himself of their ability? In the end they hoped the selection of gold and silver jewellery they had picked out would please him.

After formal introductions had been made, the three men sat with the Sheikh on brightly coloured rugs spread on the ground. An Arab serving boy waited on them, repeatedly refilling their tiny cups with thick, sweet coffee. Having told them that it would be considered rude to refuse more, David Darmon had advised them to leave some coffee in their cup when they'd had enough. That way it would not be refilled. This accomplished, their host invited them to take refreshment from a bowl of sweetmeats and another of figs. They were all silent as they ate. Murad Amrad and Abram were pleased to be able to concentrate on the constraints of not using their left hand. But once their eating was finished, the Sheikh began to make conversation, initially in the form of a barrage of questions. David Darmon translated for them all, but Murad Amrad was surprised at how much Arabic he could already understand after only a matter of weeks.

"Are you enjoying living in Jaffa?" the Sheikh asked.

"It is all very new for us but we are finding our way," Murad Amrad replied carefully. He believed the house they were renting was one of many owned by the Sheikh, and it would not do to complain about it.

"You have a wife?" the Sheikh surprised him with the personal question.

"Alas, no. I am widowed, and so is my Father."

"And not married again?"

Murad Amrad thought of the events of the past two years and shrugged. "I have been too busy. My cousin's widow looks after us."

"And you have not married your cousin's widow?" the Sheikh looked from one to the other of them incredulously.

Murad Amrad was embarrassed and clicked his tongue. The Sheikh turned to David Darmon and said something very fast. David Darmon laughed and shook his head. Murad Amrad shot him a questioning look.

"The Sheikh wanted to know if she is very plain. I told him no," David Darmon explained. He too looked embarrassed. Murad Amrad was anxious to change the subject, but felt the need to protect Sonja.

"She is a good woman," he said. "She teaches our children and looks after us all well. It is a good arrangement for us."

The Sheikh grunted, but thankfully moved on.

"You wish to trade in the market place." This was more of a statement than a question.

"We do," Murad Amrad said. "With your approval, we hope."

"Will you show me your work?" The Sheikh leant forward and directed his eyes towards the bag Abram carried. Abram duly unwrapped the jewellery and spread it gently on the ground in front of the Sheikh.

"You made all of this?" he asked, and Abram nodded, unable to keep the pride from his face. Murad Amrad wondered what the Sheikh was thinking, but he seemed to genuinely appreciate the fine work. He fingered the pieces delicately.

"And this is Russian style?"

"And European," Murad Amrad replied.

The Sheikh appeared deep in thought and did not speak for a long time. Somewhere beyond the courtyard wall, women's voices chattered softly and Murad Amrad heard one of them give a laugh. The rich smell of cooking meat hung in the air. A fly droned lazily around them and he longed to swipe at it. He became aware of the crying of buzzards and looked up. A group of the birds were swirling lazily on the thermals high above them. Even now, well into October, the sun shone out of a clear blue sky and the temperature was pleasantly warm. In Bialystok the bitter cold of winter would soon be on its way. His attention was caught by what appeared to be the head of a child ducking away from a higher window. He quickly looked away. Finally the Sheikh spoke.

"It is very fine," he said softly, almost to himself. Then he looked at Abram and Murad Amrad.

"Do you have a good workshop here in Jaffa?"

"We have not set one up. Our accommodation is very small, but perhaps we will find an area in the town that could be used as such." Murad Amrad hoped this was true.

Sheikh Abu al Khayr got up suddenly, but gestured for them to stay seated as he went inside. They remained, but were slightly at a loss as to what to do next. David Darmon shook his head and shrugged. Several minutes passed. When the Sheikh returned he was carrying a small leather pouch. Sitting back down, he opened the pouch and taking hold of Murad Amrad's hand he tipped the contents into it. Murad Amrad and Abram then looked down at the largest rough-cut ruby they had ever seen. The stone covered the palm of Murad Amrad's hand and was heavy to hold. They gazed at it in awe and didn't know what to say. The Sheikh then spoke.

"I am looking for someone to make a necklace to accommodate this stone," he said. "My youngest wife is soon to give birth to her first child. I wish to give her this as a gift. The Arab jewellers I know are not used to delicate work. But now I have seen some of your work I believe you would be able to design a piece of jewellery that is as beautiful as its wearer."

David Darmon was looking shocked and began clearing his throat a few too many times, no doubt in anticipation of Murad Amrad's reply. Murad Amrad meanwhile knew that to design and make this piece of jewellery was a task he and Abram would enjoy. But he recognised that it would also be a huge responsibility. The safety of the stone must be considered. Its value must be great and he wondered from where the Sheikh had acquired it. He was also aware of the great honour bestowed on them by the Sheikh's request and knew it was vitally important to communicate their response correctly. Having learned that Arabs love to haggle as much as Jews, he saw an opportunity and took it. He looked at David Darmon first and then at the Sheikh.

"Please tell the Sheikh we are deeply honoured," he began, and waited for David Darmon to translate before continuing.

"And my father would be proud to make him a piece of jewellery to match the beauty of his wife. But I believe we would find it difficult to ensure the safety of the stone if we were to craft the jewellery in our current accommodation. If the Sheikh could offer us alternative accommodation in part payment for making the necklace, one with a large and safe area to make into our forge and workshop, we would feel more confident in our ability to work on his stone safely."

Abram had a gleam in his eye as he looked at Murad Amrad. His son's ingenuity never failed to amaze him.

The Sheikh nodded and he too seemed impressed at the audacity of Murad Amrad's request.

"I admit the same thought had occurred to me," he said, and once again disappeared behind his thoughts. A fly landed on the white fabric of his sleeve. After a moment or two he slapped his hand down on it before replying.

"It so happens that I have a small house at the end of this road. As payment for my wife's necklace, you and your family are welcome to use it for one year. The house has a separate dwelling for animals that you could turn into a workshop. And there is space for your family to live in greater comfort."

"And after that year?" Murad Amrad was feeling emboldened by his success and knew it was expected of him to push for what he could get.

The Sheikh just shrugged. "Then we will see," he said.

Now it was Murad Amrad's turn to think. When he finally spoke, he knew he was pushing the Sheikh to his probable limits.

"I thank you for your offer of a property for us to use, but I believe it is not enough payment to merely provide us with a temporary place of work. There is our livelihood and the price of gold to consider. I will have to insist on a nominal payment as well if we are to take on this assignment."

The Sheikh's dark eyes had grown hard but he smiled stiffly. "You barter like an Arab, my friend." He paused with his hands in front of him, his fingertips touching. "I will give you a payment, half immediately, and half on completion of the necklace." He then named a modest sum, emphasising the number with his fingers. "And that is my final offer," he said.

Murad Amrad was keen to keep up appearances and refrained from replying for as long as he dared. But in reality he was jubilant. He looked forward to telling Sonja that they could at last move out of the town. This was the piece of luck he'd been praying for – a gift from God. And after a few long seconds he held out his hand.

"I agree," he said.

The Sheikh smiled. "Then you have my word," he replied, and after he'd shaken their hands, he placed his over his heart. They stood up then and Murad Amrad knew the deal was secure. David Darmon had told them that an Arab was always true to his word as a point of honour.

When the family moved out of the town and into the house the Sheikh had provided for them, they were forced to make several journeys with their handcart in order to transport all they now owned. Sonja had been a frequent visitor to the market over the past few weeks and had restocked her kitchen with cooking pots, plates and many diverse food items, as well as new rugs and cushions for their home.

The dusty track they followed took them up the hill out of Jaffa and past the collection of properties inhabited by Sheikh Abu al Khayr and his family. Half a mile further on, their new home was a traditional square building with outside stone steps leading up to the flat roof. On the ground floor of the house, the one large room had small windows all around, a substantial brick oven, an old table that needed some attention and two doors to the outside, one at the front and the other at the back. The only access to the two upper rooms was from the roof, but they were delighted to see that each of the rooms was equipped with wooden bunks.

At the back of the house, a covered well included a generously sized washing area. The rest of the back garden was edged with ancient cacti. The land was dry, barren and neglected however, and the brick built animal shelter the Sheikh had suggested they turn into their forge was half buried under a great deal of dead vegetation. But from the garden, over the tops of the houses beneath them, they could see all the way to where tiny palm trees rose up along the thin white line of gleaming beach. Beyond that was the open sea, which even at that distance was a myriad of oceanic colours. Sonja closed her eyes and breathed in deeply. She imagined a garden filled with growing vegetables and a forge up and running. She was suddenly convinced that she could even smell the sea, its salty breath carried on the westerly wind, along with the thin diluted wailing of the call to prayer from the minarets in the town below.

"We have come home," she said quietly. "This is where we will build our new life," and she opened her eyes to see Murad Amrad looking at her.

He was smiling. It was good to see Sonja so happy and he had suddenly felt a huge wave of affection for her. The wind had blown much of her hair from beneath the scarf she had taken to wearing and she looked most comely. He found himself wondering if he could think of her as someone other than a cousin. He could never replace Tamara, but Sonja would make him a good wife and perhaps it was time to move on. He suddenly realised that Sonja was looking at him expectantly. He had been staring. Embarrassed, he immediately checked his thoughts and turned away, speaking slightly more gruffly than he had intended.

"It is indeed, if only for a year."

But nothing could dampen Sonja's enthusiasm for the considerable task ahead. And there was much to do for it to be acceptable to her high standards. She and the girls immediately began to sweep away the years of dust, wash down the walls and floors and repair the shelving, shutters and cupboards. The brick oven was in good condition and once she had scrubbed it clean, Sonja set a fire and began to make bread. The family still needed feeding and her mind was busy as she mixed the dough. She must buy some chickens from the market now that they had space to keep them. And wine too. Neither the Sephardic Jews nor the Arabs drank wine and she was keen to produce her own. She must buy grapes and sugar and some more jugs.

As they slowly cleared the debris from the animal shelter and stripped away the vegetation growing over it, Murad Amrad and Abram found the building to be of a good size. It was hard work, but the sooner the task of setting up the workshop was accomplished, the sooner they could begin work on the Sheikh's necklace. They were hoping this would be the first of many such commissions.

Tomas and Utah were frequent visitors, bringing water for their father and grandfather to drink and reporting back to Sonja and the girls as to the progress the two men were making on the forge. On one such visit, Tomas made an observation.

"This is too big a building for just a workshop, Father. We should perhaps get a donkey and a cart to help us to and from the town." Tomas's desire for a replacement for Koenig was transparent and Abram caught his eye and winked.

Murad Amrad just grunted however, and Tomas knew better than to begin nagging at his father. He would bring the subject up again at a later date and was reasonably confident that his grandfather would support the suggestion. For now, he and his brother had been given the job of clearing the garden, doing what they could to turn over the stony earth. It was proving a difficult job. The ground was hard and dry, but they would do their best. Sonja wanted to plant vegetables as soon as the first of the winter rains had softened the earth. The boys were also required to build her a chicken pen.

As it happened, Tomas did not have to bring up the subject of a donkey again. On a visit to the town some days later, Murad Amrad passed an Arab peasant crouched beside the street. The man was thin and dressed in rags, and as Murad Amrad walked by he said something. Murad Amrad didn't understand his words, and in any event his thoughts were elsewhere. He just assumed the man was begging and tossed him a coin. But at once the Arab began to shout angrily. Murad Amrad stopped and turned around, now doing his best to concentrate on what the man was saying.

"I ask if you want to buy my donkey and you throw me a coin?"

Murad Amrad was confused. How could he not have understood correctly? He hadn't particularly noticed the emaciated donkey tethered at the man's side. He bent down and took the coin back, then said in halting Arabic.

"Your donkey is very thin. He will not be able to work."

"Ppff!" the Arab made a derogatory sound. "He is just hungry. He works well!"

Later, when Murad Amrad arrived home with the donkey, the children were overjoyed by his purchase. They gathered around the animal, taking turns at petting him and asking a dozen questions.

"I know nothing about this donkey," Murad Amrad said with a chuckle, handing the leading rope to Tomas, "but I was told he is hungry!"

"Is that his name?" Fanny asked. They all laughed then, but from that moment, 'Hungry' was indeed his name. They made him a stable at the back of the workshop, and in the absence of anything else to feed him, Sonja found some old bread and vegetable trimmings from the kitchen.

"We must buy grain for him tomorrow, Father," Tomas instructed. "And we must build a cart." Murad Amrad smiled in satisfaction. The boy was right. It was a reasonably large donkey and once it had recovered its health, its strength would be of enormous assistance to them all. There would certainly be no more need for him to haul the handcart up and down the hill to and from the town.

Meanwhile, Sonja was not unaware of the way Murad Amrad had been looking at her of late, and she had been giving the matter a great deal of thought. There was no denying that she was flattered by his attentions. In fact, part of her longed to encourage him. Although Isaac had been pale and learned, as was considered desirable in a Jewish man, there was something about Murad Amrad's strength and vigor that she found very attractive. She felt safe around him, comforted by his confidence and resourcefulness. She knew that should she allow it, his possible romantic notions could be nurtured and allowed to develop. But of greater importance to her was her concern for what the future might hold in store for her daughter, Fanny. And with this in mind, she had formulated an idea that made any other change to her position in the family impossible.

She had concerns for all three of the girls, of course. Thanks to her continued efforts to teach the children in a wide variety of subjects, the girls were as well educated as Tomas and Utah. But she now feared that they would find it hard to meet anyone in Jaffa who would make them good enough husbands. She had once brought this subject up with Murad Amrad. Indeed, she had felt it her duty to do so. But he had not been keen to pursue it.

"The girls are too young for us to be thinking like this," he had said severely. "When our business is more established in Jaffa, I will visit Jerusalem. There will be other Ashkenazi families there and when the time is right I will make enquiries."

He had then refused to discuss it further. She had recognised that it was hard for him to talk about things he should have been discussing with Tamara. But while Hanna and Elzbietta were Murad Amrad's responsibility, Fanny was not. It was for her to think of ways to make sure her own daughter's future was secure.

When the idea of how this could be accomplished came to her, it was such a simple solution that she wondered why she hadn't thought about it before. Of course there was a risk that Murad Amrad may not approve of it, in which case she would have to think again. But if he did, she need never worry about Fanny again. All she had to do now was to speak to him as soon as possible, before he might say something that would cause them both any embarrassment. She began to look for an opportunity to be with him alone, and when one such presented itself, Sonja took it.

"Murad Amrad, there is something I need to discuss with you that is of extreme importance to me," she began. Murad Amrad had been busy in the workshop, but he stopped what he was doing and looked up when Sonja came in. She took a deep breath.

"I remain eternally grateful to you for giving me and Fanny your protection over the past two years. But lately I have begun to fear for the future of my daughter should anything happen to me. If Isaac were still alive it would be different. But he is not here and I would like to know that an arrangement for her benefit is in place. As you know, I have been concerned about the future of all the children, but because of my position in this family it is Fanny who is the most vulnerable." Sonja hesitated before going on. She suddenly felt extremely nervous about Murad Amrad's reaction to her idea. He had been shaking his head while she spoke, and was drawing breath to say something. She held up her hand and continued in a rush. It was too late to stop now.

"I have been thinking that if Fanny and Tomas were to wed, both of them would face the future together and I will know she is to be cared for."

The silence that followed clamoured to be filled with words.

But none came. Murad Amrad's eyes stayed fixed on hers for what seemed a very long time. But still he said nothing. She searched his face, but could find no clues as to his true thoughts. He hid them well. Finally he turned away and went back to work and Sonja found that her legs were shaking as she quietly left the workshop.

It was a number of days before she received his response, but eventually it came.

"I think your idea an excellent one, Sonja," he said gently. "The future of all the children is naturally of great concern to me, and the girls especially must be taken care of. With this arrangement, I believe both Fanny and Tomas will benefit greatly, and there will only be the marriages of Utah, Hanna and Elzbietta to concern ourselves about." Sonja noticed that Murad Amrad avoided looking directly at her as he spoke. She saw hurt in his eyes and for that she was sorry. But she saw joy as well, and she knew that he, like her, was content to put the happiness of his eldest son before his own.

So the betrothal of Tomas and Fanny was agreed upon. When the prospective bride and groom were told about the arrangement they merely giggled, more interested in returning outside to continue their game. Being only eleven and ten years old respectively, they were still young enough to take little notice and carried on much as before, as childhood playmates living under the same roof.

During the weeks that Abram worked on the Sheikh's necklace, Murad Amrad took a collection of their gold and silver jewellery down to the main market square each day. He was keen to find customers for their work. Initially he encountered a certain amount of resentment on the part of the Arab jewellers. But in his halting Arabic, he did his best to reassure them that his jewellery would not compete with theirs. Showing it to the Arabs, he imagined that they found the work impossibly delicate. But they turned each item over and inspected it as the professional craftsmen they were, and eventually seemed content to accept him as a fellow trader.

Murad Amrad discovered that the traders were Bedouin, members of nomadic Arab tribes who lived in tents in the desert. Their extraordinary jewellery was made according to traditional Bedouin style; the highly ornate pieces made of silver, set with many beads and stones, with a great many dangling appendages. From what he could understand, the Bedouin traders told him that many of the stones used and the motifs engraved had healing or protective powers, a fact he privately thought was rather fanciful. They explained that it was traditional for an Arab woman to be presented with jewellery by her husband at various times in her life, such as on her marriage and each time she gave birth. He had noticed that the Bedouin jewellers were never short of customers and remembered that most Arabs had more than one wife, each of whom presumably had many children. He chuckled to himself as he deduced how many times a husband might need to buy jewellery. No wonder the Bedouin traders did so well, he thought.

It quickly became apparent however that the market for his jewellery would primarily be with the European visitors to Palestine, of which there was an increasingly steady stream. They arrived in Jaffa off the ships from Russia and Europe. Some came on a pilgrimage to visit Jerusalem and the other holy cities. Others were seasoned travellers, curious to visit what was known as the Orient. For many of them Abram's jewellery seemed to provide the right combination of what they perceived to be oriental craftsmanship and the more delicate style of jewellery traditionally favoured by European women.

But as the autumn months turned into winter and the seas became increasingly stormy, the ships brought fewer visitors and Murad Amrad found he went down to the town less frequently. For the same reason, David Darmon was not kept quite so busy offering the services of both himself and the American flag to visitors from Europe. With more time on his hands, he was a frequent visitor to the Galperin household where he began, for a slightly larger fee than before, to teach the rest of the family the rudiments of Arabic.

Although the winter was mild when compared to the harsh temperatures they were used to in Bialystok, it was still surprisingly cool with a great deal of rain. But their house had quickly become a comfortable home and it kept them dry and warm. Sonja planted her vegetables and kept her chickens as she had planned. She also bought a small olive tree from the market during that first winter, and planted it in the very centre of the garden.

On precisely the same day that the Sheikh's youngest wife Fatima gave birth to a baby boy, Murad Amrad and Abram were able to send a message to Sheikh Abu al Khayr informing him that his necklace was finished. On the following day they received a message back from the Sheikh inviting them to bring the necklace to the house that afternoon, and it was with some trepidation that they walked down the track to the Sheikh's house. They had asked David Darmon to come with them to translate.

Sheikh Abu al Khayr greeted them with his hands held together in front of him. "*Asalamu alaykum,*" (Peace be with you) he said, and they replied as they had been taught, "*Wa alaykum salam,*" (And peace be with you).

"I hope you are comfortable in my little house?" the Sheikh said. "It hasn't been lived in for a while, but it is sound enough."

"We have been very happy to make it so," said Murad Amrad. "And my family are very content there."

The Sheikh showed them into an inside room this time, a room whose ceiling was heavily beamed with timber. It was opulently and colourfully furnished. Thick cushions and rugs were arranged on the floor around a low brass table and the room was well lit by ornate lamps. At one end there was an open fire, whose smoke escaped through a chimney set into the wall. They sat at the table and the Sheikh beckoned to his young servant to bring coffee and sweetmeats. They ate and drank in silence as before. Then, with the social obligations completed, the Sheikh tipped his chin towards the serving boy who cleared the table. Finally, Sheikh Abu al Khayr indicated that Abram should open the pouch in which the necklace lay. Murad Amrad noticed that his father's hands were shaking as he unwrapped the fine leather and carefully laid his work on the gleaming brass surface.

What lay in front of the Sheikh was a pedant the size of the palm of his hand. It was a flower, created from rubies and pearls, a piece of work so intricate, so extravagant and so bold that even the Sheikh made an involuntary gasp. Abram had crafted six teardrop shaped rubies around one large central ruby. He had set each ruby in gold, and welded them together to form the flower shape. He had filled the spaces between the rubies with pearls so that it appeared the flower had been drawn in white and coloured with red. The necklace was hung on what looked like a ribbon of gold interlaced with minute pearls and rubies. It was in fact a multi-linked chain created in much the same way as some of the Bedouin jewellery Abram admired. He had taken it for granted that as the Sheikh's wife was from a Bedouin tribe, she would appreciate a piece of jewellery that was in some way familiar and in which she'd feel comfortable. At the same time, the Sheikh had wanted her to have something more delicate and infinitely more valuable than anything she already owned, and Abram now prayed that the result would be favourable to them both. He had also created a set of teardrop shaped ruby earrings set in gold and surrounded with pearls to complete the set. There was no doubt that this was probably the finest work he had ever completed.

"This is good," the Sheikh mumbled to himself, and gradually he began to smile. Then he said it again, only louder. "This is very good." He looked at Abram. "Thank you, my friend. This is indeed something as beautiful as my wife."

Following the completion of the ruby necklace, and with the arrival of spring, Abram and Murad Amrad found they were kept increasingly busy. The town was full of visitors once more, and inspired by his design of the ruby necklace, Abram was producing a new style of affordable pieces for sale in the markets. He was pleased with the results of his efforts and the sales were good, but they had not yet received another commission.

David Darmon was once again occupied by his consular duties, and although he continued with the family's Arabic lessons as often as was possible, the occasions became less and less. However, they were all gaining in confidence and ability in the language and had reached the stage when they discovered new words and phrases each time they went out.

Every day, on his way to and from the town, Murad Amrad drove the donkey cart past Sheikh Abu al Khayr's house. One evening, on his way home, he found the Sheikh apparently waiting for him. They exchanged greetings and the Sheikh invited him inside. Murad Amrad tied the donkey up and followed his host into the shady courtyard where the comparative cool was a welcome relief. After a long day in the town he was hot and thirsty and he gratefully accepted a tumbler of water from the well. The now familiar dark coffee followed, and once that had been savoured in silence, he and the Sheikh began to talk. It was the first time they had spoken together without the assistance of David Darmon and they talked slowly and carefully at first, the Sheikh enquiring as to the health of Murad Amrad's family, who in turn enquired as to the well being of the Sheikh's baby and wife. They then moved on to other subjects, and although certain words and phrases were occasionally lost to Murad Amrad, the conversation generally flowed well. When the time came to bid farewell to the Sheikh, Murad Amrad found that he had thoroughly enjoyed the meeting. From then on Murad Amrad very often found the Sheikh waiting for him on the track outside his house, and the two men began to form a tentative friendship based on mutual respect and a shared interest in precious stones and jewellery.

As the year progressed towards another autumn, Murad Amrad increasingly found the Sheikh to be a worried man, and many of the concerns he spoke of were endorsed by the whispers Murad Amrad overheard in the markets. The Egyptian Government was not proving popular.

"There is growing unrest in Syria, my friend," the Sheikh told him.

Murad Amrad replied carefully. "I have heard many people in the town say as much, Sheikh."

Sheikh Abu al Khayr tutted. "Ibrahim Pasha is his father's puppet and the puppeteer Muhammad Ali seeks to devour our country in order to boost Egypt. The Egyptian Government now demands that peasants, farmers and even Bedouin join their army. The sons of Syria enter the mouth of the Egyptian Army and are chewed up and digested and never seen again. Why should Syria have to provide soldiers for the Egyptians?"

His fervour had gathered momentum as he spoke, and he now hit his forehead with the palm of his hand in anger and remained silent for a few seconds. Murad Amrad was reluctant to enter into any political tirade against the Egyptian Government. From what he understood of everything David Darmon had taught him, the minority groups in Palestine and Syria, such as the Jews and the Christians, owed a great deal to Ibrahim Pasha. His rulings had allowed Jews like himself to trade without persecution. But it was hard not to sympathise with Sheikh Abu al Khayr as he continued. This time he sounded worried rather than angry.

"The conscription laws have caused me to have a problem, my friend. Many of my younger farm workers have been taken away to join the Egyptian Army. Meanwhile the oranges and lemons in my orchards are ripening and I have no one to harvest them. If the fruit is not picked I lose money, that is true." The Sheikh flicked up his chin and made a dismissive movement with his hand as if to demonstrate that the income was not of much consequence.

"But there is a greater danger. To encourage as many Egyptians as possible to settle here and build their houses, the government is seizing any land it considers to be lying idle, and passing it on to Egyptian farmers. Leaving fruit to rot on the trees will give the impression of untended land and I am fearful it may be taken from me. This land has been in my family for many generations, and that includes the little farmhouse in which you live. I will not let the Egyptians take it. I intend to keep it for my sons."

Sheikh Abu al Khayr paused again. He was clearly upset now, and Murad Amrad wasn't sure where this conversation was leading. Was the Sheikh about to remind him that their agreement should be terminated at this time? Would he have to break the news to Sonja that they had to find somewhere else to live? He was well enough acquainted with the Sheikh by now to know that it was unlikely he would speak before having a plan in place, and he didn't have long to wait before he learned what that was, although it came as some surprise.

"I believe we can both be of service to each other, Murad Amrad. While you are living in the farmhouse, your presence will keep it safe from the hands of the Egyptian Government, but only for as long as the farm remains in my keeping. I have few workers remaining to ensure the upkeep of my farm however, so it is in danger. In return for allowing you to remain in your home for a further year, will you and your family help to pick the harvest?"

Murad Amrad didn't need to think for long.

"We would be pleased to do so," he said.

The orange groves belonging to Sheikh Abu al Khayr were extensive and stretched far over the hills behind his house. He had seen the potential of planting the fruit trees many years before, and although he had known it would be a long time before his investment paid off, as a wealthy man he had been able to afford to wait. Much of his considerable income had come from the renting out of his properties in the town. But now that his fruit trees were mature, the oranges and lemons they bore were fast becoming an equally important source of income, despite his reluctance to admit as much to Murad Amrad. Because the new steam ships were able to carry the fruit to ports all over Europe at greater speed, the demand for the citrus fruits of Jaffa was growing with each passing year.

By taking the track outside their house up the hill rather than down towards the town, Tomas, Utah and Fanny had already discovered the Sheikh's fields while collecting firewood for the forge. When Sonja released them from their lessons each day, and after they'd finished their chores around the house, the fields had become a favourite location for their games. The previous year, soon after their arrival, they had watched the orange harvest from a distance. They had even managed to pick up some of the fallen fruit from the track to take back to Sonja.

When they learned that the whole household was to be involved with the same harvest this year, the children were thrilled. To work outside in the fields instead of doing their lessons was something to celebrate, after all. For Murad Amrad and Abram too, it was the perfect time to be doing something different. It was now late autumn and once again the markets in Jaffa were emptying of European visitors. And to know that as a result of their labours they would be able to stay in their home for another year, made the task all the more worthwhile.

They were soon to discover that stripping the oranges and lemons from the trees was a task that would continue for many weeks. Day after day they filled crates and baskets. They then loaded the containers into the donkey cart and took them down to the market in the town, from where the Sheikh arranged its sale and transportation. Their donkey wasn't the only animal working for them. The Sheikh had loaned them a larger cart, pulled by a feisty grey horse more suited to being ridden than harnessed between the shafts of a cart. But both animals eventually settled into the monotonous routine of hauling load after load of fruit down the hill into Jaffa, then carrying whoever was riding in the cart back up to the fields.

Sometimes the Sheikh's oldest son Ameen helped them. He was of much the same age as Tomas and Utah, and after an initial period of shyness between them, the three boys began to get on well. They chatted amicably as they picked and loaded the fruit, and it provided a good opportunity for Tomas and Utah to practice their Arabic. When Ameen was around however, the boys tended to ignore Fanny, who had then to be content with the company of Hanna and Elzbietta. Sonja privately thought this a good thing. Fanny had been playing with the boys consistently since their arrival in Jaffa. At eleven years old, it was time she became used to the ways of women. They, after all, were the keepers of the home.

One day in November, Tomas, Utah and Ameen returned from the town in great excitement, calling out to the family as soon as they were within earshot of the field where they were working. They had been taking a consignment of oranges down to the town as usual, but now their faces were flushed and both animals were breathing heavily. It was obvious that they had been driving the carts back up the hill fast and Abram was shocked. Tomas and Utah were usually extremely sensible. As they pulled up, he began on impulse to chastise them for their thoughtless behaviour.

"You could break a wheel driving like that. And the animals could become lame on the uneven ground. You know this, Tomas." But then he stopped. The boys seemed desperate to speak and he was suddenly aware that something must have happened.

"Forgive us, Grandfather." Tomas addressed Abram first, then turned to his father. "Father, the town is full of Egyptian troops. The roads are filled with hundreds of men on horses, long lines of camels and loaded wagons. Everywhere there are people who have come out to watch. Sheikh Abu al Khayr told us to come straight home and tell you that Ibrahim Pasha has brought the Egyptian Army to Jaffa. They are to set up camp in the hills on the other side of the town, the Sheikh said. And he told us to bring no more fruit down to the town today. The roads are too busy."

Having left two thousand of his troops to guard the city of Jerusalem, Ibrahim Pasha proceeded to set up his winter headquarters just outside Jaffa. Of the thousands of men encamped on the hillsides, many had their wives and families with them. There were also the usual camp supporters: doctors, blacksmiths, butchers, cooks and tailors, as well as thousands of horses, hundreds of camels and huge flocks of sheep, all of whom needed feeding and providing for. By the end of the winter the influx of people and animals introduced into the town with the army had pushed the town's resources to its limits. But the presence of the army also did much to boost the town's profits in an otherwise quiet time. Abram and Murad Amrad benefited every bit as much as many other merchants and traders.

By the spring of 1834, they were becoming concerned that their stocks of precious metals and jewels were running low. Sheikh Abu al Khayr told them that most Bedouin tribesmen had access to silver and copper. But if they wanted gold and precious stones, it was better to trade with the tribesmen in the Negev Desert to the South. From them they would be able to buy everything they needed and more. These tribesmen traded with merchants from India, East Africa and Iran, from whom they purchased gold, jewels and ancient artefacts, he told them. It was they who had sold him the priceless ruby Abram had worked on, and it was on such a journey to buy jewels that he had found Fatima and fallen in love with her green eyes.

Murad Amrad decided that he too needed to travel south to trade with these men, but it was not a journey to be undertaken without a guide or protection. He didn't know the land and there were many armed bandits roaming the hills. To travel on your own was not advisable. So when Sheikh Abu al Khayr suggested that he accompany him into the desert to visit Fatima's family, he felt it was the answer to a prayer. His wife was anxious to see her mother, the

Sheikh told him, and he had received word that her tribe was at Be'er Sheva, a large well on the northern edge of the Negev Desert in southern Syria.

"And perhaps you will find a Bedouin bride as well, my friend." The Sheikh laughed. He teased Murad Amrad mercilessly about his lack of a wife. But Murad Amrad now knew better than to reply to the Sheikh's comments with anything more than humour. And this time he was too grateful to the Sheikh for providing him with the protection he needed to take offence.

It would take them about a week to reach their destination, but Murad Amrad was to discover that it would take considerably longer than that to organise. There was transport to be arranged, provisions to be packed up and bearers to be chosen. Sheikh Abu al Khayr did not consider it safe for Fatima to take her baby and had instructed his mother to care for him while they were away. He was nevertheless keen to take Ameen.

"It will make a man of him to accompany us to the desert," he told Murad Amrad. "And you should bring Tomas. The boys will benefit from the journey."

Murad Amrad was surprised by the Sheikh's suggestion, but when discussing it later with Sonja and Abram, they too were very much in favour of the idea.

"The boy is nearly of Bar Mitzvah age and should be given the chance to be included in such a valuable trip," said Abram.

"He should also be attending prayer meetings at the synagogue," Sonja retorted, half under her breath. She never missed an opportunity to draw Murad Amrad's attention to what she felt was Tomas and Utah's lack of spiritual education. Although she did her best, she believed the boys should be studying in a Hebrew school and at an Ashkenazi synagogue. Once they reached the age of thirteen, they would be considered adult in Jewish law and as such should be participating in religious formalities.

Murad Amrad sighed and did his best to placate her.

"When I return from this trip, Sonja, I will make enquiries about taking the boys to Jerusalem."

He knew that in her heart Sonja understood how important it had been for them to establish a life for themselves in Jaffa before anything else. But she was right. For the sake of his children's future, he would have to seek out other communities of Ashkenazi Jews for the children to be with.

Eventually Sheikh Abu al Khayr's party was ready to leave, but not without some last minute adjustments. The Sheikh insisted that both Murad Amrad and Tomas dress as Arabs and it took them some time to arrange their clothing correctly. Murad Amrad was glad that the flowing Arab robes made concealing his purse a great deal easier than his normal belted tunic. He was carrying a considerable sum of money.

"You'll also be grateful of the cover in the hot sun, my friends," the Sheikh assured them as he watched them fiddle with their headdresses. "You can bring the sides of your scarf across your face should you need to disguise or protect yourself." He demonstrated with his own scarf. "And we will attract less attention than if we were a mixed bunch of Arabs and Jews."

He did not need to elaborate further. Murad Amrad had known for some time that friendship between Arabs and Jews in Palestine was fairly unusual.

THE NEGEV DESERT,
SOUTHERN SYRIA – 1834

It was past the middle of May when they left Jaffa to travel south, a curious caravan for all their disguises. Murad Amrad and Tomas walked alongside their donkey whose saddlebags were filled with provisions. The Sheikh had advised them that the terrain was unsuitable for a cart of any kind. Ameen and the Sheikh each rode a horse and led a third, intended for Fatima, although the Sheikh explained that she was more accustomed to camels than horses. Of five camels, two were loaded with baggage and one with bundles of fodder for the animals. Two Arab bearers led the three pack camels, taking turns to ride a large mule. Fatima and her girl servant had charge of the remaining two camels and alternated between leading the animals and riding them. The two bearers and the Sheikh carried rifles slung over their shoulders, and all wore curved knives at their waists.

Murad Amrad knew nothing about camels and he found them faintly alarming. It seemed to him that they responded to whatever they were directed to do with disapproval, gargling loudly and producing a great deal of phlegm that flew out from between their teeth in spumes of froth. Their actions on getting up or lying down appeared to him to be jerky and cumbersome. But the ease with which their riders remained on the backs of these extraordinary animals, as they bent their legs to lie down or straightened them to rise to a stand, was impressive.

This was the first time Murad Amrad had seen Fatima. As he was considered subordinate to her husband, there was no need for her to be veiled in front of him. But she wore a shawl wound around her head that could be pulled over her face should the necessity arise. She was slim and barefooted. Her long black skirt and shawl were richly embroidered, and her top and sash made from a red and gold fabric that shimmered in the light. Her arms were decorated with numerous bangles, and at her throat Murad Amrad saw Abram's necklace, which pleased him. Although he knew that it would not be polite to look at her directly or to address her, he was nevertheless able to catch the occasional glimpse of her face, framed by long black braids, and could acknowledge her fabled beauty for himself.

Each day they kept to very much the same routine. They travelled until shortly before nightfall, at which time they stopped and made camp, erecting simple canopies under which to sleep. They dined on flat bread, *labneh* (a soft white cheese), dates and nuts, after which they slept. The following day would start before daybreak when the bearers served coffee, bread and cheese. Everything was then packed up and reloaded onto the animals and, as dawn broke, they were back on their way. In the middle of the day, when the sun was at its hottest, the bearers made a fire and produced a hot meal of rice and cooked lamb. After this they rested for a couple of hours before continuing on the journey.

The tracks they followed were poorly marked, sometimes barely more than small indentations on the earth that wound their way through swampy valleys where wild flowers grew in abundance, and zig-zagged over rocky hills where trees and bushes struggled to survive in the thin soil. They occasionally passed through a village, the simple houses built entirely of mud with grass roofs. The land around each village had usually been roughly ploughed and cultivated; Murad Amrad saw one man using a camel to pull a simple wooden plough. But it was evident that the Arab peasant farmers were very poor and visitors were infrequent. When they rode into a village with the intention of filling their gourds with water from the well, their presence created a great deal of excitement. Groups of children appeared from nowhere to gather around them chattering and giggling. Women carrying pots or bundles of kindling on their heads slunk into the shadows and reached to cover their faces with their shawls. And the elders grinned toothlessly, responding to the Sheikh's greetings and requests to buy provisions with enthusiastic nods. It was usually the younger men who helped them buy what they needed, barking out instructions to the women and children who then hurried to fetch sheep's milk or bread.

Some of the villages they passed were deserted and had been left to ruin. The Sheikh explained that the area was controlled by lawless bandits, who regularly raided the settlements and drove the farmers into the hills. It was to protect the residents from such attacks that larger villages and towns were contained within gated walls, he said. But here the houses were densely packed together and connected by dark narrow alleyways where sewage flowed freely, diseases festered and plagues were born.

"It is better to be out in the open countryside," the Sheikh told him.

Tomas and Ameen talked together incessantly. After a few days, Tomas took to riding the spare horse, and he and Ameen raced each other at a gallop whenever the terrain allowed it. Tomas's riding skills were improving greatly under Ameen's tuition but he was no match for the young Arab boy, who had ridden a horse before he could walk. But in his Arab costume and with his face burned by the sun, Tomas looked every bit as comfortable in the landscape as Ameen. Only his blue eyes gave his ancestry away, although Sheikh Abu al Khayr assured Murad Amrad that many Arabs from Syria had blue or green eyes.

Murad Amrad was made very aware of the ritual of prayer among the Arabs. While Jews were required to pray three times a day, Muslims stopped what they were doing to pray five times a day and he was struck by their devotion. It brought home to him how much he had neglected his family's spiritual welfare. He realised that neither he nor Tomas would have remembered to pray had they not been with the markedly more devout Muslims. He vowed to do something about this on his return. God had given them the opportunity of a new life in the land of Israel and they had been too focused on their livelihood to grant him sufficient prayers of gratitude.

At about the same time as Sheikh Abu al Khayr and Murad Amrad were travelling south, the discontent in Palestine over compulsory conscription into the army was coming to a head. Some days after the Sheikh's party had left Jaffa, Ibrahim Pasha received information that Arab tribes as far away from each other as Nablus to the north of Jerusalem, and Hebron to the south, had come together and demanded that Syrians should no longer be forced to join the Egyptian army. They were under the command of an influential tribal leader in Nablus named Qasim al-Ahmad.

Ibrahim Pasha was furious and chose to ignore their demands, instead sending troops to the most troubled areas to disperse the rebels. This course of action was to have a disastrous effect on the already highly charged atmosphere among the local Arabs. Fired by Ottoman patriotism, the rebels decided to fight back. As more and more local Arab peasants joined the fight against their Egyptian rulers, the number of rebels grew to many thousands and they decided to march to Jerusalem, intent on taking the city from Ibrahim Pasha's troops.

Unaware of these events, or of how they were eventually to affect them, Sheikh Abu al Khayr and his party continued on their way. As they travelled further south, the heat during the middle of the day became increasingly oppressive and Murad Amrad was thankful that they rested for longer periods. Gradually the land lost its vegetation, any greenery finally confined to the banks of the streams that still flowed sluggishly down from the mountains. Eventually even these dried up and the rolling landscape turned into a wasteland. A few sparse grasses and hardy herbs struggled up through the stony ground in places, and an occasional Acacia tree broke the monotony of the desert colours. The animals now depended more and more on the fodder they carried with them, and travelling became harder for them all. The pathway was rocky and flurries of wind blew sand into their faces. Even with the protection of the Arab headdresses, the sand got everywhere, scratching their eyes and filling their mouths. By the last days of their journey, their water had finally to be rationed and they had little left to eat other than bread and dates. Murad Amrad wondered if the Sheikh knew exactly where they were, but there was no doubt that Fatima did. She seemed very much at home in the desert and spoke animatedly to her maid as they drew closer to her tribe's encampment. Seven days after leaving Jaffa, the dark tents of the Bedouin became visible in the distance. Fatima at once gave a whoop of joy and goaded her camel into a gallop. Her mount needed no encouragement and the Sheikh laughed as she sped past, her shawl flying behind her and her camel a confusion of legs and flying froth.

Fatima's tribe was a large one, consisting of many members of the same extended family and their wives and children. As they approached, Murad Amrad counted at least six tents erected side by side. He watched sheep, goats, camels, horses and donkeys around the tents scatter to avoid Fatima's camel as it galloped towards them. Then he heard the Bedouin women set up a communal whooping of welcome and Fatima was absorbed into her family.

The drinking well known as Be'er Sheva, dominated the area in front of the Bedouin encampment. It was an impressively large well, with a stone built wall around it. Buckets attached to ropes were slung along the insides of the wall ready for use, and beside it roughly constructed drinking troughs for the animals were kept full. Situated between the Negev desert to the south and Palestine to the north, Be'er Sheva was an important stopping point for the Bedouin.

The fabric of the Bedouin tents proved to be made of woven sheep's wool, a dense and weatherproof material that kept the insides of the tents cool in the summer and warm in the winter. The flaps at the front of each tent were held open and supported by large wooden poles, which provided a shady area at the entrance. Inside, hanging woven rugs in bright colours partitioned the sleeping areas and women's quarters from the main living area, where more rugs covered the ground, cushions were liberally scattered and a vast array of cooking pots and foodstuffs lay around in random piles. Murad Amrad was to learn that hospitality in the desert was taken seriously, although initially he had been at a loss to understand how the Bedouin sustained themselves while living in such a harsh environment.

He knew from Sheikh Abu al Khayr that the Bedouin tribes of the Negev Desert were nomadic. They wandered through the desert, herding their flocks of sheep and goats to wherever there was pasture and water, or travelling to where there was work. He was to learn that like all Syrian Arabs, rice was the basis of their diet. But they made flat bread every day, and cheese from the milk of their sheep, goats and camels. They also used these animals for meat. They cooked with spices and herbs, many of which could be found in the desert, together with such foods as dates, figs and berries. Grain, legumes and anything else they needed, they bought from the towns and villages they visited.

Murad Amrad was keen to begin trading with the Bedouin straight away. But first there was to be a feast, and that night they enjoyed a fine array of dishes prepared by the tribeswomen. As guests of honour, Murad Amrad and the Sheikh were given the best pieces of meat by Fatima's father. After the meal they drank sage tea and one man began to play on a loose stringed instrument. Clapping in rhythm, all the men joined in and sang songs about the desert, about beautiful women and about their camels. Then a Nargile water pipe was handed around, before the evening eventually came to an end, with promises of camel races the next day to celebrate the Sheikh's visit.

Meanwhile in Jerusalem, hearing that the rebels were approaching, the Egyptian troops closed the city gates and posted several hundred guards around the city wall. Concerned that the inhabitants of Jerusalem might rise up in support of the rebels, the guards were told to remain on duty day and night. In an attempt to intercept the rebel army before it actually reached Jerusalem, a large force of soldiers rode out of the city into the surrounding countryside. Unsure of which direction the rebels were coming from however, they were unable to find them, and as evening fell they were forced to make their way back to Jerusalem. On the way, frustrated at not being able to engage with the rebels, the Egyptian troops vented their pent up aggression on the inhabitants of a small village nearby, destroying most of the houses as a warning to the approaching rebels. But this act did nothing to deter the expected attack. Later that same night the rebels arrived under the cover of darkness and began to fire on the city walls.

The defence of Jerusalem proved to be difficult. Although the rebels were armed only with rifles, the Egyptians had insufficient weapons to defend the city to any great effect. With only two cannons at their disposal they could do no more than move these around the city walls to ward off each fresh attack, and the rebels continued their bombardment both day and night. Four days later, the ground began to tremble. The subsequent series of earthquakes continued well into the night and many buildings in the city were damaged in the process. But still the rebels continued their assault, wearing the defenders down with their determination and tenacity. The siege then impacted further on the residents of the city when food and water became scarce, and conditions inside the city walls began to get desperate.

Murad Amrad lost count how many days they remained in the Bedouin camp. The two boys joined forces with others of their own age and spent their days racing each other through the desert on horseback, creating memories for Tomas that he would always treasure. And in between being feted with daily feasts and camel races, Murad Amrad and the Sheikh conducted their business with Fatima's father and other elders of the tribe.

The business proceedings took a great deal of time and were conducted with considerable gravity and care. Every day they were invited to sit on cushions arranged in a circle, and the Bedouin would bring out a bag of uncut jewels, a nugget of gold or a piece of antiquity. They would then all discuss the merits and value of the bag's contents before a price was decided and another bag could be brought out for the process to begin all over again. Murad Amrad soon realised that each day the tribesmen offered up items of a greater value than the day before. But he was already more than satisfied with the considerable collection of gold and gemstones he had so far purchased and wondered at what point their business transactions would reach completion. But in the end this was decided for them when two Bedouin tribesmen galloped into the camp one evening and brought news from Jerusalem.

Nearly three weeks after the siege of Jerusalem had begun, the Egyptian troops had eventually retreated into their garrison in defeat, locking themselves in and allowing the rebels to break into the city. As they marched through the narrow streets, the rebels had immediately begun to single out Jews and Christians for abuse, accusing them of loyalty to Ibrahim Pasha and angry that they were not subject to the same conscription laws or the same taxes as the Arab peasants. The rebels destroyed many Jewish houses and looted their shops before they finally pulled out of Jerusalem two days later. With no food and water to sustain them, and with no concrete plan other than to try and defeat the Egyptian forces, some had marched north towards Nablus and others south towards Hebron. A considerable number however, had travelled west towards Jaffa, which was seen as the next strategic stronghold.

When the Sheikh and Murad Amrad heard about the uprising and learned all that had been going on, they were immediately anxious to return home as soon as possible. With part of the rebel army heading towards Jaffa, they assumed a battle was inevitable. Concerned for the safety of their families they began to make preparations for a hasty departure. In order to travel at a greater speed, Sheikh Abu al Khayr traded two of his camels with the tribesmen for another horse. He also made arrangements for his bearers to travel back separately. They would bring the remaining three camels and Murad Amrad's donkey.

They finally pulled out of the Bedouin camp early the following morning. Murad Amrad rode on the mule while the Sheikh, Ameen, Tomas and Fatima were all on horseback. The Sheikh was armed as before with a rifle and dagger. The maidservant sat up behind Fatima, both women astride the horse and riding like men. Their robes had caught up and exposed the lower part of their legs and Murad Amrad did his best to keep his eyes averted. This task was made considerably easier by the fact that he had to use every bit of his concentration just to stay on the back of the mule, whose movements were extremely uncomfortable despite the thick carpet saddle.

Their return journey was to be a very different experience to the one they had made three weeks before. This time they carried only as many provisions as could be loaded into the horse's saddlebags, and they planned to ride hard from early in the morning to late in the evening. By now well into June, the daytime temperature was increasing with every passing day and they were forced to stop for an hour or two during the middle of the day to eat and rest. At night they merely spread their shawls on the ground and slept where they stopped, although Fatima and her maid erected a simple canopy a short distance away from the men to provide them with some privacy.

Early on the morning of the fourth day, they were woken by the sound of distant hooves and clattering armament. Half asleep, Murad Amrad thought he was dreaming of being in Nochem Minc's wagons and listening to the Russian soldiers outside. He sprang up. Not Russian soldiers this time but a contingent of well-armed Egyptian cavalry was riding towards them at a fast trot, the low sunlight catching in the thick cloud of dust surrounding them. The Sheikh shouted an instruction to Fatima to remain hidden where she was and then ran to help the two boys who were trying to calm their frightened mounts. The animals had heard the approaching horses and were in danger of escaping from their tethers in alarm.

On seeing the Sheikh's party in front of them, the Egyptians pulled their horses up sharply and, for a few seconds, the only noise was of the horses snorting and of countless pieces of bridle jingling as the horses tossed their heads and blew the dust from their noses.

A few days earlier, Ibrahim Pasha had marched out of Jaffa towards Jerusalem with a relief force of two thousand cavalry, four thousand infantry soldiers and a great deal of artillery. His aim was to liberate the city and destroy what was left of the rebel army. On meeting the group of rebels who were on their way to Jaffa, his army had easily defeated them and most of them had been killed. Some however, had managed to escape, and while his main force continued on to Jerusalem to relieve the starving soldiers in the garrison, Ibrahim Pasha had sent several cavalry divisions to give chase, some to the north and others to the south. Their instructions were to dispatch any rebels they could find, but to inflict no harm to the Jewish population.

The Egyptian cavalry now standing in front of the Sheikh's party was one such division, and after a long idle winter in Jaffa, and a disappointingly short battle, their objective was one of revenge on the Arab population of Palestine. Their commander took in the four men, the horses and the small encampment.

"What are you doing here?" he demanded, handling the long curved sword hanging at his waist.

With no greeting offered, the Sheikh gave none in return, merely giving a curt reply.

"We are returning to our homes in Jaffa," he said. "We have been trading in the south."

"These are dangerous times to be on the road trading. We are seeking rebels who have come this way. Rebels and traitors! Are you aware of the fate of traitors?" the commander asked.

The Sheikh inclined his head and kept his voice neutral. "We are no traitors, sir. Just traders."

The commander pointed to Fatima's shelter behind a bush. "What do you have in there?"

"My wife and her maidservant are sleeping there." The Sheikh kept his voice calm, but Murad Amrad could see that he was anything but. He hoped the Sheikh would keep his distaste of the Egyptians hidden for as long as possible.

"Show me!" the commander instructed.

"They are women, sir. They are of no interest."

The commander laughed and turned his head, so that his troops could hear him.

"He says there are women here of no interest," he said, and the men nearest to him tittered. "But I say let me be the judge of that!" He turned back to the Sheikh. "Tell them to come out."

The Sheikh turned towards the women's shelter, and before he could speak he saw Fatima and her maidservant stand up. She had been listening to the conversation and had no wish for her husband to give away her name. She had covered the lower part of her face, but the dark fabric drew greater attention to her extraordinary green eyes that now glared defiantly at the Egyptian cavalry. A few of the soldiers began to make lewd remarks and the commander had a glint in his eye as he stared at the two women. Murad Amrad saw the Sheikh clench his fists.

"As you see," Sheikh Abu al Khayr said quietly, "only women."

The commander suddenly dismounted and removed a long barrelled rifle from his saddle as he did so. He clicked his fingers towards the men behind him, three of whom then also dismounted. The Sheikh immediately tensed and automatically put his hands onto his dagger, but in an instant two of the men had grabbed him, pinning his arms behind his back and holding his head back to expose his throat. At the same time, the third man lunged at Murad Amrad and held his arms so tightly that he was unable to move.

It all happened so quickly that Murad Amrad was incapable of coherent thought. The scene had taken on a dreamlike quality and he felt as if he was observing it from a distance. He recognised this feeling as his own reaction to stressful situations, but he could do nothing about it for the present. He noticed that the commander's nostrils were quivering and found himself wondering whether it was a sign of anger or desire. He glanced towards the two women. Fatima had given a short shriek when the Sheikh had been accosted, but now stood squarely facing the commander, her head held high and her stance challenging. Her maid hid behind her, visibly shivering. The Sheikh was making no sound or movement. He was being held in a vice like grip with a hand clamped over his mouth. Behind him, Ameen and Tomas were standing like coiled springs beside their horses. Seeing Murad Amrad looking at the two boys, the commander pointed at them.

"Do you not know the regulations? Those two boys must come with us. They are old enough to join the cavalry and those horses will do them well."

Murad Amrad saw Ameen make a sudden movement towards his horse's tethers, but with lightning speed the commander put his rifle up to his shoulder and took aim.

"I will shoot if you attempt to escape!" he shouted at the boys. Ameen stopped what he was doing and froze while Tomas slowly turned to face the commander. Murad Amrad could see that he had turned very pale. All at once he felt his apathy leave him, and in its place a surge of anger.

"Then you'd better shoot, Commander," he said. "Those are my sons and they are not going to join your army. But if you do fire that shot, the Government of America will want to know about it. These people are with me, and we are all under the protection of the American Government. If you harm them or us, they will hunt you down and you will be punished. I would suggest that a preferable course of action would be to release us all and allow us to continue on our way." He had suddenly remembered David Darmon's letter of protection.

"Always carry it with you, Murad Amrad," David had insisted.

"You never know when it might be needed to get you out of trouble." This was the first time he had needed it and it suddenly seemed essential to their continued safe passage.

The commander turned his head to look at Murad Amrad properly, and saw a man with blue eyes and a strange accent dressed in the clothes of a Palestinian Arab. He raised his eyebrows and his belief that all was not as it appeared to be with this disparate group of people intensified. They must take him for a fool to believe otherwise. He laughed nastily.

"And who are you?" he asked.

"I am an Ashkenazi from Russia," Murad Amrad replied.

"A Jew with an Arab companion? And one who wears the dress of an Arab?" The commander sneered and spat onto the ground in front of Murad Amrad. "And you expect me to believe you are protected by the American government?"

"Indeed," Murad Amrad replied coldly. "And if you will instruct your man to release me I will show you the proof. As I say, I don't believe that your government will want to be answerable to the Americans should anything happen to me, my family or my entourage."

The commander hesitated. His rifle was still aimed at the two boys who hadn't moved. Murad Amrad was proud of their courage but he didn't look at them, or at the Sheikh. He just looked the commander straight in the eye and waited. Eventually the commander lowered his rifle and flicked up his chin in assent. The soldier behind Murad Amrad released his arms and Murad Amrad walked over to his saddlebag, took out the letter and handed it to the commander. The letter, written in Arabic and stamped with David Darmon's seal, pronounced that Murad Amrad Galperin was an Ashkenazi Jew from Russia, and that he and his family were under the protection of the American Consul in Jaffa.

The commander was unsure how to proceed. Not only was this highly suspect man to be protected for being a Jew, but it also seemed that he was entitled to the protection of a powerful foreign government. The commander had no liking of Jews and knew his men felt the same, but this letter appeared to be indisputable.

Murad Amrad held out his hand for his letter to be returned, but still the commander hesitated. He was reluctant to lose face and was aware that his troops were watching. He looked at the Sheikh, then at the two women and finally at Murad Amrad.

"I am assuming you consider these people to be of some worth," he said with feigned disgust. "But I do not." He shook the letter in the air. "This letter makes reference to you and your family, but it is obvious that this Muslim and these two Bedouin women are not your family."

Murad Amrad was prepared for this line of argument. This was something he could understand. He reached into his pocket, but the soldier who had held him before made a sudden movement towards him and Murad Amrad felt the point of a knife at his throat. He held up his hands in a sign of supplication.

"If you will allow me commander, I will show you how much I consider the worth of my companions to be. I am unarmed."

The commander understood then and nodded, waving his hand at the soldier who released Murad Amrad straight away.

Whilst fetching the letter from his saddlebag, Murad Amrad had managed to take something else out with it, and it was this that he now retrieved from his pocket. He opened his hand to reveal a large ruby, and the commander's eyes widened in surprise. The stone was not as big as the one the Sheikh had given Murad Amrad and Abram to work on, but it was impressive all the same. The Bedouin had brought this out on the last day of their negotiations and Murad Amrad had known his father would rejoice at the opportunity to create a piece of jewellery around another ruby. But their safety was now more important and he doubted the commander could be paid off with anything less valuable.

The commander reached for the jewel, but in a final act of bravado Murad Amrad snapped his hand shut as he did so and held the other out for the letter. The commander gave it back and Murad Amrad handed over the ruby. After looking at it for a few seconds, the commander nodded, turned on his heel and shouted an order. His men then released the Sheikh, remounted their horses, and the division of Egyptian cavalry rode away at speed, leaving a thick cloud of dust in their wake.

Throughout the rest of the summer, Egyptian forces carried out a great many revenge attacks on Muslim communities, destroying village after village in their search for rebels. In Nablus, Qasim al-Ahmad was hanged, along with two of his sons. The remainder of the tribal leaders responsible for the uprising were forced to disband and leave the area. Around ten thousand Arab peasants were transported to Egypt. But as others fled further north, the anger and frustration felt by the remaining rebels accelerated and, for want of anything more than the fact that Ibrahim Pasha considered them worthy of protection, they were now intent on revenging themselves on Jewish communities around the country.

Of a series of atrocities against Jews by the Arabs, one of the worst took place in Safed, a predominantly Jewish town in the very north of Palestine near the borders with Lebanon. When Arab rebels entered the town in the middle of June, they began a sustained month long attack on the Jewish inhabitants. They raped, tortured and murdered many, destroyed properties, stole valuables and desecrated synagogues and *Torah* scrolls. The Jews that managed to escape were forced to hide in fear for their lives, and among those that stayed in the village, many incidences of bravery and heroism were documented. Eventually, details of the continued violence in Safed leaked out, and the incident began to spark off a diplomatic protest. Many of the Jews of Safed were Ashkenazi and as such were European subjects. In response, Ibrahim Pasha requested help from his Lebanese allies who marched into Safed and quelled the violence. Most of the rebels managed to escape, but the few that were captured were tried and hung. Ibrahim Pasha promised the Jews of Safed some compensation, but the amount, when it came, was considered a very small percentage of the total damage sustained. With their lives in ruins, most decided to make their way to Jerusalem where they believed it would be safer.

In the south of the country, with the last of the rebels hiding in Hebron, the Egyptian army attacked the town on the 24th July and eventually gained entry. They then proceeded to destroy everything in their path. Many of the Arab citizens of the town fled to the hills but hundreds were killed and hundreds more were taken prisoner and conscripted into the army. Having had nothing to do with the Arab peasant uprising, the Jewish citizens of Hebron assumed they were safe and stayed in the town. As before, Ibrahim Pasha had given specific instructions to his troops that Jews were not to be harmed, but the Egyptian army once again chose to ignore his command and proceeded to vent their anger on the Jews. Many Ashkenazi and Sephardic Jews escaped and they too fled to Jerusalem. Those who remained were subjected to a terrifying ordeal as the Egyptian troops raged through the town, indiscriminately murdering and raping, desecrating the synagogues, destroying property and plundering valuables. And like the Jewish community in Safed, the Jews of Hebron were left destitute.

"My friend," the Sheikh said gravely after their safe return to Jaffa. "I have been thinking a lot about this and I believe I owe my life to you. Not only that but the life of my son and my wife."

As they had done so many times before, Sheikh Abu al Kayhr and Murad Amrad were sitting on cushions in the courtyard of the Sheikh's house sharing a Nargile pipe and a pot of coffee. Their friendship was now such that it was not always necessary for them to talk. But on this day, the Sheikh had indicated that he had something he wanted to say. On hearing his opening words Murad Amrad began to remonstrate, but the Sheikh held up his hand.

"I know this to be true," he continued. "It is because of your ingenuity and speed of thought that we were all able to return to our homes here in Jaffa. I and my son will be forever in your debt."

He paused to inhale deeply from the water pipe. Murad Amrad felt somewhat embarrassed and uncomfortable. He chose to remain silent, staring instead at the swirling smoke at the top of the pipe and listening to the bubbling of the water. The Sheikh continued.

"In return for the life of my family, this is my gift to you. From now on you are Sheikh Murad. In my country that is a title of great honour. And as befitting a man worthy of such a title, I give you the house in which you live, together with some of my land." The Sheikh nodded and grunted in satisfaction and returned to his pipe.

Murad Amrad looked at the Sheikh in considerable shock. Although he kept opening and closing his mouth he could find no words to express what he felt. In the end he placed his hands on his heart and bowed his head. Whatever needed to be said to the Sheikh would have to wait. At that moment, he didn't trust himself to speak.

JAFFA – PALESTINE: 1834 – 1835

After the Arab uprising, the Egyptian Government remained deeply unpopular among the Muslim population of Syria, and the authorities were constantly challenged by regular disturbances and rebellions. Many outlying regions were under the control of dissident tribal leaders and warlords who were able to evade capture by hiding in the hills, and the Jewish population of Syria, particularly those from these lawless areas, continued to bear the brunt of Muslim anger and resentment. Fleeing repeated attacks to their properties and places of worship, a vast number continued to make their way to Jerusalem, where the rapidly expanding population of both Ashkenazi and Sephardim Jews was soon to make Jerusalem the centre for the Jewish community in Palestine, and indeed the whole of Syria.

But for the Galperin family, all thoughts of going to Jerusalem were temporarily shelved. There was an immense amount of work to do in setting up the farm, and in any event the city was subject to an outbreak of plague. To have gone to Jerusalem at that time would have been folly and Murad Amrad was glad that Sonja appeared to accept that it was not to be.

They had much to learn about farming, most especially about the growing and selling of citrus fruits. The Sheikh had promised them all the help they wanted to turn their small estate into a profitable concern and Murad Amrad and Abram threw themselves wholeheartedly into the project. They still needed to continue with their jewellery business however, so it was essential that the whole family were involved in the farm from the beginning. The boys began by teaching the donkey to pull a plough, while Sonja and the girls were to weed earth that was to house hundreds of new fruit trees. Before long, the family's daily activities centred on the many jobs that had to be done around the estate each day. But the children were not excused their lessons. Sonja insisted on teaching them for a few hours every morning, and Murad Amrad knew better than to challenge her.

Since their trip into the Negev desert, a strong bond had formed between Ameen and Tomas, echoing that between Sheikh Abu al Kayhr and Murad Amrad. Ameen was often there to help out on the farm. On occasions he even joined Tomas and Utah in some of Sonja's lessons. He attended classes at the mosque in town, but the Sheikh encouraged his eldest son to benefit from as much extra curricula education as possible. Any free time the boys had, they spent together, exploring the hills around Jaffa on horseback and hunting rabbits and small birds with Ameen's trained hawk. Sometimes Utah joined them, but he more than Tomas had become very involved with the farm and usually preferred to work at whatever needed doing there instead. And far from becoming pale and learned in the manner of Jewish scholars, as Sonja might have wished, Tomas and Utah both became strong and bronzed from all their outdoor activity.

David Darmon meanwhile, became a less and less frequent visitor to the Galperin's home. They presumed that his duties kept him busy. But then they heard he had left Jaffa for Europe without saying goodbye to anyone. Eventually they learned that he had been dismissed. The American Government discovered he had been selling American letters of protection to local people. The family were shocked, most especially because they were among those who had benefited from his administrations. But Murad Amrad would not hear a word said against him.

"Our lives were saved because of him," he would say. "And as a family we must never forget him."

David Darmon's agency duties in Jaffa were taken over by an Armenian merchant named Merad Arutin who already acted as consular agent for Sardinia, Britain and Prussia, and who was more than happy to add America to the list of countries he served. His given task was one of assisting visiting travellers from those countries he represented. But when Murad Amrad visited him to enquire as to the legality of the family's American letters of protection, he found Arutin as enthusiastic as David Darmon had been to provide alternative documents.

"I would suggest Prussian documents this time," he said. He spoke loudly, with a degree of posturing, his eyes darting around his crowded workplace, as if to see who might be listening. "I think it unlikely that America will offer protection to Russians."

Murad Amrad did not need to consider this option for long. There was no doubt that because of its geographical position alone, Prussia was a more fitting country to provide his protection than America had been. But as he watched the new agent sign the relevant document with a flourish, he did wonder fleetingly whether Merad Arutin actually had the formal authority to give letters of protection or whether, like David Darmon, he was merely revelling in the enhanced prestige his position afforded him. Such doubts were not something he wished to dwell on for very long however, and he accepted the renewed letter of protection with gratitude.

By the end of 1835, the Galperin's new farm was beginning to run smoothly. Their first harvest, although small, had been duly celebrated. They had also assisted the Sheikh with his harvest, which was plentiful. And the family had settled into a routine of work on the land that fitted well around Abram's in the forge and Murad Amrad's in the market. But as was usual in the winter, their jewellery business had slowed and Murad Amrad was able to spend longer at home.

One afternoon, Sonja found him sitting outside in the winter sunshine. He was smoking the clay pipe he was rarely without and appeared to be deep in thought.

"Is all well with you, Murad?" Sonja asked. It was rare to see him idle, and she was unable to keep a note of concern from her voice.

"Ah, Sonja!" He turned to her and smiled. "Indeed, never better. I am merely planning how and when we might extend our house."

Sonja's eyes widened, in pleasure.

"I am thinking of a house built around a courtyard," he continued, thoughtfully. Then he stood up and walked over to the olive tree that Sonja had planted during their first winter in the house. "And in the middle of the courtyard an olive tree to give us shade in the summer, and for me to sit beneath smoking my pipe when I'm old." As he said this, he put his arms over his head to imitate a tree, and they both burst out laughing.

"That's a wonderful idea," said Sonja.

Murad Amrad was still laughing as he came back to stand beside her. He suddenly reached for her hands and held them in his. He seemed about to say something else, but after a moment or two of awkward silence between them Sonja gently withdrew her hands and patted his arm.

"Well, the olive tree is a bit small to give much shade right now," she said with a smile. "But the children are growing and there is no doubt that we could do with more space."

She found it easy to laugh the incident off at the time, and indeed had been anxious to alleviate any embarrassment on Murad Amrad's part. His actions, she was sure, had been based on affectionate impulse. Her own however, caused her greater concern. Her heart had thumped and her stomach fluttered as Murad Amrad had held her hands. And later she could not stop wondering what it was he had so obviously wanted to say. There was no future in these thoughts however. They could never forget that their children were betrothed, and it was to this end that she brought the subject of Jerusalem into the conversation one evening, when she, Murad Amrad and Abram were together.

"With your affairs in Jaffa now in order, Murad, would it not be a good time for you to take the boys to Jerusalem?"

Murad Amrad was caught unawares and didn't reply immediately.

Abram too appeared surprised, but then he began to nod in agreement.

"It would certainly be good to get established in the city before the spring when the new visitors and pilgrims arrive," he said. "And Jerusalem is clear of the plague now. We've done what we can to develop the land here, but it is after all our jewellery and money-lending business that earns us the most money."

"Be that as it may," Sonja went on gently. "I believe it just as important that Tomas and Utah should receive some spiritual education before it is too late. They are almost young men now. I'm also concerned that Tomas and Fanny should spend some time apart. They need to grow and develop separately. It is not right for them to spend the whole of their childhood in each other's company before they reach adulthood and are married."

141

Murad Amrad still hadn't said anything and Abram watched as his son looked at Sonja for a fraction of a second longer than was necessary. He had noticed other such looks between them in the past year and felt saddened for them both. With their children betrothed, there was no future for any relationship between them other than one of decorum. He gave a little cough.

Murad Amrad looked away from Sonja abruptly, and sighed. "You are right, both of you. I'll speak with Merad Arutin tomorrow. I believe most of the housing in Jerusalem is owned and rented out by Muslims and Merad Arutin has many influential contacts in the city. He may be able to help us find accommodation."

"Will you take Hanna, Murad?" Sonja asked. "She can keep house for you and the boys. And you can look for a suitable husband for her among the community. You'll meet many people at the synagogue."

"What of Elzbietta?" he asked. He could see that Sonja had been planning this for a long time and her idea seemed a good one. But the two girls were very close and he could not imagine separating them.

"She will stay here," Sonja replied. "Abram will be working hard in the forge and Fanny and I will need some help to run the house and farm."

And so it was decided.

Over the next few weeks, Sonja continued to supply Murad Amrad with a seemingly endless list of instructions.

"The man you find for Hanna should be a good man, Murad, from a good family," she stressed repeatedly. "And you must make sure the boys attend their studies every day."

He tutted and nodded good-naturedly, arranging his face in what he hoped was a suitable expression of agreement. In reality he was unable to take in everything she said. There was a great deal to prepare, and his mind was full. He preferred it that way. He was anxious to keep his many conflicting emotions at bay, not least the huge weight of responsibility he felt at breaking up his family. It was a momentous occasion for them all, especially for the children who were all affected by the preparations in different ways. Tomas and Utah were beside themselves with excitement; Fanny was inconsolable that she was to lose her playmates; Hanna became pale with nerves and trepidation; and Elzbietta spent a great deal of time angry that it wasn't her going instead of her elder sister. Murad Amrad knew their leaving was the right thing to be doing on many levels, and he knew they would return on a regular basis. But nevertheless, their departure marked the end of an era for them all.

JERUSALEM – PALESTINE: 1835 – 1848

Of the many people who entered the city of Jerusalem each day, most came on foot, balancing their belongings or wares on their heads, their children clutching at a spare hand or the folds of a robe. Others came by donkey, horse or camel. Some came to live, some to trade and a great many more to visit, but nearly all of them had travelled a great distance to get there.

From their first sighting of the holy city, those walking or riding towards it had spoken of little else, whispering to one another, 'It's Jerusalem, it's Jerusalem', such was the city's legendary lure. And with no other buildings in the barren landscape around it, Jerusalem from a distance was an impressive sight; a vast walled city on the top of a hill in the Judean mountains – a city whose lofty walls and towering parapets had defied a thousand years of battles, bombardment and siege – a city of such religious importance to Christians, Jews and Muslims alike that it attracted visitors and pilgrims from all over the world. As they drew nearer, the travellers had increased their speed, desperate to climb the last rubble-strewn slopes in daylight. Each of the city's six massive gates was closed and locked at nightfall. If they timed it wrongly, they would be forced to stay out in the open until the following day. When they finally reached the end of their journey, market stalls selling food and drink outside the gates offered them refreshment, and all but the very poor were glad of it. Their journey had often been arduous and long.

Once inside the city walls, the travellers were not immediately aware of the sacred monuments that vied with one another for space and privilege among the ruins of predecessors and the scars of ancient battlegrounds. Their first impressions were merely of noise and competing smells as a kaleidoscope of differing religions and nationalities jostled for space in the narrow streets. But the city was divided roughly into four quarters, and the new arrivals would discover that the populations of each lived around the sacred monuments of their own religion. In the Muslim Quarter, Palestinian, Turkish and Egyptian Muslims represented the authoritative Islamic faith. Their holy shrine, the imposing Dome of the Rock, dominated the Jerusalem skyline. In the Christian Quarter, the Greek and Russian Orthodox, the Copts, the Maronites and the Roman Catholics all took turns in presiding over Christianity's holiest site, the Church of the Holy Sepulcher. The Armenians meanwhile, although also a Christian people, remained as separate and distinctive in their quarter as the Jews. And in the Jewish Quarter, where the housing was cramped and the synagogues were built into the ground to ensure they rose no higher than the Muslim mosques, Sephardim and Ashkenazim prayed at their holiest site, the Western Wall of the Temple Mount.

Most visitors to Jerusalem began by making their way to the market. Central to the daily life of all the inhabitants of the city, irrespective of their religion, the market was where people came together to eat, drink, laugh, smoke and trade. With its unique blend of noise, colour and smell, it was here that the city's global influences merged and became one. And it was here in the main street of the market that Murad Amrad first set up his store and began to build a business his sons would be proud to inherit.

Merad Arutin had found them accommodation in the Jewish Quarter straight away, and their apartment proved to be comfortable and reasonably spacious. It was situated in one of the outer walls of the quarter, which meant it had windows looking out over the rest of the city and remained free from the smells of sewage and slops that came up from the streets below.

Surrounded at last by other Ashkenazi Jews, Murad Amrad was glad to be able to report back in letters to Sonja that they were being welcomed into the religious and social life of the Jewish community. He also did his best to describe the quarter in which they lived. The crumbling multi storey buildings that leant into each other, attached and shored up by terraces, archways and buttresses. The way the echo of footsteps and voices carried far down the dark interconnecting alleyways. The long flights of stone steps that led to crooked doorways sitting above and below street level. The

145

families and holy men who lived under arches or in open cellars begging for money and relying on charity for food and clothing.

What Murad Amrad didn't tell Sonja however, was that for Tomas and Utah it was perhaps too late for them to be the religious scholars she had hoped for. Without the strict adherence to their faith being instigated by Sonja and Abram on a daily basis, he found the boys took their studies less than seriously. He knew he was a poor mentor. He put most of his energies into setting up his business instead of praying, but this was something the boys inherently understood. More important to them than learning the *Talmund* was the task of helping Murad Amrad at his new store in the market, and they wasted no time in joining him there each day after school.

Hanna fared less well. She missed the companionship of her sister and felt homesick for Jaffa and all that she knew. She was a shy girl, and although adept in the home she found it hard to leave the house without the companionship of another woman. Despite being a year younger than Hanna, Elzbietta had always been the more outgoing and Hanna had grown up relying on her confidence. Now on her own, when she needed to visit the well for water or the market for food she would wait until one of her brothers was around to accompany her. She became pale and withdrawn and was obviously not happy in her new role as sole housekeeper.

In the market, Abram's Judaica silverware began to be noticed and coveted by many among the wealthier Ashkenazi population of Jerusalem, and his jewellery began to attract customers from as many different nations as visited the holy city. Murad Amrad had persuaded Abram to produce a selection of gold crucifixes decorated with jewels. He had explained that these would be worthy souvenirs for the many Christian pilgrims who visited the holy city each year, especially during the times when the birth, crucifixion and resurrection of Jesus were observed. Abram had been somewhat reluctant at first, but had eventually seen the financial merit of such items. For although the quality and workmanship of the ceremonial silverware and the jewellery pieces alone would have been enough to make Murad Amrad's store unique, by selling the Christian symbols as well, the store immediately stood out from others by being the only one of its kind to specifically attract both Jews and Christians.

As his sales increased, Murad Amrad found it necessary to make the journey back to Jaffa more frequently in order to collect his father's latest pieces of work. This he did with a glad heart. Although he was reluctant to leave his store for very long, and would travel back to Jerusalem at the earliest opportunity, he nevertheless cherished the brief time he was able to spend with Sonja and Abram on each visit.

The journey there and back was not without its dangers however, conceivably more so for Murad Amrad who carried a valuable load with him each time he returned to Jerusalem. Despite the best efforts of the Egyptian Government to impose law and order on the land, anyone making their way alone along the rough track between Jaffa and Jerusalem was in danger of being attacked and robbed by bandits, or caught in the crossfire of warring tribes. Luckily for him, a group of far-sighted businessmen had recently begun offering the services of a regular guarded caravan for those travelling between the two cities. The long line of camels, horses and donkeys, together with the presence of armed drivers, had so far proved a strong deterrent to would-be bandits, and by riding in one of these Murad Amrad felt confident that he and his precious cargo would remain safe.

On his return to Jerusalem after each trip, the children would want to know every detail of his visit. What was happening on the farm? How were the animals? What had been planted in the garden? What had Sonja cooked while he was there? Had Fanny grown? Had Elzbietta written Hanna a letter? The questions always went on for hours. Murad Amrad could see how much they all missed their home and the rest of the family, and it saddened him. But after one such visit to Jaffa, he had a surprise for them. Worn down by Elzbietta's pleas to join her sister and the others in Jerusalem, Sonja had finally relented and asked Murad Amrad to take her with him. When he arrived back in Jerusalem with Elzbietta at his side, the children were overjoyed. After talking well into the night, they all promised to show her 'everything there is to see and more' the following day. Although Murad Amrad worried that Sonja and

Abram were now without any extra help, he knew that to have his children around him once again was as it should be.

Made bold with her sister now beside her, Hanna showed Elzbietta the markets, and together they began to acquaint themselves with the best places in which to buy their provisions. They were given much culinary advice by the women folk of other Ashkenazi families living around them, all of whom seemed keen to share their favourite grocer or butcher, or to tell the girls what they should be cooking that week. This made them feel embraced and accepted by the Jewish community, and they knew Sonja would be proud of them. Conditions within the Jewish Quarter may have been somewhat cramped compared to the space and fresh air of Jaffa, but the girls loved keeping house for their brothers and father, feeling nothing but pride in the collection of small rooms and steep steps that made up their home.

Meanwhile, Murad Amrad's store was so often filled with customers that he increasingly needed Tomas and Utah's help. At first they took turns in helping on a daily basis, but very soon business was such that both boys ceased attending school completely and worked full time with Murad Amrad. But this was something none of them admitted to Sonja until sometime later.

By early 1838, it was becoming clear to Murad Amrad that among the ever-mounting volume of foreign visitors, a great many were British. Not only that, but whichever European country they were from, it seemed to him that all educated people were able to communicate with one another by speaking English or French, neither of which he had any knowledge of. When customers came to his store, he liked to offer greetings in all the languages he knew until he found one in which they could converse. This habit usually caused the customer to smile. But it was not only done for their amusement: Murad Amrad considered it a necessary courtesy, and one that appeared vital for good business. On finding they could communicate in a foreign land, his customers immediately relaxed and seemed more comfortable about buying from him. But he increasingly found no common language with customers from England and this troubled him. Anxious not to be perceived as backward, and keen to be able to talk with all his customers, Murad Amrad decided that it was no longer sufficient to speak only Russian, Arabic and Hebrew. He and the boys would have to learn English as well, and to this end he began to look around for a possible tutor.

The only British resident he could think of in Jerusalem was the missionary John Nicholayson, who lived and worked at the Protestant Mission in the Armenian Quarter. With growing British interest in the Holy Land, the absence of Protestant representation in Jerusalem had become the catalyst for a recent surge in missionary activity in the city. The Protestant Mission had been founded by The London Society For Promoting Christianity Among The Jews, and its aim was to develop a Protestant community of converted Jews in Jerusalem. Murad Amrad knew that Nicholayson spoke Hebrew, but he was reluctant to approach him. Although not fully aware of the motives of the mission, he knew that it attracted a great deal of antagonism on a daily basis, not only from the Muslim authorities and members of the other Christian denominations in the city, but most especially from the Jewish rabbis. He had no wish to incur the wrath of the latter by visiting the mission. He would have to think of something else.

In a city rife with rumours and gossip, news carried fast through the streets of Jerusalem. He had recently heard that Britain was setting up a consulate in the city, with an appointed British Consular Agent as its representative. He doubted however, that such an esteemed man would be able to help. Certainly not immediately, and Murad Amrad was anxious to begin English lessons straightaway.

But fate was on Murad Amrad's side one morning, when a young man wandered slowly past his store dressed in European clothes and seemingly with time on his hands. Murad Amrad greeted him tentatively in Hebrew and was delighted when the man replied. Murad Amrad then asked him if he needed any help. The young man replied that he was new to the city and thought he might be lost. He smiled apologetically as he said this. He had an open trusting face, the sort that was immediately likeable, one that reminded Murad Amrad of an eager child. They began to converse. The young man's name was Joseph LaRosa. He had recently arrived from Malta to join the Protestant Mission in Jerusalem. He was a convert from Judaism, he said, which was why he could speak Hebrew. And as a citizen of Malta, he was also a British subject. Murad Amrad suddenly concluded that here was a gift sent from heaven. Although a Christian (and intriguingly, one who'd been born a Jew) Joseph LaRosa would obviously be able to speak English. Without hesitation he invited the young man to his home that evening to share their meal. For Joseph LaRosa too, this was an unexpected stroke of luck. As a new and untried missionary, with an assignment to convert Jews to Christianity, he was thrilled to accept.

After they'd parted, Murad Amrad hurried home, leaving Tomas and Utah to run the store. He wanted to give the girls as much notice as possible that they were to entertain a guest that evening. But on hearing the news, Hanna was immediately thrown into a panic.

"We haven't prepared enough food for a visitor today, Father," she lamented. "Oh how I wish we'd known earlier. The market will have sold out of so many things by now."

Elzbietta on the other hand was very excited at the thought of entertaining a young man. She was the more efficient of the two girls and began to make plans straightaway.

"Nonsense, Hanna," she said sternly. "There will still be product available. We can welcome this man with a good meal." She removed her apron and put on her shawl. "You must make more bread while I go down to the market to see what I can find."

By the time she returned with armfuls of vegetables and the carcass of a newly slaughtered chicken, Hanna had calmed down and the smell of baking bread was filling the apartment.

"Look what I found!" Elzbietta said happily, showing Hanna a large bunch of parsley. Herbs were hard to come by in Jerusalem and they missed all those grown in Sonja's garden. Hanna smiled.

"You're right to be pleased, Sister. All this will make an excellent soup. It was childish of me to panic so."

They both worked hard for the remainder of the afternoon, and by the time Tomas and Utah came home from the store, and Joseph LaRosa had found his way through the narrow streets to their home, the table was laid with the best linen, and the pots on the stove steamed invitingly. After introductions and pleasantries had been exchanged, they all sat to eat. Murad Amrad then gave the blessing and broke the bread, welcoming their visitor in the customary way.

It was only once they'd started eating that he remembered Joseph LaRosa was a Christian. Speaking with him in Hebrew had caused him to forget completely. He started to offer an apology of sorts, although was at a loss to know what to say. The young missionary made it easy for him, however.

"Please don't feel uncomfortable giving thanks for this delicious food," he said, smiling across the table at the two girls. "We have the same God, and this food deserves His blessing."

Murad Amrad was amused to see both Hanna and Elzbietta colour up and look down at their laps. It was a reminder, if one was needed, that the girls were now of an age when they would be susceptible to a young man's attentions. He wished Sonja was there to help them with the correct advice, but Joseph LaRosa's behavior seemed quite proper as he turned to Murad Amrad to spare the girls any more discomfort.

They dined on a rich chicken and vegetable soup, flavoured with the precious parsley, and with plump dumplings floating on top. A salted fish dish cooked with onions, parsley and lemon juice followed, served with rice and almonds. Finally, little pancakes with cinnamon and raisins completed the meal.

"I must compliment you on your cooking," Joseph LaRosa said, once again making the girls blush. This time Elzbietta was a little bolder however, and was able to hold his gaze as she replied. She had her mother's eyes, very dark and heavily lashed. Her usually pale face was delicately flushed and a lock of her dark, wavy hair was slipping from her scarf. Murad Amrad was suddenly aware that his daughter had grown into a lovely young woman.

"The fish is from Jaffa," she said proudly. "Father brings some back each time he goes there. And Hanna is the best bread maker among us. Don't you think it the lightest you've ever tasted?"

"There I must agree with you," Joseph LaRosa said enthusiastically. "I haven't eaten this well since leaving my home in Malta."

The girls looked at each other and smiled and Murad Amrad felt very proud of them. It was good for them to have entertained a visitor, and it had obviously made them happy. But now he had to put his proposition to Joseph LaRosa.

"I have to tell you, Joseph, that I have an ulterior motive for inviting you to dine with us."

Joseph LaRosa looked rather startled and Murad Amrad laughed. "Please don't be alarmed, my friend. I merely wanted to ask if you would be prepared to teach the boys and me to speak English. I will pay you whatever you wish for your services."

Joseph LaRosa looked relieved. "I would be delighted, of course. But why don't I teach you all?" He looked at the girls questioningly and was rewarded with their enthusiastic nods. "And it would be my pleasure to come here once a week and give you a lesson in exchange for a meal. That would be all the payment required."

So it was settled. Joseph LaRosa began to visit the family once a week to instruct them in the English language, and on the allotted day the girls worked feverishly to make increasingly ambitious meals. Murad Amrad was very quickly forced to accept how much more receptive a younger brain was when learning something new. While he struggled to get his mouth around the English words and remember the vocabulary, Tomas, Utah and the girls absorbed the language far more quickly. He'd noticed the same when they'd all started to learn Arabic. But he was determined to conquer this new language, and he worked hard to keep up with the young.

As the weeks went on, he began to notice that Elzbietta, more than any of the others, seemed especially keen to impress their young tutor, flushing up readily when he addressed her and smoothing down her skirts a great deal more times than was necessary. Murad Amrad was not sure what to think about this and wondered whether it was appropriate for the girls to have such a young male tutor. He made a mental note to ask Sonja for her opinion.

Joseph LaRosa had never spoken to the Galperin family about his religion and for that Murad Amrad was grateful. But one day in October he hesitantly asked them if they'd like to visit the mission's temporary chapel in the Christian Quarter that evening. It was a special event, he told them, a Christian service to be conducted in Hebrew, and he wondered if they might be interested. Murad Amrad was shocked, and as politely as possible declined for them all. The last thing he wanted was trouble from the rabbis. They viewed the British missionaries with great suspicion and would no doubt be concerned for his family's spiritual welfare should he visit a Christian church. He was surprised to see Elzbietta looking slightly crestfallen however, and he frowned at her. But Joseph LaRosa seemed not to take offence, and for that he was relieved. The young missionary just smiled and shrugged his shoulders.

As it turned out, Murad Amrad's decision was fortuitous. The rabbis heard about the service and decided that the plan to hold Christian services in Hebrew was the final insult to what they perceived as the mission's meddling in Jewish affairs. They turned up at the chapel in force that evening and confronted John Nicholayson, demanding not only an end to all missionary activity among the Jews in Jerusalem, but that all the British missionaries should leave the city immediately.

John Nicholayson had to think quickly. It was important to keep as much on the right side of the Jewish religious leaders as possible, at least until the new British consul for Jerusalem arrived. He knew this should be imminent, for the rumours circulating in Jerusalem were indeed correct and a man named William Tanner Young was on his way to begin his duties in the city. But until then, he needed to play for time. He decided therefore that his best course of action was to agree to the rabbi's demands. He deduced that it could only be a matter of days before Mr. Young arrived to give the mission his protection, and the missionaries could then return.

John Nicholayson's overriding ambition in life was to oversee the development of a Christian/Jewish community in Jerusalem, and he was willing to do anything to achieve it. He had long been of the opinion that without the protection of a British consulate in Jerusalem he would remain powerless to defend his mission against the hostility it encountered. He was encouraged by his belief that once a British consulate was in place to provide increased security, more Jews from Britain would want to settle in Palestine. Many considered Palestine to be the Jewish ancestral homeland of Zion after all and once they were here, he had every confidence that many could be persuaded to embrace Christianity. With all this in mind, he was in the process of purchasing land in Jerusalem on which to build a Protestant church, as well as a cemetery and housing for a permanent mission, and he was anxious to see the process finalised. It was for this reason that he himself insisted on being allowed to remain behind in Jerusalem, and the rabbi's eventually had no option other than to agree.

In the event, the missionaries weren't the only inhabitants of Jerusalem to be forced to leave the city. An epidemic of cholera sweeping through Palestine had recently reached Jerusalem, and the numbers of new cases reported in the city each week was beginning to mount. Hearing of this, Sonja had sent a letter insisting that the young came home to Jaffa for the winter, where she believed they'd be safer. The family needed no second telling. Although they had as yet seen no cases of cholera for themselves, memories of their mother, sister and cousin's deaths still haunted their nights. They packed quickly, although not without some excitement. The thought of spending the winter in Jaffa thrilled them all, and it was in more of a holiday spirit than in panic that they locked up their home just after dawn and walked towards the Jaffa Gate. This, like all six of the city's gates, would be opened just as the sun rose. Not wanting them to travel on their own, Murad Amrad had decided to close his store for a few days and accompany them on their journey.

Despite the early hour, the Jaffa Gate was already crowded with people. Some were coming into the city to trade, but a great many others were leaving, all equally keen to depart the disease-ridden city. Once outside, Murad Amrad guided his family through the crowds towards the waiting caravan. It was to be a long one judging by the number of animals involved. At least a dozen camels lay with their hobbled legs folded beneath them, their cud chewing interspersed with irritable gargling and spitting every time a load was placed on their backs. A long row of donkeys and mules, attached to one another by ropes, were harnessed up with thick, padded saddle-rugs over their backs. They brayed impatiently, pawing at the dust or kicking out at a passing stray dog, their irritation increased by the swarms of flies attracted to the piles of steaming dung. The drivers shouted instructions to each other, or to the waiting passengers who stood in a huddle to one side until commanded individually to come forward with their luggage. It was a scene of intense activity, backlit by the low sun whose rays shone through swirls of sand picked up by a frisky wind. Only the guards were idle. They rode their prancing mounts up and down and waited to leave, talking and laughing amongst themselves, admiring one another's weapons and eying the Arab girls who had set up their stalls to sell provisions outside the city walls.

"Look over there," Tomas said suddenly. "It's Joseph."

Following his gaze Murad Amrad could see that the expelled missionaries were riding in the same caravan. He had heard late on the previous evening that they had all been instructed to leave the city. Elzbietta flushed and Utah nudged her in the ribs. The boys had begun to tease her about her obvious infatuation. Murad Amrad frowned at Utah pointedly as Joseph LaRosa came over to speak with them.

"This is well met, Murad Amrad," he said, lifting his hat to them all in turn. "Perhaps an English lesson on the journey would help pass the time?"

They all laughed. "Indeed it would, Joseph," Murad Amrad replied. "But I hope you'll visit us in Jaffa? We can continue our lessons there, and in greater comfort."

"I would be delighted," he said, and giving them a wide smile, he returned to his group.

Finally, with most of the passengers mounted on mules, some perched on the top of camels, and the luggage loaded onto the donkeys and remaining camels, the caravan was ready to leave. They each had parasols and gourds of water, but it was going to be a long, hot day. The track they would shortly follow wound down the hill, away from Jerusalem, and over the rocky hills beyond, until it disappeared into the hazy distance. They would not arrive in Jaffa until nightfall.

It was to be a lot longer than a few days before Murad Amrad returned to Jerusalem to reopen his store, however. As news of the rising death toll in the city spread, Sonja remembered the horror of having watched Isaac die of the disease. She began to suffer from nightmares that the same fate would befall Murad Amrad. He had always seemed so irrepressible and strong but she knew that no amount of strength would keep cholera at bay. Her fears caused her great anxiety that only abated once she had persuaded him to remain in Jaffa until the danger had passed.

As the winter progressed and the number of cases in Jerusalem increased still further, the Egyptian Governor eventually resorted to locking the gates of the city in an attempt to contain the epidemic. Soldiers were posted outside to prevent anyone leaving, and food for the city was dropped outside the gates. In a further attempt to halt the spread of the disease, all new visitors to the country were required to remain in quarantine for twenty-one days. So when the ship carrying William Tanner Young eventually arrived in Jaffa from Alexandria, it was forced to stay at anchor with all its passengers on board until the allotted time was up. After that, Young had to remain in Jaffa and wait there until the gates of Jerusalem were reopened.

The inhabitants of the Jerusalem were nothing if not fatalistic, and they carried on with their every day lives for as long as they could. But as time passed, and resources ran low, conditions in the city inevitably worsened. The city gate nearest to the Jewish Quarter was the Dung Gate, so called because the city's refuse was taken through it on horsedrawn trailers to be dumped in the hills beyond. But as this gate too was locked, there was no other course of action than to let the sewage and garbage pile up on the inside. Here the cholera bacteria multiplied, and the inhabitants of the Jewish Quarter were the first to fall victim. As the epidemic continued to spread, and the death toll rose to thousands, pits were dug in all four quarters of the city in which to bury the dead, and this practice and the lack of religious observance it necessitated, caused frequent riots. As the situation deteriorated further, those who hadn't died of cholera began to die of starvation and other related diseases. Most susceptible were the very young and the very old.

For the Galperin family, although concerned for those of their friends left in Jerusalem, their enforced time in Jaffa continued to feel like a holiday. They were happy to be together again, and after an initial new-found shyness between Tomas and Fanny, who were suddenly aware of their advancing years and future marriage, they were soon back to their normal relationships. Sonja was still fearful of the cholera risk however, and made them promise not to eat or to drink anything that was not prepared at home. She was unwittingly giving them sound advice. Although she would not yet have known that cholera was spread by contaminated food and water, as well as unsanitary conditions, her instinctive directives did much to ensure their safety.

Throughout the winter, Joseph LaRosa visited them a great many times. Like the rest of his fellow missionaries, he was waiting for his next instructions from the mission and was delighted to be able to spend time in a family home. In return, he continued to teach them English. Sonja and Fanny too joined his classes, although Abram declined, declaring that not only was he far too old to learn another language, but he didn't think there was any point in learning English.

As the weeks passed, it was obvious to both Murad Amrad and Sonja that Elzbietta and Joseph LaRosa were forming a strong attachment to one another. This made them very fearful: with mixed marriage at best an extremely controversial subject in any Jewish community, they had no idea how to react. Murad Amrad remembered the story Valvel told him about the daughter of Levi and Anna Rosen. She had fallen in love with a Christian, whereupon the community, including her parents, had run her out of town. He knew his response would not be as harsh, regardless of what his rabbi in Jerusalem would instruct him to do. But Murad Amrad felt the most concerned for Elzbietta. She would be ostracised in any Jewish community and probably unaccepted in a Christian one. He continued to worry about this, and between them he and Sonja decided to keep a close eye on his daughter, making sure she and Joseph LaRosa were never left alone.

By the end of the winter, the Governor of Jerusalem acknowledged that the suffering of the city's inhabitants would only be alleviated once he'd allowed the gates to be unlocked. This done, the city was at long last able to get help from outside. In response to a request for urgent medical supplies from John Nicholayson, the mission in London sent a Jewish convert named Doctor Gerstman who, on arrival in Jerusalem, immediately set up a free clinic for the sick and dying. Despite the continued danger of cholera in the city, William Tanner Young too made the journey from Jaffa to Jerusalem and, on 16th April 1839, finally opened the first British consulate. A few days later, Young was an honoured guest at the baptism of the first Jewish family in Jerusalem to convert to Christianity and John Nicholayson prayed they would be the first of many.

Although representative of the British Government, Young was nevertheless the sole European authority in Jerusalem. There were no other consuls in the city and his responsibilities included the provision of aid to all European travellers and visitors. Previously, there had been nowhere for foreigners of any nationality to go should they get into trouble of any kind. In the absence of any hotels, most European visitors stayed in one of the Catholic convents or monasteries where they had at least been able to make use of the resident interpreters and guards should it have been necessary.

But Young's most immediate instructions were to offer assistance and protection to Jews, regardless of nationality. At the mercy of countless repressive regulations, and persecuted on a daily level by both Muslims and Christians, the Jewish community rejoiced that at last they had someone they could go to for help, and they welcomed the new British consul with open arms. Young found himself to be deeply shocked by the poverty and daily humiliation affecting many Jews. Straightaway he began to involve himself with cases of persecution presented to him, from fighting for the rights of an innocent Jew condemned to death by torture, to defending another from Europe in his request for exemption from taxes due to poverty.

With Jerusalem now accessible, Murad Amrad began to think about going back. He was concerned for the safety of his store and wanted to assess conditions in the city. For this reason, he decided to take only Tomas and Utah with him on his first trip back. There would be much to do before their store could reopen, and he wouldn't know if the city was safe for the girls until he had been there.

A few days before he was due to leave however, his worst fears were realised when Joseph arrived unexpectedly and asked to speak with him alone.

"I have been called back to Jerusalem, Murad Amrad," he began. "Now that the British consul is established, the mission considers our position in the city to be safer." It was clear that he was ill at ease. He was twisting his hat around in his hands and beads of perspiration were appearing on his forehead. He took a deep breath. "I would like to ask for your permission to marry Elzbictta."

Although having feared this scenario, Murad Amrad was nevertheless completely unprepared in his response. He found himself merely staring at Joseph in some horror, not knowing what to say.

"I love your daughter, Murad Amrad," Joseph continued, "and I wish to care for her all my life."

Murad Amrad eventually found his voice and asked hoarsely, "Does Elzbietta know of your intentions, Joseph?"

"She does, sir. And I am lucky enough to know that my feelings are returned." He stared intently at Murad Amrad, still twisting his hat, all the fear and longing he clearly felt expressed on his face.

"Elzbietta will have to become a Christian!" Murad Amrad said, and paused as he took in the magnitude of the words. He suddenly felt incredibly sad more than anything else, and wondered how Tamara would have reacted. She had been as devout a Jew as Sonja and Abram, and not for the first time he felt ashamed of his comparative lack of piety. Was it his fault that Elzbietta now wished to turn her back on her faith out of love for a man? Given the events of the past six years, he knew he had prioritised on work for the sake of his family. He wondered whether Tamara would have been changed by everything they'd all been through. He thought of Sonja's unswerving faith and decided not. But for him, the Jewish faith was just a way of life. He had never questioned his own beliefs, or lack of them. He sighed and turned his attention back to his daughter's suitor.

"Does Elzbietta understand what a big step that would be? Would she be accepted by other Christians?"

"Oh yes! Of course she would be accepted." Joseph LaRosa had been unnerved by Murad Amrad's long silence and was now relieved by his question. "We owe our faith to its Jewish roots, Murad Amrad, which is why we at the mission worship in Hebrew."

He paused to try and find the right words to explain the unique beliefs of the mission to Murad Amrad. "We believe that God has not forgotten his promise to the people of Israel and that Jews will return to the land of Israel. We also believe that by introducing the Jewish people to the message of Jesus Christ we are offering them the greatest gift of all."

Murad Amrad was silent again as he took in what Joseph LaRosa had said. The rabbis had preached that the teachings of the mission were sacrilege, but on hearing the passion in this young man's voice he couldn't help but question their condemnation. Who was to say what was right or wrong?

"Let me think about your proposal, Joseph," he said eventually. "Let me talk with Elzbietta, and with Sonja, who is as much a mother to her as any could be. I too will be travelling back to Jerusalem in a few days, and I'll let you have my answer when we meet there."

Later that day he called Elzbietta to him. He wanted to do this before he told Sonja and Abram about Joseph LaRosa's proposal. She appeared calm and rational, but her hands repeatedly scrunching up her apron betrayed her nerves. He found it in his heart to be amused at the similarity between the nervous mannerisms of his daughter and the man of her choice. And when she spoke, it was with similar passion.

"I love him, Father. And I am willing to go to the ends of the earth and to do anything to be with him. But I don't want to go without your blessing."

As she waited for his response, he could see her once again as a little girl, assessing him to find out what mood he was in before telling him of some misdemeanor. This time however, he wasn't at all sure himself. There was no doubting that she and Joseph were deeply attached to one another. And the family had got to know Joseph LaRosa well and had become very fond of him. He was a good man, but to undertake such a commitment as changing your religion required a great deal of courage. But as his daughter's dark eyes stared steadily back at his, he recognised in some deep part of his being that she of all people possessed that courage. She was his daughter after all. She knew her own mind and would face whatever life threw at her with great tenacity. And whatever any of them thought about the union, there was not much he could do other than forbid it, and that was something he suddenly knew he had no wish to do.

Before returning to Jerusalem some weeks later, Murad Amrad visited Sheikh Abu al Kayhr. He had grown to value the Sheikh's opinion on most things and he now, more than ever, wanted to hear what his friend would say about recent events. They were, as usual, sharing a pipe in the Sheikh's courtyard, a place where he had always felt at peace. But he failed to do so today.

"Something is troubling you, my friend!" It hadn't taken the Sheikh long to notice that Murad Amrad was not himself.

"I am just concerned for my daughter," Murad Amrad said. "She wishes to become a Christian."

The Sheikh's initial response did little to offer him comfort however. The Arab merely tutted and shrugged his shoulders, as if it was not of much consequence.

"To become a Christian is not much different to being a Jew!" he said with a slight sneer. "Was their prophet not Jewish also?"

Murad Amrad was momentarily taken aback by the connection of his comments to those of Joseph LaRosa, and didn't reply.

"Perhaps it is the work of your Christian friend from Jerusalem!" the Sheikh continued, chuckling quietly.

"Well he has asked for her hand in marriage as well," Murad Amrad replied miserably. "That is why she wishes to convert. He is a missionary and it would not be good if his wife remained a Jew."

The Sheikh then looked at Murad Amrad in some surprise.

"Marriage!" he exclaimed. "You will allow her to marry a stranger? And someone of a different race?"

"He is not really a stranger any more," Murad Amrad said quietly, justifying a situation he himself was not yet used to. "And he seems a good man."

Sheikh Abu al Kayhr was fairly open-minded about other religions. They all believed in one God after all. But each had a different Holy Book, and each had separate sacred laws, and this seemed most unsatisfactory to him. As he saw it Islam was the only true path to God. After that, whether Christian or Jew was hardly of any consequence. But he could see that his friend was in some turmoil, and he had no wish to be offensive.

"Where is he from, this missionary?" the Sheikh asked, and his voice was slightly gentler.

"He is British," Murad Amrad replied, and could not help but feel a certain pride as he said this. "He is from Malta."

The two men were silent for a while. The early summer sunshine filtered through the trees causing dappled shadows to flicker on the ground all around them. Murad Amrad looked across at the Sheikh, whose face was shaded by his headdress. Sheikh Abu al Kayhr appeared deep in thought, maintaining one of those silences that had once so unnerved Murad Amrad, but that he had come to know preceded intelligent observation. Eventually the Sheikh spoke again.

"Allah is good and we must submit to His will. But this seems a good thing to me, my friend. At least, it is not as bad as you make out. Be glad for your daughter. Married to this British missionary, will she not also be a British subject? You Jews are a people without a nation. She will now have a nation as well as a husband." The Sheikh smiled. "And it is a good thing after all that you are learning the language of Britain. It will be the language of your grandchildren."

When Murad Amrad eventually arrived back in Jerusalem with Tomas and Utah, he found the city subdued and impoverished after its long confinement. The huge death toll had left a deep sense of sadness in its wake, and there were few families who hadn't been touched by loss. Despite this, the city appeared to be slowly coming back to life, much like someone waking from a long sleep. Refuse had been cleared, roads swept, shops and kitchens restocked and the residents of Jerusalem at long last free to come and go. Murad Amrad was gratified to find his store much as he had left it, apart from the presence of a great deal of dust. And as the foreign visitors slowly started to return he, like all the other market traders and shopkeepers in the city, was glad of the much-needed business.

While the city recovered it was, for the most part, the Jewish community who remained the worst off. Although there were a considerable number of successful Jewish traders and businesses in Jerusalem, the majority of Jews in the city were refugees from Europe, with little or no chance of employment. Those who had escaped the cholera epidemic still lived how and where they could in abject poverty, forced to rely on charity for food, clothing and fuel, and repeatedly victimised or abused by the authorities. The reputation of the mission had much improved since the epidemic, and as more and more Jews availed themselves of the charity and free medical care on offer, even the rabbis acknowledged their good works. But the persistent persecution of the Jewish community continued throughout the holy land, and no single incident served better to alert the rest of the world to their situation at this time, than a much-publicised case of blood libel.

The history of blood libel in Europe went back to the Middle Ages, from which time Jews were regularly accused by Christians to have been involved in the supposed act of killing young Christians and using their blood in Jewish religious ceremonies. There had been other instances of blood libel in Palestine, but it was this particular case that finally highlighted both the implausibility of the accusations and the oppression of the Jews.

In February 1840, following the murder of a French monk in Damascus, the Christian population accused the town's Jews of his death for such purposes. The Egyptian authorities, keen to maintain the approval of France, accordingly imprisoned and tortured thirteen prominent Jewish merchants. Four of them died, and one became a Muslim to escape the torture. But the blood libel charges remained and they were sentenced to death, after which the population of Damascus ripped the synagogue apart and destroyed the sacred scrolls.

Backed by the British Government, a delegation of influential Europeans, including John Nicholayson from Jerusalem, was sent to meet with Muhammad Ali. At their head was Sir Moses Montefiore, a wealthy and highly influential British Jew, who had devoted his life to helping the Jews of Syria and Palestine. Their goal was to force the Egyptian leader to order an investigation, and in that they were successful. As a result of their efforts, those of the imprisoned Jews from Damascus who had survived the torture were declared innocent and released. Eventually a new edict was put in place in an attempt to prevent further blood libel accusations. But just as importantly, the plight of the Jewish community in Palestine and Syria had become of prime concern to the British Government, and they instructed Young to increase his efforts to provide British protection for as many Jews as possible.

Murad Amrad however, gave no thought to the British protection on offer. His business concerns in Jerusalem and Jaffa were sufficiently profitable to allow his family to live well. If he'd thought about it at all, he would have assumed his Prussian letter of protection from Merad Arutin was enough to provide him and his family with all the security they needed. In any event, he had not personally experienced any trouble in Jerusalem. In fact, as a result of his knowledge of the ways of the Arabs, and his ability to converse with them, he had a good relationship with most of the Arab traders in the market. For this he knew he had David Darmon and Sheikh Abu al Kayhr to thank. His knowledge of Christians however was limited to Merad Arutin, who was Armenian, and Joseph LaRosa who was soon to be his son-in-law. Murad Amrad had finally given Elzbietta his blessing, and she and Joseph were to marry the following year. They would then live in Jerusalem where Joseph worked. But until that time both Elzbietta and Hanna were to remain in Jaffa, where Sonja felt they would be safer and better chaperoned.

A few months later, Murad Amrad's complacency over his security was considerably shaken when a man named Constantin Basilly visited Jerusalem. Basilly was the newly appointed Russian Consular Agent for the area, sent to Palestine by the Russian government to lay claim to the European Jews, the majority of whom at that time were from Russia. Wanting to establish a strong influence in Palestine, Russia had seen an opportunity in its estranged Jewish population, and felt it essential to challenge Britain's self appointed role as defender of the Jews. Basilly duly announced to the Jewish population that they were now under his jurisdiction, and that anyone found seeking alternative protection from Britain would be sent from the country.

Hearing this, Murad Amrad suddenly felt alarmingly vulnerable. It was as if Igor Sigorski was once again at his heels. Even if he had wanted to, seeking protection from Britain would now be too dangerous. He cursed himself for being a fool in not gaining the British protection previously provided so freely. However, he could not risk being sent back to Russia by applying for it now, and he could not risk seeking Russian protection for fear of discovery. He had the safety of his family to think of. There was no choice in the matter. He would have to keep a low profile and hope that his Prussian letter of protection continued to afford them all some security.

In the meantime, Muhammad Ali and Ibrahim Pasha were growing increasingly determined to control a greater area of the Levant. With this in mind, they had now moved their army to the border in the north of Syria. The Ottoman Turks were equally determined not to concede any more of their territories to the Egyptians, and military confrontations between the two began to develop into ever more violent clashes. Concern mounted among the European powers as to the effect on Europe should there be all out war between the Egyptians and the Turks. It was in Europe's best interests to preserve the boundaries of the Ottoman Empire as they were. For this reason, Britain, Austria, Prussia and Russia decided to intervene in the gathering crisis.

Faced by their combined power, and threatened by the might of the British navy, Muhammad Ali and Ibrahim Pasha requested military support from Egypt's historical ally, France. When this failed to materialise however, they were forced to accept defeat and they had no choice but to agree to the demands of the European allies. Accordingly, Muhammad Ali and Ibrahim Pasha retreated to Egypt and, in November 1840, control of Syria and Palestine was returned to Turkish Ottoman rule.

William Tanner Young left Jerusalem during the last days of the Egyptian Government. But after Turkey was forced to accept European influence in the area in return for their assistance, he was able to return at the beginning of 1841. He found Palestine much changed. Following the handover, law and order had broken down completely. Local Sheikhs battled for supremacy in the hills and villages around Jerusalem. In the city itself, the administration and security was in chaos. To make matters worse for Young, he found himself challenged on a daily basis by the Turkish Governor, who resented his presence and questioned his authority at every level.

In the spring of 1841, Elzbietta and Joseph were married in the mission's temporary chapel in the Christian Quarter of Jerusalem. The service was conducted in Hebrew, and contained scripts from both the Torah and the Christian Bible. Sonja, Abram and Fanny remained stony faced throughout the service, as if fearful of absorbing some essence of Christianity. Murad Amrad was thankful that Tomas, Utah and Hanna were more polite and cultivated a degree of interest in the ceremony. He had to admit that he was moved, despite himself. The service was simple and the vows brief, but Joseph spoke them with such sincerity, and Elzbietta was obviously so much in love with him, that it was hard not to be affected. A year later however, when Tomas and Fanny were married in a Jewish ceremony, Murad Amrad found greater comfort in the familiar words, and acknowledged that the ceremony felt more valid because of it.

Tomas and Fanny wanted their wedding to take place at their home in Jaffa. Murad Amrad's planned extension onto their house had been completed some months earlier, and they now had ample room to accommodate such a celebration. So the *chuppah,* the wedding canopy, was erected in the garden, and a great many wedding guests were in attendance. Murad Amrad led Tomas to stand beneath the canopy and Sonja led Fanny. Murad Amrad noticed that his future daughter-in-law was shaking as she took the customary walk around Tomas three times before coming to stand beside him. Then, as the rabbi began to recite the seven blessings, the words suddenly transported him back to his own marriage ceremony, and he remembered how nervous Tamara had been on that day. He looked across at Sonja and wondered if she too was thinking of her wedding day. She would undoubtedly be wishing Isaac could see their daughter today. Fanny had grown into a fine girl, with the stature and strength of character of her mother. She was still inclined to be rather serious, much as she had been as a little girl, and although she was only eighteen, a small frown line had already etched itself between her eyebrows. But her tendency to give a great deal of thought to a subject before she spoke was a characteristic that encouraged the family to value her opinion on most matters, and she increasingly displayed a maturity beyond her years. And as she stood beside her new husband, with her straight dark hair secured simply behind her head, and a flush visible on her cheeks through the fine fabric of her veil, she looked as comely as any bride should on her wedding day. Murad Amrad noticed Tomas gazing at her with great tenderness and pride.

Tamara would have been proud of Tomas. He may not have been as pious as she would have wished him to be, but he was a hardworking young man with strong principles and great determination. He and Elzbietta were similarly high-spirited and outgoing, both full of energy and drive. Utah and Hanna on the other hand were more introverted, preferring the security of their home to the company of strangers. When he looked at Hanna now, she appeared ill at ease in her fine clothes and in such a large group of people. She avoided eye contact with all but family, and was covering up her shyness with practicalities. She, Sonja and Fanny had been working in the kitchen for days in advance of the wedding feast. Now, as the ceremony drew to a close and the traditional dancing and singing began, he saw her hurriedly turn away and make her way back to the kitchen.

A little later, Murad Amrad caught Sonja's arm as she too rushed towards the kitchen to begin serving the food. She was flushed from dancing and exhausted by days of preparation, but she was euphoric, and she impulsively reached up and kissed him on the cheek.

"We have done well by our children, Murad Amrad," she said. "We can be proud of that. Now I must get back into the kitchen. Hanna will be needing my help."

Murad Amrad smiled as he watched her go. They had indeed done well by Tomas and Fanny. But at what price to themselves, he wondered? He had known for some time that he was very much in love with Sonja, and the thought that they could never be together as man and wife was almost unbearable. It had been for the best that he didn't have to live beside her in Jaffa any longer.

After Elzbietta's marriage, Hanna had decided she would prefer to remain in Jaffa with Sonja, which left Murad Amrad, Tomas and Utah living on their own in the apartment in Jerusalem. With no one to cook for them, they had perfected the art of tossing chunks of meat and vegetables into a cooking pot with some water, and taking it to one of the Arab public ovens on their way to the store in the morning. On their way back home in the evening, they would then collect the fragrant steaming pot. But when Fanny moved into the apartment, after she and Tomas were married, there was a communal sense of relief among the men. They could once again enjoy all the benefits of having a woman around the house and a meal waiting for them on their return from the market.

In Jaffa, Abram was beginning to have health problems. He had suffered from arthritis for some years, but by 1846 his joints were giving him such pain and his hands were so swollen that he could foresee a time when it would be impossible to continue working in the forge. He was already finding it hard to beat the sheets of silver into shape, or to solder the finer pieces of gold. And on the farm, he was having to leave more and more of the heavier work to Sonja.

When Utah asked if he could go back to Jaffa and help out, it was an arrangement that suited them all well. While Tomas was as passionate about their jewellery and silverware business as his father and grandfather, Utah had always been happiest working on the land. There was also no doubt that his departure from the apartment would release some much-needed space. Tomas and Fanny already had one child, James, and Fanny was pregnant with another. But that didn't solve the problem of who would help Abram in the forge. Murad Amrad discussed this dilemma one day with Sheikh Abu al Khayr. After accompanying Utah back to Jaffa he had, as usual, stayed on for a few days. He and the Sheikh were sitting in the Sheikh's ornate beamed room beside the open fire sharing a pipe. It was a wet and windy day, and it was good to be inside.

"It may be that I can offer you something of a solution, my friend," the Sheikh suddenly announced, and Murad Amrad raised his eyebrows in surprise. "My youngest son, Khaled, has inherited my interest in jewellery and precious stones. He is now thirteen, and although still studying, he needs to work. I want him to learn about making jewellery the fine way, not just the Bedouin way." He paused to inhale noisily on the Nargile pipe, allowing Murad Amrad time to reflect on what his friend was saying. The Sheikh continued. "Would Abram be willing to take him on as an apprentice, do you think? Khaled could help with the heavier work once he knows what to do."

Murad Amrad was amazed that they had never before thought of taking on an apprentice, and Abram was delighted when Murad Amrad told him the news. Neither of his grandsons were interested in working the forge, and it was somehow fitting that he should pass on his art to the boy whose birth had marked the beginning of so many blessings for the Galperin family. It seemed only yesterday that he had made the ruby necklace for Khaled's mother, Fatima.

With Utah there to help run the farm, Abram was able to throw himself into the task of teaching Khaled everything he could about the creation of fine jewellery. He found the boy a quick and willing learner. But as a Muslim, Khaled had no interest in the Judaica silverware, or indeed in working with silver at all. Silver was for the Bedouin to craft, he said. Abram was disappointed of course, but he realised this was probably for the best. It was, after all, their gold jewellery that attracted the greatest number of customers these days. And as if to compensate, Khaled proved himself to have a natural affinity with gold and precious stones, with an excellent eye for design and style. Within a year, he was able to tackle much of the finer work that Abram found increasingly difficult to do.

Over the next decade, France, Prussia, Austria, Spain, Greece, Sardinia and finally Russia and America all joined Britain in opening consulates in Jerusalem. Each of the consuls enjoyed a considerable degree of authority. They expected to be treated with deference, and vied with one another for power and supremacy in the city. Despite this, their task of encouraging the Ottoman authorities to acknowledge and respect the rights of foreigners and minority religions was often very frustrating. The Turks remained highly suspicious of increasing Western presence in Palestine, and regularly did what they could to challenge the jurisdictions of the consulates.

And it was the British consul's involvement in one such occasion, many years later, which marked a turning point in the destiny of the Galperin family. But that time was still to come.

In 1846, William Tanner Young resigned and was replaced by James Finn, a devout Christian who had previously been involved with the London Society for Promoting Christianity amongst the Jews in London. Although as British Consul he was forbidden to sanction the work of the mission, he openly approved of its endeavours to build a strong community of Jewish Christians in Jerusalem. Much like John Nicholayson, he also supported the ideology of Jews returning to their homeland, the land of Zion, and he hoped to make Jerusalem a better place for them to live.

On his arrival, much like his predecessor before him, Finn was deeply affected by the conditions under which many in the Jewish community currently lived. Much of the housing in the Jewish Quarter of Jerusalem was derelict, overcrowded and unsanitary, the inhabitants severely impoverished, without employment and subject to frequent incidents of injustice and violence. He immediately vowed to place as many Jews as he could under British protection. And from personally helping the mission to distribute food, clothes and fuel to starving Jewish families, to intervening and defending Jews in legal disputes and acts of violence against them, Finn went on to prove himself inexhaustible in his efforts to help the Jews of Jerusalem. Fearless, passionate, zealous and dogmatic, he let nothing stand in his way, and he very quickly began to make as many enemies in the city as friends. Many in the Jewish community mistrusted him, taking their lead from the rabbis who were suspicious of his motives, suspecting him intent on converting the Jews to Christianity. He always maintained that his intentions were fired by a genuine philanthropic interest in the Jews, but his relationship with the Jewish leadership was a bad one throughout his time in Palestine.

In 1847, Fanny gave birth to a second son, Nathaniel. Elzbietta and Joseph however, had no children as yet; something Murad Amrad imagined was a source of great sadness to them. But Elzbietta gave no indication of regret. She remained cheerful and optimistic, and in between helping her husband in the mission, where they administered what aid they could to the poorest Jews of the city, she was a constant help and companion to Fanny. She poured a great deal of affection onto her nephews, and Tomas would jokingly chastise her for spoiling them. But he didn't begrudge his sister access to his boys. They considered her a second mother, and Fanny loved having her childhood friend around her. By the time her third son was born a year later, Fanny could not imagine coping without her.

The baby was only a few days old when a horseman arrived at their store in the market and handed an urgent message to Murad Amrad. Sonja had written that Abram had collapsed that day and was asking to see his son. The horseman was a servant of Sheikh Abu al Kayhr, she wrote, and would accompany him back to Jaffa. Leaving Tomas to run the store, he lost no time in hiring a horse for himself and a fresh one for the servant. The two men then managed to leave the city before the gates were locked at dusk. They rode throughout the night, and as the dawn was beginning to glow on the horizon Murad Amrad arrived at their home. Sonja met him at the doorway and took his hands in hers.

"Murad! I thank God that you have come. Your father still lives," she said and led him inside.

Murad Amrad found his father propped up on cushions in his bed. His breathing was shallow and one side of his face drooped downwards, pulling his mouth into a lopsided grimace and closing one eye. The other was open, staring at the doorway. He was an ashen grey colour, and there was a film of sweat on his forehead. When Murad Amrad walked into the room, Abram lifted the fingers of one hand.

"My son. You are here,' he said. His speech was slurred and little more than a whisper. It was obviously a huge effort for him to talk. Murad Amrad took his hand and sat beside him.

"Hush, Father. Do not try to speak just now. I am here and all is good."

Abram's good eye sought Murad Amrad's and he looked at his son for a few long seconds before giving him a crooked smile. "Now

I am content," he whispered. Then he turned his head slowly and looked beyond him towards Sonja, who was still standing in the doorway to the room. "Szejna?" he said suddenly, his smile widening. "Is that you?"

Sonja was unsure of the kindest way to reply, but Abram closed his eyes then, and appeared to fall into a deep sleep. Those were the last words he spoke. A short time later he stopped breathing and died, very quietly, with no struggle or noise, and seemingly at peace.

Afterwards, it seemed the most natural thing in the world for Murad Amrad and Sonja to embrace, holding onto one another in their shared grief. They remained that way beside Abram's body for a very long time. Eventually Sonja looked up and wiped Murad Amrad's tears from his cheeks with her fingers.

"Abram is with his beloved Szejna now, *Bubbala*," she said softly.

"That is what I will pray for," he replied. "Mammeh and Father gave up so much to be with us. It is right that they should be reunited somewhere."

Then he looked down into Sonja's eyes and saw, as if for the first time, the love she felt for him. Beyond his grief he suddenly knew, with something of a shock, that from then on their relationship would never be the same again. There would no longer be any need for him to keep running away. They held each other's gaze for a few seconds more, as if sealing an unspoken vow, before moving gently apart.

After the period of mourning for Abram had passed, there had seemed little reason for further discussion between Murad Amrad and Sonja on what had previously appeared to be an insurmountable moral dilemma. They were both of the same opinion that with Abram gone, and Tomas and Fanny married, what felt so right between them could no longer be considered a sin against God's laws. If Utah and Hanna observed that when their father was in Jaffa, he and Sonja lived together as man and wife, they gave no sign of it. When the rest of the family was home, they too seemed barely to notice. On the surface, the relationship between Murad Amrad and Sonja was much as it always had been – one that had evolved from adversity, hard work and a mutual love for their family. If any of the family had looked more deeply however, they might have seen the lingering glances between them that left Sonja's cheeks pink. Or the unnecessary brush of hand against hand in passing. Or how much more relaxed they both appeared to be. And if they had asked, Murad Amrad would have told them that he was happier than he had been since Tamara's death, and that he knew she would have approved. His place was now beside Sonja. This was where he was meant to be. But none of the family thought to question the way things were. They just accepted them.

JERUSALEM – PALESTINE: 1849 – 1862

Following Abram's death, Murad Amrad decided to make Jaffa his permanent home. The family's apartment in Jerusalem didn't seem to be as big as it once had. James and his brother Nathaniel, now four and three years old respectively, were as active as all small boys were. And the new baby, who they had named Abraham in honour of Abram, seemed to cry a great deal. Much as he loved his grandsons, Murad Amrad had to admit that he gave thanks every time he returned to the comparative peace of life in Jaffa. But he still travelled regularly to Jerusalem. With income from their jewellery business growing rapidly, he and Tomas had recently begun offering a banking and money lending service in the city, much as he and Abram had done in Bialystok. The service had already been taken up by a number of small businesses eager to expand, as well as by a few private individuals in financial difficulties. Although he had the utmost confidence in Tomas's capabilities, running their business concerns on his own, as well as the store, would be a great deal of work for one person. In any event, Murad Amrad had no intention of relinquishing his hold on the business he had worked so hard to build.

Tomas was a heavier man than his father. He carried himself with dignity and authority, and appeared older than his twenty-seven years. Despite his youth, he was as much respected by all the other traders in the market as his father. Like Murad Amrad, his ability to converse fluently in Arabic, Russian, English and Hebrew meant that he was frequently sought after to translate, or to mediate in a dispute or a discussion. And he was always happy to oblige. His father had taught him well, and he knew how important it was to keep on good terms with every one of his fellow tradesmen. Business was often to be found from a surprisingly diverse number of sources, Murad Amrad had always told him. So he would take time to share a pipe with an Arab carpet seller, joke with a Christian hawker selling rosaries, or haggle with a Jewish collector over the price of a gemstone. But all the time he would be listening. The market was the beating heart of Jerusalem, the source of all information.

Murad Amrad wasn't in Jerusalem on the day Tomas met the new British consul, James Finn. Tomas was alone in his store when he was suddenly made aware of a growing sound of animated voices. He stepped out of the doorway, and looking down the street saw James Finn, accompanied by his Arab dragoman (his interpreter and guide) and a noisy crowd of Jews. Tomas and Murad Amrad had often seen the British consul about in the city, but there had never been an opportunity to meet him. They had heard a great deal about him, of course. His efforts to help the Jews of Jerusalem had created considerable interest in the city, and Tomas had been curious to know what he was like. He had quizzed Joseph and Elzbietta on several occasions. They had not only met Finn and his wife Elizabeth at the mission, but had been guests at a reception at the consul residence.

Finn had recently begun to organise members of the Jewish population in public relief work. New drains, water systems and home repairs were just a few of the essential amenities in the Jewish Quarter that urgently needed attention. Finn had argued that there was no one better to get paid for those jobs than the unemployed amongst the Jewish residents. Tomas remembered that the Governor of Jerusalem had been reluctant to finance the work at first, but that Finn had publicly challenged him and had won his case. No doubt many of those now clamouring around the British consul were keen to offer their services in the much-anticipated building work. But Tomas thought James Finn looked hot and slightly irritated. He didn't hesitate. He stepped straight out and spoke to James Finn in English. Although unsure of how to address a British consul, he decided on the spur of the moment to use the title 'sir' and hoped it showed sufficient respect.

James Finn had studied Hebrew for many years and spoke it well, so language was no barrier. But Tomas's English took him by surprise. It gave every indication of an educated man and his reply, in turn, was instantaneous. He was beginning to feel uncharacteristically bothered by the excited crowd around him. To accept Tomas's invitation to have coffee with him in his store would provide some much needed respite.

Feeling deeply honoured to be entertaining so distinguished a guest, Tomas led him to the back of the store and invited him to sit. While he poured the coffee and made polite conversation, he surreptitiously took in the appearance of the British consul. James Finn had long side-whiskers and a generous moustache. He sat very upright on the stool provided for him and Tomas wondered whether this was because his starched collar was too high or his short waistcoat too tightly buttoned. But then he decided that James Finn was obviously dressed in the mode of an English gentleman and as such his attire should be beyond remark. There was no doubt that he presented a grand and imposing figure and Tomas found himself lifting his ribcage in a subconscious effort to emulate his visitor's impressive bearing.

At the entrance to the store, Tomas could hear the excited chattering of the gathering crowd. The dragoman was doing his best to prevent them from entering, but he suspected Finn's respite would only be short. Word got around quickly and there were always Jewish supplicants asking for his help. He had become their ardent champion. With this in mind, it seemed fitting for Tomas to refer to Finn's benevolent activities.

"My father and I have heard many stories of the good work you are doing amongst the Jewish community," Tomas began. "Your efforts are to be applauded."

"Thank you," Finn replied, and smiled stiffly. "My only desire is to do what I can to help. I see so much suffering among the population here. There is much to do I fear. And much to be gained by providing British protection."

"That is very commendable," Tomas mumbled, although the British consul didn't seem to hear him and continued speaking.

"It is unfortunate however, that so many amongst the Jewish population of Palestine are originally from countries within the Russian Empire, and as such have been forbidden from accepting British protection." Finn spoke with considerable feeling, and it was obvious to Tomas that he felt the injustice of this situation very strongly. But he was slightly embarrassed by the British consul's candor.

"May I ask if you and your family have diplomatic protection, Mr. Galperin?" Finn asked suddenly and with genuine concern. "Where did you come from originally?"

Tomas now felt himself colouring. This was not a subject his father would wish him to dwell on. But he also believed it was important to give Finn enough of the bare facts to avoid further explanation.

"We came from Russia," he answered. "We have been here for fifteen years and are under Prussian protection. Before that the agent for America provided us with protection. In fact, our American documents once saved our lives."

James Finn raised his eyebrows and nodded. "Then you will understand my desire to see every Jew protected in the same way," he said. "You are lucky to have Prussian documentation, although I have to say I am surprised. Most Russian Jews I know have been forbidden from accepting protection from any other country. We are currently negotiating with Constantin Basilly and trying to get him to lift this ridiculous dictate. But for the present it is enforced."

Tomas was anxious to change the subject.

"What other plans do you have for the Jewish community?" he enquired.

"I'm glad that you ask, Tomas. I'd be interested to know what you think. I can see that you are an educated man."

Tomas could not help but feel pleased at this compliment, and knew his father would be proud when he told him.

"I have a plan to establish a Jewish factory producing high quality soap to sell to tourists," Finn continued. "As well as many other ideas. But I must tell you that my eventual dream is to establish a Jewish farming community somewhere outside the city walls." He waved his hand in the air to indicate the area he referred to. "All that land is lying at waste. It could be cultivated and farmed." His enthusiasm was tangible. But Tomas had never heard of such an extreme idea. It had to be impossibly ambitious.

"Outside the city walls?" he exclaimed. "That will be hard to protect from bandits. And who will fund such an enterprise? I hope you won't mind me saying, sir, but you are going to need a great deal of money to fulfill your dream."

"Ah, Mr. Galperin. Spoken like a man with an eye for finance. There you have hit upon the problem. All my enterprises have to be paid for from my own pocket, and that of my wife. And my salary is not yet as much as I would wish."

Tomas had been trained well and, as an inveterate salesman, he now made full use of the opportunity presented to him, as his father would have wanted him to do. He lowered his voice and leaned in closer to James Finn.

"Well, sir. My father and I may be able to help you," he said. "If you ever have any need to use our banking or money-lending services, you would be an honoured customer. And I can tell you that our loan rates are the best in the city."

James Finn looked momentarily shocked. It was his turn to feel ill at ease. He shuffled on his stool. But he also felt a stab of relief. He had not imagined finding financial assistance so easily. If the British Government didn't increase his salary soon, or at least agree to pay something towards his efforts to help the Jews, he would be forced to borrow money until they did so.

"That is most kind, Mr. Galperin," he said gruffly, and stood up. "And I will remember your offer. But now I must leave you. I've enjoyed our conversation, and the excellent coffee, and I hope to see you again soon."

Over the next few years, James Finn continued to throw himself wholeheartedly into his benevolent enterprises. His negotiations with Constantin Basilly were eventually successful and he was permitted to give British protection to Russian Jews, but with one proviso: they had to obtain a letter of dismissal from the Russian consul first. With no Russian consulate in Jerusalem, Jewish families were often forced to travel great distances to wherever Basilly was stationed in order to gain the necessary documentation. But this proved no great deterrent, and gradually the number of Jews under British protection in Palestine grew into thousands. Many years later, the number would exceed that acceptable to the British

Government and new laws were required to introduce limitations on those eligible. But that too was in the future.

The legacy for which Finn was to be most remembered however, was the establishment of Karm al-Khalil, or 'Abraham's Vineyard'; his much dreamed of training farm where a community of Jews lived and earned a wage by working on the land. He bought several acres of uncultivated land just outside Jerusalem in 1853 and, by putting the name of his dragoman on the deeds, he was able to circumvent the ban on Europeans owning land. Over the following two years, he first built a summerhouse there for his family, and then began to develop his training farm, employing only Jews to help in the construction, development and maintenance of both projects. It was a brave thing to do. As one of the first developments outside the walls of Jerusalem at the time, the risk of attack by bandits and Bedouin tribesmen was very high.

Financing his Jewish projects remained an ongoing predicament for him during the whole of his time in Palestine. The salary for a British consul was not very high and despite his repeated requests for an increase in consular income, the British Government refused, accusing Finn of failing to manage his finances correctly. As a result he ran up huge debts over the years, and his later involvement in another farming venture further north of Jerusalem, near Bethlehem, eventually compounded his financial problems. The shortfall increased each year and Finn was obliged to borrow increasingly large amounts of money from a variety of moneylenders in Jerusalem. Many of these were Jews who were so dependent on consular protection that they could not refuse the loans. But one of his main creditors was Tomas Galperin.

James Finn began borrowing occasional sums of money from Tomas fairly soon after their initial meeting. Before long he was coming to the store every time he needed help to finance one or other of his projects. He and Tomas would conduct their business at the back of the store, then take some time to talk over coffee. Finn would animatedly describe to Tomas all the details of his current endeavours and Tomas began to feel that the British consul regarded him as a friend, as well as a source of funding.

"I need your help again, Tomas," Finn would say with a wry

smile, and immediately Tomas would feel as if he was integral to the current project.

It had to be said, that James Finn was not often able to keep up to date with his repayments, and more than once Murad Amrad threatened to demand immediate repayment if Tomas didn't. But Tomas argued that in the face of Finn's efforts to help the Jews of Jerusalem, it was an unworthy thing to do. They should concentrate instead on feeling proud that their money was helping to finance new employment or material assistance for the Jewish community, he told his father, and the subject was usually left in abeyance.

By 1858, Tomas and Fanny had been blessed with five children. Four years after Abraham, Fanny had given birth to a daughter, Sarah, and two years later to another, Anna. With their business concerns going from strength to strength, Tomas had recently secured a larger property for his growing family in the main street of the market, one that also provided more spacious accommodation for the business. His eldest sons, James and Nathaniel were now of an age to help in the store when their schooling permitted, and Tomas was pleased to see that they both took a keen interest in all aspects of the family business. Their store was now one of the largest and most successful of its kind in Jerusalem.

Since Abram's death, the store had traded for the most part in gold jewellery and precious stones rather than in Judaica silverware. Khaled still worked Abram's forge in Jaffa and made much of the jewellery for the store. At the same time however, with their money lending business proving to be extremely profitable, Tomas and Murad Amrad had begun to invest in antiquities. There was a vibrant trade in artifacts throughout Syria if you knew the right people, and a good market for them amongst the ever-increasing number of visitors who flocked to the city each year. The Arab and Bedouin contacts who provided Murad Amrad with supplies of gold and gemstones now frequently produced findings from sites of ancient civilization, many from as far away as Egypt and Persia. He had become an avid collector and there wasn't much he refused to purchase. Each time he arrived in Jerusalem, he and Tomas would lock the door of the store and go through the contents of the carpetbags in which he had transported his treasured acquisitions.

As well as Khaled's jewellery, there would be gold and lead coins, lead seals, bronze bowls, clay lamps, and sometimes a marble head or an elaborate piece of ancient jewellery. They would carefully catalogue and label each item, discussing its merit and worth before displaying it in the store. It was a long and painstaking job but one the two men enjoyed. And it was on one such occasion that Murad Amrad and Tomas were interrupted by a knocking on the door.

"We are closed!" Tomas shouted, irritated by the intrusion.

"It is I, Tomas," a voice from the other side of the door called. "Elzbietta."

Tomas opened the door then, and was surprised to see Joseph as well as Elzbietta. In itself, there was nothing unusual about a visit from his sister and brother-in-law. Elzbietta and Joseph had continued to live in Jerusalem and were frequent and welcomed visitors to their home. But Joseph would normally have been working at that hour, and he noticed that they looked very glum.

"We would like to speak with you and Father in private, Tomas. And Fanny too, of course."

Tomas and Murad Amrad exchanged a quick look, puzzled by the formality of her request. Elzbietta's relationship with her brother was normally very easy.

"Are you quite well, Elzbietta?" Murad Amrad asked.

Elzbietta nodded, but continued to look serious.

"Let us go upstairs, sister. Fanny is up there, and the children." Tomas said, hoping this might cheer her up. He knew how she adored her nieces and nephews.

Fanny was sitting at the table teaching Sarah and Anna to sew. James and Nathaniel were studying, somewhat reluctantly it had to be said, and were thrilled when their father asked them to reopen the doors of the store and mind it for a while. Abraham was still at school. He was a studious boy who took his studies very seriously, in stark contrast to his brothers who were always more keen to play with their friends or help their father in the store than to stay on at school.

"We have something we wish to discuss with you," Elzbietta then said, sitting very upright in her chair and smoothing down her apron. Murad Amrad recognised this nervous mannerism and wondered what was coming next. Elzbietta had always had the ability to surprise and even shock. Her next words were no exception to the rule.

"Joseph has been posted back to Malta."

Fanny looked up sharply and gasped. Her sister-in-law was her childhood friend and she could not imagine life in Jerusalem without her.

"When?" she asked, and Tomas heard the catch in her voice.

"We leave in three weeks," Elzbietta replied sadly. "Joseph has been offered a position at the Malta Protestant College."

"Is that a school?" Tomas directed his question at Joseph.

"It is," Joseph replied. "It's a fee-paying boarding school for boys up to the age of seventeen, and its education is of the highest caliber. It's a great honour for me to have the opportunity to teach there. The pupils are mostly Europeans whose families live in countries around the Mediterranean." He paused then and looked at Elzbietta, whose nod suggested he should continue. "The school takes in scholarship boys from around the world, if they are clever enough." He swallowed and paused again. This time however Elzbietta interrupted in a rush, all the while looking at Fanny as her words came tumbling out.

"We were wondering whether you would allow us to take Abraham with us to attend the school. He is such an excellent scholar and it would be an incredible opportunity for him to receive the best education. He could make his home with us and…" She trailed off. Fanny had put her hand up to her mouth in shock but remained silent.

Murad Amrad cleared his throat. "What would the college get out of this arrangement?" he said. "They are Christians. Why would they want to educate a Jewish boy?"

Joseph took a deep breath. "Abraham would have to become a Christian to receive this education, Murad Amrad," he said quietly, glancing briefly at Tomas. "He would then have the opportunity to return to Jerusalem at the end of his education and work for the mission. His career and salary would be assured for the rest of his life."

The fact that Elzbietta and Joseph were Christians had never been a subject of contention in the family before, and indeed had rarely been talked about. Elzbietta had worked alongside Joseph in the mission since their marriage, and together they had administered what help they could to the poorest Jews of the city. But she had made no attempt to convert her family. Indeed, Fanny would not have heard of it. She was as devout a Jew as anyone could be, and despite what she believed to be her husband's lack of piety, she did her best to make sure her children received the correct tuition in the Jewish faith.

Murad Amrad was at a loss to know what to say, but Tomas stood up and began to pace the floor. Downstairs, James and Nathaniel looked at each other in some alarm as they heard their father speak in a raised voice.

"So it is a choice between being a Jew or receiving a better education?" Tomas sounded incredulous. "The boy is only ten. How can he make such a decision?"

"He can't. It is for you to decide for him, Tomas." Elzbietta stood up and faced her brother, her cheeks becoming increasingly flushed as she spoke. "And I ask you to think carefully. He will be given the best education money can buy. He will mix with the sons of missionaries, chaplains, military and naval officers and merchants. He will become a gentleman. And yes, a Christian! But what is the alternative? You know how it is for you. So far you have not been challenged. But should you be so, you do not have protection from any country. We watched all the Russian Jews arriving in Jerusalem to escape the war in the Crimea receive British protection. And we watched Jews from all over Europe being granted British protection. But throughout all this time, Consul Finn has not been able to help you and our family."

Tomas frowned and opened his mouth to say something, but his sister put her hand up as if to stop him, giving him no time to speak.

"Yes, yes! I know Mr. Finn would be willing to give you British protection. You have told me that much. But you and I know it would be impossible. Despite having been here for most of your life, without a dismissal notice from the Russian authorities even Finn is powerless to help. And if you were to approach the Russian agent in Jaffa and ask for such a document, you would be putting

Father in danger of discovery. So instead, you have assured Mr. Finn that you have Prussian protection. You even *believe* you have Prussian protection. But I don't think you have, Tomas. Nor you, Father. I don't believe old Merad Arutin's letter of protection was intended to be a long lasting legitimate document. I doubt he ever had the authority to provide such a thing. Yet you both refuse to face the truth. Father has not sought to update his papers and you, Tomas, are trapped into living a lie. As a result, your family must remain stateless and without protection. Do you want this for your children as well? Here is a chance to do something about it, for Abraham at least. If he were to become Christian, and live in Malta, he would become a British citizen, as I am. And Joseph and I believe that, as his family, you would all stand a greater chance of being protected and defended by Britain if you too chose to convert."

But she had gone too far. Fanny stood up abruptly.

"That is enough, Elzbietta," she said. "We cannot let this come between us. I thank you for your offer to take Abraham to the Malta College. Tomas and I will discuss it later, but I must tell you that I do not think it a good idea." She had gone quite white.

As Elzbietta and Joseph got up to leave, Murad Amrad noticed Elzbietta was doing her best not to cry. Sarah and Anna, who at six and four years old were too young to understand the words that had been spoken, recognised all the same that everything was not as it should be. They consequently responded to their aunt's departure with some caution, a far cry from their usual enthusiastic embraces. Tomas and Fanny were stiff and silent, and even Murad Amrad could find no words to say to Elzbietta as she left. He was too shocked by what she had suggested. For the family to become Christian was not something he had ever imagined them considering. Would she have dared suggest it as a solution to their problems if Abram had still been alive? The prospect would have destroyed him. And he knew that Fanny and Sonja would not condone it still. But he felt threatened and disturbed nevertheless, and considerably shaken. He suddenly longed for Sonja, and the reassurance of her strength of faith.

Tomas too was haunted by Elzbietta's words. He knew her tirade was born out of genuine fear for them all. He also understood that her reasons for suggesting they become Christian were for their safety rather than from any religious zeal. She had been right on all counts. The family's lack of diplomatic protection was indeed cause for considerable concern. And his inability to do anything about it had resulted in a lifetime's habit of suppressing his very real fear of discovery and persecution. Conversion to Christianity had never entered his head as a solution, until now. It seemed an extreme course of action, and one he knew Fanny would find intolerable. But for Abraham, presented with such an unparalleled opportunity, did they have the right to deny him? Did it really matter if he became a Christian when he was twelve, rather than a Bar Mitzvah Jew? He had to admit that to him it didn't. But it did to Fanny. When they discussed the matter, she acknowledged that Abraham would benefit hugely from a European education, and that it would be an excellent opportunity for him. But she remained extremely distressed at the thought of his having to give up the Jewish faith. Up until then, it had been the cornerstone of his learning. And with only three weeks in which to make a decision, the pressure between them mounted with each passing day.

Meanwhile, as was now usual at this time of the year, Jerusalem was crowded with visitors. It was the pilgrim season; the time between Christmas and Easter when the city was overrun by thousands of Christians visiting the Holy Land. The greatest number of pilgrims came from Russia, the majority of who travelled overland to reach Jerusalem. But the steamship companies were now offering organised trips to the Holy Land on specially commissioned steamers, sailing from Odessa. Those arriving by steamer were permitted only to stay for three weeks however, after which time they were required to return home to allow another shipload of pilgrims the opportunity to visit. This had become a big business concern, and the number of Russians making the journey to Jerusalem in the past few years had dramatically increased. This year was no exception. As they always did, the Russian Ecclesiastical Mission had set up a vast encampment outside the city walls to accommodate the pilgrims, but this year Tzar Alexander II of Russia had become involved in concerns for their greater comfort and safety. With that in mind, he had obtained permission to purchase a large area of land on an adjacent hill to Jerusalem, on which he had already begun to build permanent accommodation and facilities for the Russian pilgrims.

As the first foreigners to own land in Palestine, the proposed development had caused quite a sensation, as well as the promise of much local employment. The walls encircling what had become known as the Russian Compound had already been completed, and excavation work within the compound was well under way. Tomas had heard they were planning to build a Russian Orthodox Church, hostels, monasteries, hospitals and a great deal more. Also that the architecture was going to be European in style, and that much of the stone and building materials were being brought all the way from Russia on the steamers. He remembered the majestic buildings in Odessa and wondered if these were to be as grand. Not to be outdone, the sultan had announced the planned construction of new roads to replace the rough dirt tracks that criss-crossed the hills around Jerusalem. Tomas especially welcomed the one planned between Jerusalem and Jaffa. It would considerably speed up the journey. In an attempt to protect travellers from the still too frequent risk of attack from bandits, the sultan had even promised to erect small forts at intervals along this road, to be manned by armed guards.

Tomas, like most of the other citizens of Jerusalem, had initially observed these developments with some interest. But since the issue of his family's protection had been resurrected by Elzbietta's outburst, he had begun to feel nothing but concern at the thought of greater Russian presence in the area. To compound his worries, news had recently filtered through the market that Russia was about to open a consulate in the city, the last of the European powers to do so. Of the vast number of Russians who made the journey to Palestine each year, most were no doubt greatly relieved to hear that their interests were at last to be protected by a consul in Jerusalem. In the past, their only representation had been by an annual visit to the city by a visiting consular agent. But this knowledge did nothing to allay Tomas's concerns.

Murad Amrad, now back in Jaffa, wrote to Tomas of his fears that with Russian documentation better organised in the city, the name Galperin would stand out and finally be condemned. He cautioned Tomas to be extra vigilant. This thought had already occurred to Tomas. He began to be revisited by childhood nightmares. In these as a child, the family would be discovered and his father taken away. This time however, it was Abraham who was taken, by an unknown and sinister cloaked figure. He would wake after these dreams in a sweat and then be unable and unwilling to go back to sleep. After a week of sleep deprivation, Tomas began to suffer such bad headaches, that once they started he was unable to withstand bright light or even to think very coherently.

It was during one such episode that the British consul arrived at Tomas's premises. He wanted to secure a further loan. James Finn's debts were increasing each year and Tomas had recently been forced to increase his interest in order to provide greater protection. He hadn't liked doing it. The British consul was someone whose friendship and good opinion was worth a great deal to him. But Murad Amrad had been insistent that Tomas should put the business and the support of his family first. Tomas hadn't seen Finn since he'd sent the letter to inform him of the new interest rates, and he was relieved to see that the consul appeared to be his usual friendly self. Given the severity of his current headache however, he was pleased that they were able to conclude their business quickly.

"You look unwell, Tomas," Finn remarked as he got up to leave.

Tomas had been doing his best to maintain a sense of normality despite the pain in his head and behind his eyes, but he did indeed look ashen, his mouth set in a thin line and deep frown lines on his brow.

"Oh, I get these confounded headaches," he said, attempting a smile, hoping he could soon go back upstairs and lie down. "They last for days sometimes."

"Well why didn't you say, Tomas. I'll go now and leave you in peace. But you must go to the English hospital and see Dr. Mendelsohn. In fact, I insist."

"But I am not a Christian," Tomas pointed out. "Nor am I under British protection."

"That is of no consequence," Finn told him. "Just give my name and tell Dr Mendelsohn that I sent you."

Dr Mendelsohn was a progressive thinker for his day, and on being presented with a case of severe headaches, was prompted to ask the patient if there was anything that might be causing him undue concern at the present time. Tomas looked at him blankly.

"Forgive me, Dr. Mendelsohn. But what might that question have to do with my headaches?"

"Ah, you'd be surprised, Mr. Galperin. I am of the belief that circumstance has a great effect upon health."

Tomas was tempted to excuse himself and leave straightaway. He'd never heard of anything so ridiculous. But remembering James Finn's act of kindness he decided he should remain. He shrugged his shoulders and, somewhat hesitantly, began to unburden himself of his worries instead. There was something about the doctor's quiet attention that encouraged openness, and he began telling him about Abraham, about the opportunity being presented to him, and about Fanny's reluctance to allow their son to go, on account of his having to become a Christian. He did not however, discuss the fears he had for his family's safety or the issue of British protection.

"What is your own opinion of your son going to Malta and becoming a Christian?" Dr. Mendelsohn asked.

"I feel we would be wrong to prevent it," Tomas replied immediately. "And as to the issue of his religion, I can't believe Christianity is any better or worse a faith than our own. But I must confess to not having my wife's piety. To me, being Jewish is more a way of life, and I know no other."

Tomas suddenly felt he had said too much. Dr. Mendelsohn was, after all, a Jewish convert to Christianity. But the doctor did not seem unduly concerned.

"I have to tell you that I still consider myself to be a Jew," he said. "A Christian Jew. You are right when you define Judaism as a way of life. It is the way of our ancestors and I would have it no other way. Which is why, when we worship in the mission's church, we continue to observe the Jewish calendar and adhere to many Jewish laws and customs. But we combine them with those of Christianity. I have come to believe that there are many pathways to God. Once I had heard the teachings of Jesus, who was also a Jew, I decided that particular path was right for me. I am confident that were you to send your son, Abraham, along that path, it would not lead him away from all that your family hold true."

Tomas found himself speechless. The fact that the doctor then went on to prescribe a concoction of herbs, as well as recommend that he cease wearing too tight a hat, almost passed without him noticing. Dr. Mendelsohn had made it all sound so simple. When looked at like that, Christianity didn't seem such an alien concept. If only he could present the argument for Abraham having to convert to Christianity to Fanny with as much inspiration and clarity.

By the time he arrived home, he imagined the pressure in his head was already beginning to lessen. Perhaps Dr. Mendelsohn was right, and his recent worries were indeed the cause of his headaches. He had to admit that he felt more hopeful that the dilemma regarding Abraham might not be that insurmountable after all. He hadn't admitted to himself, until speaking with the doctor, how much he wanted his son to have this chance. But he was not prepared to give his permission without Fanny's blessing. And to this end he did his best to describe to her the beliefs of John Nicholayson's Jewish Christians – the way in which to be both Jewish and Christian.

"Elzbietta still thinks of herself as a Jew, Fanny. I hadn't appreciated how much until now. And if Abraham went to Malta and became a Christian, he too would remain a Jew. A Christian Jew. And we would be giving him an unparalleled education. I don't believe we would ever forgive ourselves if we denied our boy such a chance in life!"

He and Fanny stayed awake talking through most of that night. Finally, as the sky was beginning to lighten, he held her as she sobbed in defeat. But he felt no triumph. They would be losing their son after all, albeit for a good cause.

Ten days later, the family travelled to Jaffa with Joseph and Elzbietta. Their ship to Malta was leaving the following day, and they were to stay overnight at the family home where Sonja had prepared a huge farewell feast. Although they were all heartbroken at the thought of being parted, and Joseph in particular felt nothing but guilt at having to wrench Elzbietta away from her family, they wanted the evening to be one filled with laughter and joy. It was going to be the last time the family would be together for some time and they were determined it would be memorable. So they sang and danced, laughed and shared memories of the past, made promises to visit one another frequently, and planned what they would do the next time they were reunited.

The next morning, just before dawn, the whole family left the house and set off down the track to Jaffa. There was a strip of lighter sky in the East, streaked with dark clouds that promised rain, and a chill in the air. Murad Amrad and Tomas led the way, holding a lantern whose services were not needed for long. Sonja followed in the donkey cart with Sarah, Anna and the luggage. Their first donkey, Hungry, had died some years before and had been replaced by another they had rather improbably named Freeda. On this morning, Nathaniel and James walked on either side of Freeda, occasionally making encouraging noises to her. She was inclined to walk rather slowly. Abraham and Fanny walked immediately behind the cart, the boy holding tightly onto his mother's hand, while Utah, Hanna, Elzbietta and Joseph brought up the rear. They were a subdued party, and for the most part silent, each of them with their own thoughts, their faces set grim in the early morning light. The rumbling wheels of the donkey cart and the padding of Freeda's hooves on the rough ground soon sent Sarah and Anna back to sleep. It was early for them to be awake and they'd been up till late the night before. But Abraham, at ten years old, announced that he was too old to accept a lift in the cart. He wanted to walk, he said. Fanny smiled down at him and squeezed his hand. The next time she saw him he'd most likely consider himself too old to hold her hand, she thought. She blinked back the tears that flooded into her eyes. She wanted to be as strong as he was being.

When they reached the beach, several rowing boats were pulled up onto the shore. A number of other passengers were standing around, most looking apprehensively at the choppy waves. There was some conversation about the advisability of taking to the boats if there was a storm approaching. The boatmen seemed unconcerned however. They had rowed through much rougher seas than these, they assured the crowd, before drawing away and talking quietly among themselves. They would wait for the full consignment of passengers to arrive before loading them onto their boats and beginning the long pull to the waiting ships lying at anchor beyond the reefs.

The time to say goodbye eventually came and went all too quickly, before the family was left on the beach watching the rowing boats' slow and turbulent progress away from the shore. In the bow of one of them, Joseph sat looking resolutely ahead. Beside him, Elzbietta returned their waves, frantically at first, then more slowly. Before long she stopped altogether and wrapped both her arms protectively around the small figure sitting beside her.

On the beach, Fanny could no longer hold back her sobs. Tomas folded her into his arms, Sarah and Anna held onto her skirts, and Sonja stroked her back. Nathaniel and James kept their eyes on the sea. But they were all crying. They stood in a tight group for what seemed like a very long time. Long enough to see the rowing boats reach the ship, although it was too far away to see the passengers climb the gangway. And long enough to see the fishermen arriving back on the beach to unload their night's catch.

"Come now," Murad Amrad said gently. "It is time for us to leave. A new day has begun for them and for us, and we must make the most of it."

Back in Jerusalem, although the family settled back into their normal routine, they felt Abraham's absence keenly. Fanny became so quiet and withdrawn that, after a few weeks had passed, Tomas began to be worried about her, most especially as she continued to lay a place for Abraham at the table. He knew she missed Elzbietta as well, and decided that perhaps it would be good for her to return to Jaffa for a while. She could at least then get comfort from her mother and Hanna. But one day, before he could suggest it, Fanny suddenly asked whether they could visit the Christian church. She was preparing their meal at the time and spoke as if it was the most normal thing in the world to suggest, continuing with her preparations without a pause. Tomas felt rather alarmed at her request.

"Why do you want us to do that, *Bubbala?*" he said.

191

"I would like to know what Abraham is learning," she told him. "When he comes home, he'll tell us all about his studies and I want to understand what he's talking about. I don't want him to feel too different to us. I don't want to lose him." She choked back tears and increased the speed at which she was cutting up vegetables.

"Then we will go this Sunday," Tomas said soothingly, after only a short pause. And seeing the look of horror on James and Nathaniel's faces, he told them, "You will both stay here and mind the girls and the store." Then, ignoring their relieved expressions, he returned downstairs to the safety of his store. He needed a few moments to recover his composure.

The market was quiet that day and business had been slack. Torrential rain had turned the myriad of narrow streets into rivers and he was glad not to have to go out. But all at once, he was startled by the sound of shouting outside. He looked out and saw one of his fellow tradesmen struggling with three Turkish guards who appeared to be trying to escort him away.

"What's going on here, Levi?" he called to his friend in Hebrew.

"These men have accused me of stealing a loaf of bread from the market, Tomas. Have you ever heard of such nonsense? It is the young Arab boys who steal the bread, not I. This is because I remonstrated with them when they hit an old Jewish man out of their way. This is their reprisal. I am just yet another scapegoat, and they know it."

Levi was a successful cloth merchant, a good man, and their two families were friends. There was no reason or likelihood for him to steal bread. But the Turkish guards had twisted his arms cruelly behind his back as he had been speaking and were marching him off down the road like a common criminal. Tomas felt a surge of anger.

"This is wrong! You are making a mistake!" he shouted in Arabic to their retreating backs, but he was powerless to do anything else to help.

"Don't get involved, Tomas," Levi called out. "Or you will be next."

Tomas knew he was right. Levi and his family had British protection, and for that reason the Turkish authorities wouldn't dare keep him on a trumped up charge. He would soon be freed, unlike other Jews he knew of who had no representation and still languished in the Turkish dungeons for no particular reason other than they were Jewish. There had been no need for him to get involved in Levi's situation at all, and the reality was that he had placed himself in danger by doing so. He just hoped the Turkish guards didn't speak Arabic, or hadn't heard him. He did not want to put his Prussian letter of protection to the test. They had all managed to keep away from any conflict with the authorities up until now. He turned back into the store and decided he wouldn't tell Fanny about the incident. It was, after all, only one among many other similar injustices handed out to the Jewish population by the Turks, many far worse it had to be said, and she had enough to worry her at the present.

When Tomas and Fanny arrived at the mission compound near the Jaffa Gate on the following Sunday, Fanny was clearly nervous. Tomas wondered if she was regretting her request to attend a Christian service. He, however, was curious. Although he came to the compound fairly frequently to see James Finn, whose consul residence was nearby, he had never been inside the church. This was Nicholayson's Protestant church for the Jewish converts, named the Christ Church. It had taken over nine years to build, and had not been completed until 1849. The Turkish authorities had feared that the British were intent on turning Palestine into a Christian state and done everything they could to block its construction. In actual fact, Joseph had told Tomas that the rate of conversion from Judaism to Christianity was not as high as the mission would have liked, and the Apostate congregation still only numbered a few hundred. But those few welcomed Tomas and Fanny warmly as they stepped through the doors of the imposing building.

They found the inside of the Christ Church to be filled with Jewish symbols and texts alongside the Christian ones, with reference made to many Jewish traditions and values. As the service began, they were surprised by the Hebrew prayers, and by the gospel preached in such a way as to place emphasis on the Jewish cultural heritage of its congregation. Tomas saw Fanny look startled at first, then visibly begin to relax. He felt enormous relief. Their experience of Christianity was to be far less stressful and unfamiliar than either of them had feared. And when they stepped out into the sunshine after the service, he saw that Fanny was smiling.

Some days later, when Murad Amrad was once again in Jerusalem, Tomas was able to tell him about their visit to the church and the reasons why Fanny had wanted to be there.

"What did she think of it?" Murad Amrad asked.

"She hasn't said much about it," Tomas replied. "I asked her what she thought, of course, and she just said it was interesting. She hasn't mentioned it since."

Murad Amrad raised his eyebrows. "And you, my boy? What did you think?"

Tomas didn't say anything for a minute or two. The experience had left him with many conflicting feelings, and he welcomed the chance to discuss them with his father. But he needed to assemble his thoughts first. He was frowning when finally he spoke.

"I felt safe, Father! For the first time, I felt totally safe. And to tell you the truth, I didn't want to leave," he gave an embarrassed laugh. "It was strange. James Finn was there of course, with his wife Elizabeth and their children. Dr Mendelsohn, too. And John Nicholayson. Everyone was very warm and inclusive. I felt as if we were being welcomed into an elite club. I then found myself thinking that to be in that club, surrounded by all those people, would be the safest place to be. It was a place where I, and the family, would be taken care of, a place where no one could harm us. In fact, I found myself thinking that I would be a fool not to..." he hesitated then, finally reluctant to give word to thought.

But Murad Amrad had anticipated his son's meaning, and broke in somewhat sternly.

"If you were to convert, Tomas, you would still not have British protection."

"But I would have the protection of the English church, Father. And that must count for something."

Murad Amrad grunted. "Does Fanny know your thoughts?"

"No, she doesn't. But I feel we must discuss them soon, and it is not something I relish."

Murad Amrad nodded grimly and sighed. The outcome of this

issue suddenly seemed inevitable. If Tomas and his family had to become Christians in order to be protected, then so be it. The most important thing to him was their continued safety. Elzbietta's outburst had shaken his confidence in their Prussian documents as much as it had Tomas's. He just prayed that Sonja would be able to come to terms with her daughter renouncing her religion.

"I do understand, Tomas," he said. "And if that is what you think is best for your family, then I will speak with Sonja and make sure she understands as well."

When Tomas eventually found the courage to tell Fanny that he thought the family should convert to Christianity, her initial prolonged silence unnerved him to such an extent that he found himself justifying his reasons over and over again.

"It is the most sensible solution open to us all, Fanny. Elzbietta was right. We have fooled ourselves for too long. Our documents are dubious, and our chances of getting British protection very slim. But this is one way we just might be protected, or at least treated with respect. Did you not feel safe in the English church?"

When finally she spoke, her response surprised him. "You are right, Tomas. But I only agree because of Abraham. I don't want to be alienated from his beliefs and it will gladden my heart to know that we will all be members of the same church. In my heart however, I will always remain Jewish. I'll still light the Sabbath candles at the proper time, I'll still keep a kosher kitchen and I'll still attend synagogue. In that way I'll remain true to what I believe."

The ceremony to baptise them all into the apostate community of Jerusalem was a simple one, made more meaningful by the knowledge that Abraham was himself being baptised by the principal of the Malta Protestant College on the same day. The congregation, being made up of men and women who had themselves converted from Judaism, had a great deal of understanding of the pressures placed upon new converts, and one by one they came forward to offer Tomas and Fanny their help and support.

From then on, Tomas and Fanny incorporated the daily life of the English church into theirs, and Tomas threw himself wholeheartedly into the task of becoming an active member of the small community of converted Jews. Fanny meanwhile, was content with her decision to tread a path between both faiths. In deference to her Christian friends, she reverted to holding her neatly contained hair in place with a modest net instead of the shawl or wig she had worn before. But although she and the children had the freedom to dress in a far greater range of colours, she was unwilling to abandon her Jewish sobriety of taste, and continued to wear primarily dark clothes. As for the children, they appeared remarkably unaffected by their conversion to Christianity. James and Nathaniel, after an initial period of horror at what their father was making them do, were old enough to recognise the pragmatism of the decision. Sarah and Anna seemed able to take it in their stride. Tomas assumed they were too young to understand it, but one evening, soon after their baptism, Anna asked: "We're still saying our prayers to the same God aren't we, Mamma?"

He and Fanny both looked at her, and then at each other, in some wonder. Their youngest daughter had put the whole business into perspective with just a few simple words. She had also somehow cleared the air and Fanny laughed properly for the first time since Abraham had left.

"Indeed we are, *Bubbala,*" she chuckled. "And aren't we lucky to know two ways to reach Him?" She then smiled at Tomas, who all at once felt happier and more relaxed than he had in a long while.

The most difficult aspect of converting from Judaism to Christianity, especially for Fanny, was the loss of many of their friends. While some understood the political and social pressures surrounding the family's decision and remained as friendly as before, the more pious among them renounced their former friends without a backwards glance. A few maintained a sympathetic relationship with Fanny alone, the fact that she still considered herself a Jew being applauded by those who supported her open duality. Tomas was just glad he had moved his family into their new property when he did. It would have been far more difficult for them if they had still lived among their erstwhile neighbours in the Jewish Quarter. As it was, surrounded by the vast diversity of religions and races in the market, they were free to establish new relationships based on their position as Christian converts.

In Jaffa, when Murad Amrad told Sheikh Abu al Khayr about Tomas's conversion to Christianity, he took care to emphasise the reasons behind the decision. The situation was one he and Sonja were finding hard enough to come to terms with themselves, without the added weight of censorship from the Sheikh. But Sheikh Abu al Khayr knew Murad Amrad only too well and sought instead to defuse what he took to be his friend's feelings of shame with some playful goading.

"Ha! Now a second one of your children has distanced themselves from the Jewish faith! Does that not tell you something, my friend?" He grinned mischievously at Murad Amrad who duly snorted in amusement. But then the Sheikh continued in a more serious tone of voice. "Tomas must be cautious, however. This protection he speaks of? It is merely a veil. It can easily be torn away, and behind it, everything will be as it always has been."

Murad Amrad looked at the Sheikh quizzically, and then pointedly changed the subject. He had no wish for his head to be filled with doubts. Two years later however, he was given cause to remember the Sheikh's words.

It was a day in May 1860, and Tomas was returning from a meeting with James Finn at the consular residence in the mission compound. Never had he seen the British consul so agitated. He had been pacing up and down his chambers when Tomas arrived, and had immediately launched into such a tirade that it was hard at first for Tomas to understand what he was talking about. He learned the reason soon enough. James Finn and his family had been given notice to vacate their property in the mission compound, and not only was James Finn beside himself with anger, but he wanted to know if Tomas could help them find somewhere else to live.

James Finn was prone to tirades. He was well known as having many thorns in his side and he had no hesitation in voicing them to whoever would listen. One of them was the failure of the British Foreign Office to allocate funds for a specific property in which to house the British consulate and consular residence. Other consuls had their own premises, Finn had often told Tomas. But despite Britain being the first consulate to open in Jerusalem, he was forced to move from pillar to post in rented property. Did they expect him to live in a tent, he would ask? Another frequent source of his anger was the meager allowance on which he was supposed to support his family. The Bishop of Jerusalem, Samuel Gobat, received over twice his salary, he once informed Tomas, who sympathised and assured him that he would always be there to lend him further funds as and when they were needed. Tomas had also, on several occasions, offered help in other matters should they arise. This was now one such occasion.

Tomas was well aware that the cause of today's problem was most likely to be the continued enmity and apparent competition for status between James Finn and Samuel Gobat. The mission was subordinate to the bishop, and it was hard not to imagine it was he who had instructed them to issue the eviction order, possibly exacting some sort of revenge in doing so. But Tomas was of the opinion that James Finn continually asked for trouble by being so confrontational. Despite being forbidden to do so, Finn persisted in trying to interest Jews in Christianity. The bishop viewed this as gross interference in the activities of the Mission, which he considered to be his domain. Their relationship had worsened over the years, and their enmity was compounded when Finn had publicly accused the bishop of being anti-British and of plotting against him with the Prussian consul, Dr. Georg Rosen who, like Bishop Gobat, was German. Finn's relationship with the Prussian consul was also very strained. Finn argued with many people it had to be said. And after more than a decade of hearing about hostile confrontations between Finn and various high-ranking dignitaries, Tomas felt it all to be extremely tiresome. Right now he was glad to be able to take his leave and give himself time to think about where James Finn and his family could live.

It was a glorious morning, the air in the city still comparatively fresh, free from the odious smells so prevalent during the summer months. But summer was not far off and Tomas felt a small thrill of pleasure at the thought. He and Fanny always took the family to Jaffa during the hottest weeks of the year. With the pilgrim season then at an end, and the heat in Jerusalem insufferable, there were fewer visitors to the city and it was a good time to take a break. He always looked forward to working on the farm and spending time with family and old friends in Jaffa. He ran a finger around his collar. The day was hotting up and he had been walking briskly in his eagerness to put distance between himself and the consular residence. He slowed his pace slightly, in an attempt to cool off.

There was little difference in the way Tomas dressed since his conversion, although he had shaved his beard and now wore only a heavy moustache – the black trousers and frock coat worn by Ashkenazim was a dress code similar to that used by the Europeans. But he had swapped his skullcap for a European top hat, an article of clothing he wore every day and of which he felt secretly rather proud. He now lifted it slightly to let in a brief waft of air. In Jaffa, he sometimes wore the clothes and headdress of an Arab, especially when he and Ameen went out on horseback. The garments were a great deal more comfortable and considerably cooler in the heat than the ones he wore in the city. In them, Tomas felt himself to be no more conspicuous in the Palestinian landscape than Ameen. Those were good times.

He had been surprisingly reticent about telling Ameen of his conversion. But when he did, his Arab friend had just shrugged.

"My father has already told me, my friend. But Jew or Christian! What is the difference? You are still a non-believer, an infidel." Then he had laughed, slapped Tomas on the back and changed the subject. But Tomas knew he'd understood.

Dragging himself from his recollections, Tomas returned to the problem in hand. It was to be hoped that the British Government would decide to build a British consulate and residence one day soon, he thought. He had to admit that these temporary housing solutions did little for the consul's standing. As it happened however, he remembered a small house high up in the city that had recently become empty. He decided to walk up and take a look at it before returning home. The rent would probably be greater on account of its position, but it would be a cool house in which to live.

A small commotion on the road ahead of him caught his attention. A group of men in Turkish dress walking towards him had been brought to a halt. A collection of shabbily dressed men had thrown themselves onto the ground in front of them and now appeared to be pleading and making requests. Although Tomas was slightly too far away to hear exactly what they were saying, he was near enough to identify one of the Turks, and he gave an involuntary gasp. Here was no less a person than Sureyya Pasha himself, the Ottoman Governor of Jerusalem. Tomas hesitated for a second. He would normally prefer to avoid walking directly past the governor, who was well known for making trouble with Jews. But then he remembered he was a Christian now, a member of the English church, and as such he had nothing to fear. He composed himself and continued to walk on.

As he got nearer, he observed a tall, studious looking man with round spectacles who stood beside the governor, his body inclined towards him as if grafted into constant attention. This was undoubtedly the governor's secretary, who was known to go everywhere with him. Another man, presumably a servant, hovered behind them both. He looked nervous and kept his eyes averted from the scene in front of him. As well he might, Tomas thought, as the two Turkish soldiers with them began to kick the supplicants on the ground until they got up and ran away. The whole scene had only taken a few seconds to act out, but the random brutality of it left Tomas considerably shaken. The men on the floor had been Jews.

The governor's group then continued on their way, walking sedately towards him. Their paths were going to cross, and as they neared, Tomas moved aside to allow them to pass. The governor however stopped, and Tomas felt his stomach give a small lurch of alarm. As much to keep the upper hand as to instinctively instill calm, he greeted the governor's party in Arabic, a language he knew the governor spoke well. Sureyya Pasha was a tall, good-looking man with a neatly trimmed beard, but his eyes were hard and the greeting was not returned. Instead he said something to his secretary in Turkish. The secretary turned to Tomas, held out his hand and asked in Arabic for his papers. He felt the rate of his heart speed up. This was the event he had dreaded for so long. The event he had so far managed to avoid. He had never been asked to show them before and he wondered what had initiated the request now. He pulled Merad Arutin's somewhat ragged document from his pocket and presented it to the secretary, who then handed it straight to the governor. Sureyya Pasha looked at it briefly and a look of amazement spread over his face. He snorted in derision and said something that made the secretary smirk and titter behind his hand. The governor then addressed him directly, this time in Arabic.

"This piece of paper has no authority. Where are you from?"

"I came originally from Russia, but I have lived in Jerusalem since I was a child. I am a member of the English church here in Jerusalem," Tomas replied, trying to keep the concern from his voice. "I am also a personal friend of the British Consul Mr. Finn, who can vouch for my character if that is what is needed."

The governor curled his mouth in derision as he spoke. "That may be the way it is. But the facts with which I have been presented are conclusive. You are not a subject of any other country; therefore you are a Rayah, a person of inferior status without European protection. And as you have just assured me that you are a resident of Jerusalem, you are therefore under my jurisdiction."

He spoke the last few words slowly and loudly, almost as if he was talking to a person with limited understanding. Tomas understood only too well but thought it best to remain silent. There was no arguing with the governor's logic, although his mind was racing as to what the outcome of this conversation might be. The governor didn't keep him in suspense for long.

"I must remind you that our sultan, in his infinite wisdom, has decreed that all his subjects are to wear the Fez."

Tomas was completely unprepared for this apparent diversion in topic and his face must have portrayed his confusion. The governor indicated his own cylindrical red hat and those of his companions as if in explanation. Suddenly Tomas understood. He remembered that the sultan had indeed issued this decree, some years ago, not only in an attempt to modernise the Ottoman Empire, but most probably to try and prevent the headdresses of non-Muslims living in Ottoman territories from being more flambuoyant than those of Muslims. He remembered the wildly extravagant turbans worn by many citizens of the Ottoman Empire in his youth.

The governor spoke again. "You are wearing a headdress that has no place on the head of a Rayah. I must insist that you remove it immediately and replace it with a Fez."

Tomas was at a slight loss as to what to do. He had no Fez with him and had to think quickly.

"If Your Excellency would permit me to explain myself, I have been directed by Dr Mendelsohn at the clinic not to wear a Fez on account of my liability to severe headaches. My current hat affords me some shade from the sun as you see. I believe you can find the certificate pronouncing it improper for me to wear a Fez at the English hospital."

Tomas tailed off. The sudden change in the governor's countenance was rather alarming. He had gone very pale, his eyes had narrowed to such an extent that they had almost disappeared and his mouth, under his beard, had become a hard line. He was not used to having his orders questioned or contradicted and he suddenly barked out an order. Tomas embarrassed himself by jumping. He was shocked even further when the two soldiers jumped on him, holding his arms on either side in a vice like grip. He remained silent however, feeling nothing but complete disbelief at how events had unfurled. He found himself noticing that the secretary was blinking rapidly behind his round spectacles, and that the servant was employing the same distant gaze that had accompanied the soldiers' previous assaults. The governor then spoke to Tomas in a hiss, as if through clenched teeth.

"You insult the sultan with your words. His decree is not to be questioned or excuses found to ignore it. You obviously need time to learn respect and obedience to the words of the sultan."

With that he turned on his heel and strode away, his secretary still moulded to his side and his servant padding after him with rapid steps.

Tomas cast around for help. He had been aware of a group of Arab boys watching the proceedings from a safe distance and he now quickly called out an instruction in Arabic to the nearest of them. The soldiers responded by twisting his arms sharply behind his back and, as he was marched away, he had no idea whether or not his words had been heard.

Some time later, Tomas doubted that the tiny room into which he had been thrown had seen much use as a prison. With little evidence of past human occupation on display, he thought it had perhaps once been a storeroom. But whatever its history, it had until now long been abandoned. The walls were crumbling, long cobwebs hung from the ceiling and the floor was deep in loose rubble. He had fallen and cut his knee when the soldiers pushed him in and his wound now throbbed. He was aware that his trouser leg felt sticky with blood and he looked around for somewhere to sit. The only available place was on a pile of large stones in one corner, and he lowered himself down on these carefully to examine his knee and consider his predicament.

His prison cell was at the very end of a long tunnel in what appeared to be the dungeons of the old garrison. He and the two soldiers had entered through a heavy door set into a portion of the city wall he hadn't known existed. They had then descended steep steps and continued along the tunnel in virtual darkness, heading towards an area of dim daylight ahead of them. It was many degrees colder than it had been outside, and the walls smelled musty. Eventually the tunnel opened into a long chamber, and Tomas saw that the light by which they had been guided came through rectangular apertures along one of the walls at ceiling level. He had craned his neck to try and see outside, but could make nothing out. The openings were too small and too high up. Ahead of him, to the right and left of the chamber, rows of barred cages faced each other, and inside each an indistinguishable number of ragged human shapes were slumped on the ground.

Tomas assumed his own destination had been reached, but to his surprise the soldiers had marched him between the cells towards another entranceway beyond them. As they did so, the other prisoners suddenly mobilised themselves and, as if on a signal, surged against the bars, dirty hands reaching out towards them and disembodied voices calling for news and food. The sudden noise was deafening and Tomas had found it a greatly unnerving experience. He wondered how long and why these men had been incarcerated. But the overriding impact had been the stench of unwashed human bodies and excrement that emanated from each cage as its occupants moved. It remained with him even now, seemingly impregnated into his clothing, despite his own solitary cell being some distance away at the end of a second tunnel.

Similar apertures to those in the main chamber, along one wall of his cell, provided sufficient light for him to discover fairly quickly that he was not alone. He was sharing the small space with a great many rats. As time went on, it became apparent that these rodents were unafraid of human contact, and he lost count of how many times he kicked out as they ran over his feet or up his legs. He noticed that the rodents were free to come and go as they pleased. They had a route in and out of the cell through a gap under the door, where the wood of the door and the stone of the floor had worn away. He watched them for a while. Apart from their scuffling and squeaking and the occasional muffled shouts of the other prisoners from way down the tunnel, the silence in his cell pressed in on his ears.

He wondered what Fanny was doing. When would she discover he was missing? She would be too busy with their baby to notice for a while. David James had been born at the beginning of the year. Tomas had been pleased that Fanny had given birth to another son. He knew she still missed Abraham enormously and hoped this new baby would help in some small way. Thinking of Fanny caused him to feel even more distressed. She was going to be worried sick when he failed to return home. He closed his eyes and tried to stay calm.

A noise in the tunnel outside caused him to start. He must have fallen asleep. A hunk of bread and a shallow dish of water were being pushed through the gap under the door by an unseen hand. Tomas jumped up and shouted out, asking how long he was to be held. But there was no reply and he was left feeling horrified at how quickly he had become like the other prisoners. He tried to focus on the food provided. But with his mother's death from cholera often in his mind, together with Sonja's incessant instructions on how to avoid the disease, he was reluctant to drink the water. He was determined that the rats would not have it however and covered it up with the offending top hat. He might need it for washing later. The bread too was stale and seemingly filled with grit. Having assessed it as inedible, he amused himself by throwing small pieces at the rats to see how often he could hit one. He was able to account for his successes by the number of corresponding squeaks at the other end of the cell.

It had been morning when he'd been taken prisoner and brought to the garrison. He now saw that what little light had filtered in before was fading, and that his cell was rapidly descending into total darkness. He could only pray that his family, in missing him, would somehow find out where he had been taken and try to secure his release. If they spoke to James Finn he was sure that the British Consul would speak for him in defense of whatever crime he had been accused, despite his not being under British protection. But he felt totally defeated by the knowledge that he was powerless to do anything to help himself. His role as a member of the English church had counted for nothing after all. And all his past fears of having no diplomatic protection were summarised by his current position. He was trapped. Whatever social or financial standing he achieved in Jerusalem, he and his family would never be any different to thousands of other Jews in Palestine; inferior citizens of the Ottoman Empire, totally dependant on the whims of a tyrannical leader. It was a destiny that filled him with huge despair.

Unaware of Tomas Galperin's plight, James Finn sat at his desk and began a letter to the Foreign Office. He wrote regularly, as indeed he was expected to do, reporting on the state of affairs in Palestine. But his letters most often exceeded that expected in the course of duty by including a long list of his complaints. On this day, as he faced eviction from his current home, he had cause to write about the immediate problem his family faced in a lack of accommodation. He followed that by criticising the British Government's failure to sanction the construction of a British consulate building in Jerusalem and a permanent consul's residence, despite his repeated requests. He made sure to detail all the properties obtained by the governments of every other nation represented in the city for their consulate's usage. And, as was usual, he made an impassioned request for a rise in salary. Still on this subject, he was in the middle of citing the dramatic rise in the cost of rent and the depreciation of the currency in Jerusalem, when a commotion outside his door caused him to put down his pen and investigate. He found his dragoman holding the arm of an Arab boy.

"This boy has something to tell you," the dragoman said. "And I am trying to find out if he is telling the truth."

The dragoman was being somewhat heavy handed and the boy was looking scared. James Finn spoke many languages including Arabic and had no need of the dragoman's interpretation services, except in matters of writing and formality. He indicated that the boy should be released.

"The man said you would give me money if I told you," the boy whined, rubbing his arm vigorously and glaring at the dragoman.

"What man? Told me what?" James Finn asked gently.

"I do not know his name." The boy sniffed loudly and wiped his nose on his sleeve. "But he told me to tell you that he had been taken by the Pasha's men."

James Finn was anxious for the boy to give him further details. What had the man looked like? What words had been said between the man and the governor? But even given this information he was still not entirely sure who it was that had been abducted. The wearing of European hats was becoming increasingly popular as a headdress in Jerusalem among men of other nationalities. But when the boy remembered, as an after thought, that the governor had called the man a Rayah, Finn concluded that the unfortunate captive would have no diplomatic protection, and that was enough to spur him into action. He thanked the boy, paid him a few coins and went immediately out, striding furiously towards the governor's residence with the intention of demanding an explanation of such arbitrary behaviour.

Once he discovered who the Pasha's prisoner was, Finn's further intervention in the affair was inevitable. Tomas was a Christian convert and a member of the English church in Jerusalem and as such deserved his help. Arguably, added motivational force behind Finn's involvement in the case was the fact that Tomas was by now his primary moneylender, and as such was of vital importance to him. To challenge the Pasha on the legality of his conduct however, was undoubtedly beyond the jurisdiction of his role as British Consul. But the Pasha, when faced with Finn's wrath, indignation and threats, nevertheless backed down and, after twenty-four hours, released Tomas without further charge.

Walking back towards Tomas's home the following morning, the two men were silent at first, unspoken questions hanging awkwardly between them. Finally Finn broached the subject of Tomas's Prussian protection.

"It seems that the confidence you had in your Prussian protection was unjustified after all," he began, and his dislike of the Prussian Consul was such that he couldn't keep a note of triumph from his voice. "Perhaps you will now allow me to grant you and your family British protection."

Tomas knew the time had come to be as honest as he dared with the man who had probably just saved his life and whom he liked to consider a friend. He took a few moments to choose his words carefully. The events that had so changed the fortunes of his family had happened nearly thirty years ago, but they were still events for which justice could be demanded.

"When my family first came to Palestine, we left Russia without the necessary documentation," he began. "We left in such haste that certain of our affairs remained unsettled." James Finn glanced at him questioningly and Tomas hesitated. He took a deep breath before carrying on. "To settle those affairs might have taken a long time and we were reluctant to delay our departure." He was sweating now and he wiped his hand across his forehead. "We have always been of the opinion that were we to approach the Russian Consul, they may insist we return to Russia to complete our affairs. This is something we all still wish to avoid at any cost. When we were offered Prussian documentation from the agent in Jaffa some years ago, we presumed we could rely on that country's protection should it become necessary. Now that we know the documentation is invalid, we must presume to be without European protection."

James Finn was silent for a while. "And are you still reluctant to approach the Russian authorities?" he asked.

Tomas nodded. He was suddenly exhausted. He hadn't eaten or drunk anything since the morning of the previous day when he was taken prisoner, and one of his headaches was threatening. More than anything else right now, he wanted to be home with his family.

"This is indeed a problem, then." Finn inclined his hands as if in defeat as he walked. "And I'm at a loss to know how to help. It is a pity that you became Christian as late as you did. In the past, Jews who converted to Christianity were automatically offered British protection, as you would have been a few years ago. But as you know, the law has changed since then and the British Government has placed many more restrictions on who can and can't obtain their protection. If I granted you British protection without the necessary documentation from Russia, my government would demand an explanation." He paused for a while and appeared to be thinking the problem through. When he spoke again he sounded weary and discouraged. "I would strongly suggest that you cast your fears behind you and pay a visit to the Russian Consulate after all. And in some haste! I cannot say too much, but I believe the government to be planning further new legislation regarding British Protection. Certainly the numbers of Russian Jews offered British Protection are to be reduced at some stage in the future."

Tomas was shocked to hear this. And he knew that James Finn would be taking this proposal very personally. His mission to help as many Jews as possible by providing them with British protection, with or without encouraging them to convert to Christianity, would be seriously challenged.

The two men were silent for a while, and then talked briefly of other things. Tomas was thankful that the subject had been changed. When they parted, he shook the British consul's hand and declared himself deeply indebted to him.

"You have my word that I will do everything in my power to be at your service," he said.

There was little doubt that James Finn welcomed Tomas's gratitude. Already heavily in debt from financing all his Jewish projects, his newest venture, the farm for Jewish workers at Artas near Bethlehem, had been incurring massive losses. Incessant raids by local tribes regularly destroyed all the crops, and much publicised arguments and legal battles over control and ownership of the farm had undermined its success as well as his reputation. Having borrowed money from a number of moneylenders in the city, the majority of them were now refusing him further credit. Worse still, many had started to demand immediate repayment. Tomas's ongoing willingness to accommodate his frequent requests for money was therefore critical to him right now. Without it, James Finn could envisage a time ahead when he would be unable to even buy food for his family.

In the face of growing criticism from the Foreign Office for his frequent interference in local affairs and his incessant quarrels with local dignitaries, James Finn felt the need to justify his every action in his letters. His involvement with Tomas Galperin's release from prison was one such occasion, and Finn used the incident to illustrate the unreasonable behaviour of the governor, another man with whom he had frequent disagreements. As his debts spiraled out of control, his letters became more desperate. Hearing that a branch of The Bank of Turkey had opened in Constantinople, he suggested that a branch be opened in Jerusalem as soon as possible. He listed the many establishments in the city that would benefit from such a bank. He pointed out that all those in financial distress at the present time were forced to borrow money from small firms of Jews who transacted their business at enormous interest. A bank would improve credit and encourage financial confidence and trade in the area, he wrote.

But neither The Bank of Turkey nor the British Government had any such plans for the present, and James Finn meanwhile was heading for bankruptcy. Once again, he prepared to make a visit to Tomas to ask for his help. But it was to be his last. The intricate thread of obligation now tying James Finn and Tomas Galperin together was to be tested one final time, with life changing results for them both.

By the beginning of 1861, much of Palestine was suffering from a severe economic crisis. After two years of drought, crops had failed in the normally fertile plains in the south of the country. Thousands of livestock had died during the winter and the rural population was starving. Without grain, many of the Arab peasants were being forced to abandon their villages, and the streets of Jerusalem had become crowded with poverty-stricken families dressed only in rags and existing on such scraps as they could find or were given by others. In Jaffa, and subsequently in Jerusalem, imported grain from Odessa meant that bread at least was available, although it was considerably more expensive. But this disturbance in the price and availability of that most vital of commodities, flour, meant that the price of everything else had gone up to meet the rising cost of living. Even the pilgrim season this year had been affected, and the numbers of visitors to Jerusalem were greatly reduced. Merchants and traders were struggling to make ends meet and many had been forced to sell personal possessions and even property. The only people profiting from this sequence of events were the wealthier Jews, Christians and Muslims who took the opportunity to buy property at vastly reduced prices.

Tomas's business was suffering as much as everyone else's. The value of jewellery was at an all time low and his livelihood of late had been almost solely dependent on his moneylending services. Given that many people were in financial difficulties his help was much in demand, despite it having been necessary to increase his interest rates to cover the risks and shortfalls in income. But since his arrest and imprisonment the previous year, he had not been sleeping well and his headaches had returned. He could not shake off a feeling of vulnerability and fear, and he was no longer able to push the problem of his family's lack of protection to the back of his mind. To make matters worse, he had seen Turkish soldiers wandering past his premises on a number of occasions recently. Fanny told him it was his imagination, but he firmly believed they were spying on him. He could see that the Pasha might be intent on getting him arrested again for the sole purpose of saving face, after having had his actions publicly challenged and defeated by the British consul.

In Jaffa, Murad Amrad decided to take things into his own hands. Increasingly worried about Tomas's state of mind, he wrote suggesting that Tomas, Fanny and the children take a short break in Jaffa. It would do him good, he said. But he had another motive for his invitation. Tomas's arrest had deeply disturbed the whole family, forcing them to acknowledge their vulnerability and the reality of living without diplomatic protection. Nearly a year had passed since then, but their situation remained the same. Now Murad Amrad decided the time had come for them all to get together and discuss what, if anything, could be done.

Tomas had never felt so much in need of his father's council, and replied by return of mail. They would close the store for a while, he wrote, and would come to Jaffa. But on the day they were preparing to leave Jerusalem, James Finn visited. Tomas hadn't seen the British consul for a few weeks and was shocked by his appearance. He looked extremely strained and rather ill. Finn was brief. He told Tomas of the problems he'd experienced recently at his farm in Artas and expressed his optimism that he would soon see them resolved. He then mentioned the sum of money he believed he needed to help him do so.

Notwithstanding his pledge to help his friend, Tomas was considerably shocked by the size of loan James Finn was now requesting. It was certainly a far greater amount than he had ever borrowed before, and Tomas felt a sudden wave of apprehension. Finn already owed him a great deal of money. And with certain rumours in circulation regarding both his increasing unpopularity as British consul and his dire financial situation, Tomas wondered whether Finn would ever be in a position to repay his debts. His optimism for the ultimate success of his project was commendable, but his request for such a large loan spoke also of desperation, and for the first time Tomas felt uneasy about his financial entanglement with the British consul.

"My friend," Tomas said after some hesitation. "We are leaving today to visit our family and property in Jaffa, and will return in a week. Come to me then, and I will do what I can to help."

Two days later, when the family was reunited in Jaffa, the subject of their apparent lack of diplomatic protection was initially left hanging in the air. Murad Amrad and Sonja were mindful that Tomas and Fanny needed time to rest and recuperate after the journey before the subject was broached. So the conversation settled amicably instead on family matters, before moving on to the situation in Jerusalem. To Tomas's surprise, he found that the affairs of the British consul were as much on everyone's lips in Jaffa as they were in Jerusalem.

"They say James Finn owes a fortune to a great many moneylenders, Tomas. I am concerned that you will not get any return on your investment," Murad Amrad began, and Tomas was thankful for the turn of conversation. The problem of James Finn's escalating debt had been compounded by his most recent request and he was looking forward to hearing what his father had to say about it.

"I've had similar concerns of late, Father," Tomas admitted. "His debts are the talk of the city and he has since asked me for another advance, this time a vast sum." He named the figure and his father whistled through his teeth. Tomas continued. "I've delayed granting it until my return. He's desperate and I owe it to him to help of course, but I'm not entirely sure I can raise the amount he asks for immediately. I'm at a loss as to what to do."

"He could become bankrupt at this rate!" Murad Amrad said, and began to look concerned. "Will the British Government allow that to happen? As their representative in Palestine, would they not be responsible for his debts?"

"I don't know, Father. But given that they would, at what point would they step in? From the information Finn himself gives me, it would seem that his government do little to accommodate him. Even if I were to agree to this most recent loan, the amount is considerable and I need to be sure of when I'll see a return."

"I have heard that he might even be dismissed," Fanny put in. "He has made a great number of enemies and many would be glad to see him go. If that were to happen, the British Government would have to honour his debts before he left, would they not?"

They were silent for a while then, all pondering on the problem of their involvement with the British consul's debts. From around the house came the sounds of the younger children playing and exploring, no doubt noting the changes that had taken place to their home in Jaffa since the family last visited. The adults and older children meanwhile, were sitting at the table in the kitchen. Sonja had prepared a great feast to welcome them all home, and they were now replete and content. Outside it had grown dark and cold, but inside the log fire in the kitchen grate glowed and crackled and Tomas thought how good it felt to be surrounded by all that was most loved and familiar. He could already feel the tension in his head lessening. He looked around at his family. The lamp on the table lit their faces from underneath and cast long shadows on the walls around them. A few of them were missing of course. Elzbietta, Joseph and Abraham were in Malta; Abraham with another four years at the Protestant College before he returned to Jerusalem. But their places around the table would always be preserved in the hearts of the family. And in each of the faces of those present, in some way, his mother and grandparents too remained alive.

It was Sonja who finally introduced the subject they'd all been avoiding. When she did so, she couldn't keep a note of disapproval from her voice.

"You turned your family into Christians because you hoped it would provide you with protection," she said. "But it was proved not to be. Nor, seemingly, has it increased your chances of being given British protection. Why is that? Why do you still need a certificate of dismissal from the Russian consul?"

"It seems that the British Government have tightened the law on the granting of British protection," Tomas said gently, and he told them of his conversation with James Finn a year earlier, and the advice the British consul had given him to go to the Russian consulate. He had kept it from them until now.

"Impossible!" Murad Amrad said fiercely, bringing the palm of his hands down on the table and making them all jump.

"I know, Father." Tomas put a hand on his father's arm. "I know."

"Perhaps we should have maintained our faith after all," Fanny said, somewhat bitterly. "I believe it has done us no good to become Christian, and that our conversion has been in vain. And if Finn leaves, we may never be able to get British protection."

"I don't believe we would be in any better position had we remained Jews than we are now," Tomas said quietly. "And perhaps our conversion will count for something one day."

"Tomas, I want you to think carefully," Murad Amrad suddenly said. "Is there any other house of finance in Jerusalem who would be able to lend Finn the amount he now requires?"

"I don't believe so," Tomas replied. "And in any case, if what I hear is true, no-one else will lend him money now. Why do you ask?"

Murad Amrad appeared to be deep in thought and ignored the question, as if he hadn't heard it. Then he murmured, as if to himself.

"I wonder how desperate the British consul is for this loan? How much would he be prepared to pay for it do you think?"

"What have you in mind, Father?" Tomas asked, but once again his father ignored his question, staring instead into the lamp with a deep frown on his face. Tomas and Fanny exchanged a look, she raising her eyebrows questioningly. He shrugged, and gave her a little smile. In the meantime, the conversation continued to flow and change around them, as conversations do. The talk turned to the poverty in the countryside.

"The peasants we passed on the road were digging for roots this morning," Fanny said. "And there were no camels or cattle or sheep anywhere to be seen. Their situation is very bad."

"What is happening in Jerusalem to help the poor?" Hanna asked.

"Well, the Pasha has made no effort to give aid," Tomas retorted. "He refuses even to lessen the taxes."

"The Latin convents have been giving food to the poor," Fanny said. "And the mission too has been generous in their administrations. There is still a great deal of poverty in the Jewish Quarter."

"I hear that in Bethlehem people are dying in the streets from starvation," Hanna said, with a look of horror on her face.

Fanny did her best to reassure her. "The situation is indeed very bad. But I believe a great many peasants have travelled north to the area around Nablus where such severe conditions do not exist."

"And many have been fleeing to Egypt," Utah added. "They come through here on their way to Gaza."

"And what of our land, Father?" Tomas enquired anxiously and turned again towards his father.

Murad Amrad left his thoughts behind then and answered his son.

"Well, as you know, our grain harvest was badly affected this season by the lack of rains, Tomas. Much like everyone else's," he said. "But our oranges and lemons are doing well and the harvest will be good this year. Competition is high now that there are so many other growers in the area. But so is demand. The buyers cannot get enough of our fruits and the steamships ply backwards and forwards to take them all over Europe. It would seem that the whole world has developed a voracious appetite for them!" He chuckled. "There is also talk of a railway line being constructed between Jaffa and Jerusalem, and a harbour to be built in Jaffa. Commerce will benefit greatly by these developments and the future looks good for us all."

"Well the authorities will no doubt do what they can to delay such progress, so we will all have to exercise patience," Utah added, and they all laughed.

The following day, Murad Amrad asked Tomas to sit with him outside. A strong wind was blowing, whipping up the dry earth and creating swirling dust that made it extremely uncomfortable to be anywhere else but in the courtyard of their home. Here, it was sheltered from both wind and dust and they were able to feel the warmth of the sun.

"Perhaps there'll be rain later," Tomas said, looking up at the high white clouds streaking the sky.

His father grunted in a non-committal way as the two men sat themselves down on the stone bench beneath the olive tree.

"I have been thinking hard about the British consul's recent request for this latest loan, Tomas," he began instead. "And I believe this is an opportunity for you, for us all, that must be made use of." Tomas raised his eyebrows briefly and waited for his father to continue.

"If the British consul is as desperate for this money as you imply he might be, he will be prepared to give anything in order to get it. It has to be said that charging greater interest will in all probability do you no good. I believe you must be prepared to accept that Mr. Finn is unlikely to be able to repay you all that he owes you anyway. But if he was to agree to give you something else, something of far greater value, then a certain loss of money on your part is small payment."

Murad Amrad turned to his son, took his hands between his and looked deep into his eyes. "I'm talking about British protection, Tomas, something that will change our lives forever. And you hold all the strings in your hands. Another opportunity like this may never present itself again. The stipulation you must place on granting Mr. Finn this loan is that he gives you and your family British protection in exchange. If it is the only way he can get his hands on the funds he needs, I believe he will not be in a position to refuse. No-one else will lend him this much money."

Tomas had begun to nod slowly while his father spoke. He stared back at Murad Amrad now, not daring to hope. But there was one major flaw in such a seemingly simple course of action.

"He would be breaking the law to give us protection without Russian dismissal, Father," he said slowly.

"It is amazing what a desperate man will do, Tomas," Murad Amrad replied.

"Yes, indeed," Tomas said thoughtfully. He stood up and began to pace up and down the courtyard, hitting the palm of one hand with the fist of the other. "He gave me the impression that if he could settle affairs at Artas, he would gain the approval of the British Government. He can't do that without this loan and, for that reason, he may indeed be prepared to take a risk. As you say, it all depends on how desperate he is and I'll not know that until I speak with him. But if his position as British consul is in danger, it is vital that I get to him before anything happens to remove him from office." He stopped suddenly. "But we are forgetting one thing Father." He returned to his father's side and sat down again heavily. "I have no way of raising that much money so quickly. And by the time I do so, it may be too late."

"There is a way," Murad Amrad said quietly, and he pulled a rather dirty leather pouch from his pocket. He handed it to Tomas who looked at it quizzically before gingerly undoing the ties and tipping the contents into the palm of his hand. It was the diamond.

Tomas was shocked into silence. The stone was almost blinding in its purity, the sunlight on its faceted sides shattering into all the colours of the rainbow. He had not seen the diamond for nearly thirty years and had, since then, become extremely knowledgeable about precious stones. But in all his dealings, he had never before handled a jewel of such astounding beauty and value. More than anything else however, he felt completely overcome by the gravity of the situation. This exquisite stone had, until now, remained in its pouch, bearing testimony to an old contract for which the family had already paid a huge price. Since that time, the Galperin family had forged a successful life for themselves, and their determination to succeed without the need to sell it had been fed to some extent by their belief that the jewel might be cursed. But ultimately, the diamond had always been there as security, something to fall back on should all else fail. Could this really be the time to cash it in? He was battling with conflicting emotions and was thankful when his father spoke again.

"I remember sitting here one day with your grandfather, Abram, shortly before he died. And he said something all those years ago that until now has puzzled me. He told me to remember that although the diamond was the family's safeguard, if ever we had need to sell it, we should only do so provided the value of what we got in return was greater than the value of the stone. Last night I suddenly knew that this was such a time."

He put his hand on his son's arm. Tomas had begun to cry unashamedly, the tears falling down his cheeks and onto the diamond still resting in his hand. The two men remained that way for some minutes, before Tomas sniffed loudly, took out a pocket-handkerchief and wiped his face. Murad Amrad then continued gently.

"I have arranged for Sheikh Abu al Khayr and Ameen to come here later to discuss its sale. Once we have agreed upon a price and a market, you must present your terms to the British consul. Upon his agreement, the sale of the diamond will be completed and the money brought to Jerusalem."

The following day, Tomas knew that he could wait no longer to meet with James Finn. Having received assurances from the Sheikh and Ameen that they would easily be able to sell the diamond for its true worth, it now seemed imperative that he should return to Jerusalem immediately. Until he had spoken with the British consul, he had no idea whether or not his father's plan was feasible. It was arranged that he would make the journey back to Jerusalem the following morning, leaving Fanny and the children in Jaffa until his return. The Sheikh offered him the loan of a fast horse and insisted on providing him with one of his mounted guards. Tomas could not have been more grateful.

The next morning the two men left long before dawn and rode hard. Tomas travelled in Arab dress. His return was not something he wished to broadcast for the time being. They arrived in Jerusalem just as the gates were about to close. Leaving the guard to arrange the stabling of their exhausted mounts, he made his way straight to the British consul's residence rather than going first to his own. It was dark as he made his way through the narrow streets and up the hill to the house he had obtained for the Finn family the previous year. He was amazed that they were still able to afford the considerable rent he knew the landlord of this property demanded. Remembering the British consul's desperation a few days before, he realised of course that they couldn't. There was no doubt that trying to live in a house befitting his station was one of the many reasons that Finn lived well beyond his means. Other reasons were more charitable it had to be said, but now was not the time to let his resolve be softened by sympathy for James Finn's predicament. He had arrived at his destination.

Adjusting his headdress he glanced around him. There were very few people around at this time of the evening, this being mostly a residential area. This suited him well. He opened a metal gate in the high wall that ran along one side of the street. Closing it behind him, he walked across the small courtyard towards the house. A British flag was hanging limply from a white post beside the entrance. The previous day's wind had either dropped or been defeated by the high walls and narrow streets of the city. He saw a light on behind the window that he knew was Finn's study. His heart was beating fast and he paused for a moment in an effort to compose himself. He then took a deep breath, pulled back his shoulders and knocked loudly on the wooden door.

Despite the hour, Tomas was expecting the dragoman to answer. When the British consul himself opened the door it caught him by surprise. But he had a few seconds to collect himself. James Finn didn't realise it was him immediately, and Tomas was able to take in the unkempt appearance of the man standing in front of him. He looked thin and hollow-eyed, his hair upended and his clothing in disarray. As recognition dawned on his face, his expression became one of surprise and then, very rapidly concern.

"Come in, Tomas, come in," he said, and hurried him inside. He led Tomas into his study, which also served as the consulate office. Somewhere in the house a child cried and Elizabeth could be heard chastising either it or someone else. Once the study door was shut however, all sounds in the house were obliterated and Tomas was only aware of the loud ticking of a carriage clock on the British consul's desk.

"Are you in danger?" James Finn asked, pointing at the Arab robes.

Tomas shrugged by way of explanation. Finn raised his eyebrows but made no other comment. He scooped up a pile of papers from a leather chair.

"Sit. Please sit," he said, indicating the now empty chair. He cast around for somewhere to relocate everything he held in his hands. He finally placed the papers onto his desk which was already well covered with stacks of documents, pamphlets and what looked like half written letters. He then sat down on the chair behind the desk. He appeared nervous, his body tense and uncomfortable, and he didn't seem to know what to do with his hands. He got up again and began to pace the room, stopping to pick up certain objects, a paperweight, then a book, before putting them down again.

Tomas was determined not to be the first to speak and contented himself by looking around. He had been here several times before of course, and each time it was never clear whether Finn was in the process of packing or unpacking. His books were always stacked on the floor, and several wooden crates around the edges of the room had become a permanent feature. Today a woven rug spilled over the edge of one crate and a black umbrella stuck incongruously out of another. Finally Finn cleared his throat.

"You are back sooner than expected, Tomas. Do you have good news for me? Can I assume that you bring the funds I wish to borrow?" He was unable to keep a note of desperation from his voice, and Tomas now chose his words carefully in reply.

"It is a very large sum of money that you have requested," he began slowly, and before he could continue with his planned speech, James Finn interjected.

"And you stand to make a great deal from the rates you charge!" Sensing refusal of his request, he was suddenly on the defensive.

Tomas frowned and expressed his reply with some indignation.

"You and I both know that business throughout the city is suffering this year," he said sternly. "The city is bereft of visitors and sales in my shop have fallen sharply. The reason I have been forced to increase my interest rates is that I need to make sure I get a sufficient return for my needs. Furthermore, this is the only way I can guarantee my continued ability to assist those less fortunate than I."

Remembering how much he still owed Tomas, James Finn had the grace to nod his head and mumble an apology. He sat down heavily at his desk.

"But I have a problem with the sum of money you require," Tomas continued. "What you are asking for will represent a substantial proportion of my available funds." He paused for a while and stroked his moustache absent-mindedly. He knew that he must present his argument clearly, but was anxious not to offend. He of all people knew of James Finn's quick temper. He had no idea how the consul was going to react to the terms he was about to set, but he knew he would be advised to keep the upper hand in the discussion.

"With due respect, and despite your assurances to the contrary, I would suggest that your current situation may not be secure. I have to tell you that default on repayment of such a large sum of money would represent a substantial loss to me."

Tomas then ceased speaking. James Finn cast around for a suitable response and found none. He had been sitting upright in his chair, but now allowed himself to slump back and let his arms fall limply to his side. All at once he had no words to parry Tomas's arguments. He felt instead that he was backed up against a wall with no escape. The British Government was assessing his every move and it was vital to his continued position as consul that he present himself in the best light. For this reason he was desperate for them not to become aware of the full extent of his debts. But he knew there was no one else he could turn to in his ongoing financial crisis. He had assumed Tomas could be relied upon to help him, as he had done many times before, and his apparent reluctance to do so this time was a great shock. He had sworn his indebtedness after all. He felt a tightening in his chest and his left arm began to tingle. He flexed his hand a few times. He'd been troubled by such sensations a lot recently.

Tomas meanwhile allowed the short silence to settle over them before he spoke again, and when he did so, he leant forward in his chair and looked directly at his erstwhile friend.

"There is a way in which we can both take benefit from this situation, however," he said. "Notwithstanding my reluctance to do so, I may in fact be prepared to lend you the funds you require after all."

James Finn sat up sharply, not believing he had heard correctly. It was as if Tomas was playing with his emotions, like a cat with a mouse.

"But I have to tell you that my willingness to do so comes at a price," Tomas went on. "There is something I require from you in return."

As he listened to the terms Tomas laid out before him, James Finn knew he was no longer in control of his own destiny. Whether he agreed to Tomas's proviso to his lending him this sum of money or not, he was destined to give the Foreign Office further cause to condemn him. If either the true extent of his debts became known, or if it was discovered that he had gone against the law and given unauthorised British protection not just to one, but to a whole extended family of Russian Jews, his credibility would be in tatters. Either revelation would be sufficient reason for the British Government to question his continued role as British consul, and he would assuredly be dismissed. But his creditors were waiting for him, and his financial obligations were great. He believed he had no real options left other than to accept those presented to him by Tomas. Either way his fall from grace was likely to be absolute.

The excitement engendered by Tomas's news on his return from

Jerusalem was unparalleled, and it set the whole family on a course of high activity. Their first and most important task was to sell the diamond, a thought that had been causing Murad Amrad some sleepless nights. Although many years had passed since the Russian diamond had made its way into their possession, he was still concerned that it might be recognised. But Sheikh Abu al Khayr came to his rescue by insisting that he would be honoured to take upon himself the task of selling the stone. He had been sufficiently overawed by the beauty and quality of the stone to want to make sure his friend received its true worth in payment. Although unaware of the true reason for Murad Amrad's fears, he had nevertheless understood that this was a momentous time for the Galperin family and was genuine in his reasons to help. Murad Amrad was overcome with gratitude and relief. This arrangement would not only provide him with the necessary anonymity, but there was no one he would rather entrust with the task of selling the diamond. The Sheikh was well known among the traders of gemstones in Syria and beyond, and there was no doubt that he would get a good price for it. And as a regular dealer in high value items, he was also well used to the responsibility such a deal entailed.

The Sheikh lost no time in setting off on his mission. Accompanied by Ameen and two armed guards he immediately headed south on horseback, with the diamond concealed within his clothing. Despite his advancing years, he remained lean and fit and was well accustomed to travelling great distances to trade. The Galperin family meanwhile, had no choice but to wait for his return. They tried to keep the household running as normal, but as the days passed they all became increasingly jumpy and nervous. Tomas was often to be found pacing the courtyard, and even Murad Amrad, who had the utmost confidence in his friend and did his best to instil calm into the household, could not settle to anything in particular. It was as if they'd been left in a vacuum.

It was a full week before Sheikh Abu al Khayr returned to Jaffa, and when he did, he came straight to their home before going to his. He had been riding hard and the dust from the journey was ingrained into the deep lines around his eyes and on his forehead. He staggered a little as he dismounted from his horse and was very obviously exhausted. But he was triumphant.

"Allah is good, my friend," he announced to Murad Amrad as he entered their kitchen. With his strong personality and flowing robes he always seemed to take up more space than any other person. On this occasion his arrival caused a palpable shift in the atmosphere of the house. It was certainly enough to alert the rest of the family, all of whom managed to reach the kitchen from wherever they had been in time to see him place several large moneybags onto the table with a dramatic flourish. He looked at Murad Amrad as he did so and grinned like a little boy. As promised, he had indeed obtained an excellent price for the diamond. It was an amount that far exceeded the sum required for James Finn's loan. But of the greatest importance for them right then, was the fact that the deal with the British consul could now be completed, and it was for this reason alone that they celebrated that evening.

A day later, having closed up the house in Jaffa, the whole family made the journey to Jerusalem. What was needed of the money to service the loan was divided between the adults. In ways reminiscent of their flight from Bialystok all those years ago, Sonja had spent a greater part of the previous day sewing leather pouches to be concealed under their clothing.

There were many other travellers making the journey to Jerusalem that day, and their long caravan of camels, horses, mules and donkeys had left at dawn. Sonja, on account of her age and generous proportions, and Hanna, who was to keep her company, were mounted on a camel, whose handler rode beside them on a donkey. They had ridden on camels before when travelling to Jerusalem, but never ceased to find the behaviour and movements of the animals alarming and disconcerting. Fanny, who had an even greater aversion to camels, was relieved to find herself on a mule. She rode sidesaddle, her legs on one side of the animal and the baby, David James, reclining in a woven carrier suspended from the other. The two girls, Sarah and Anna, sat one behind the other on another mule, while James and Nathaniel each had a mule to themselves. At fifteen and eighteen the boys had felt this to be somewhat of a slight and they had scowled when they saw that Murad Amrad, Utah and their father were given horses to ride. But their discontent was short lived. It was enough of an adventure to be travelling together and they were in good spirits. The Arab guards rode ahead of them on fine horses, which they handled with great skill and dexterity. They were well armed and happy to fire their rifles at anything suspicious along the pathway, but although it was difficult for the family not to feel more concerned than usual about bandits, the likelihood of them attacking such a large group was negligible, and the day-long journey passed without mishap.

By the time they presented themselves to the British Consul later that same evening, they were tired, dirty and travel-weary. But Tomas was not prepared to delay the proceedings, or to keep that amount of money on his person, a moment longer than he had to, and had no compunction about once again breaking the restraints of convention by calling at such a late hour. For her part, despite being disturbed in her preparations for bed, Elizabeth Finn managed to keep up the pretence of normality as she showed Fanny, the children, Sonja and Hanna into her small sitting room. While the men went into the consul's office to finalise their business dealings, she did her best to make polite enquiries as to the well being of their family, and even took a turn at holding the baby, who was beginning to fret and whine. But she looked pale and strained and the prime reason for the Galperin's being there at that hour hung unspoken between them, like an unwelcome guest, making their conversations stilted and forced. Fanny complimented her on the charmingly furnished room and they discussed the price of fabrics. But as the minutes ticked by, the silences between their sentences lengthened to such an extent as to make them excruciatingly uncomfortable, and there was an audible communal sigh of relief when they were finally summoned into the British consul's office.

The room was not large, and by the time the family was inside there was little room for any of them to move freely. Here, one by one, they were all at last to be registered as British subjects and, over-awed by the experience, they stood still until called forward. Even the baby seemed to sense the importance of the moment and ceased its complaining. James Finn presided over the signing of the necessary papers with a grim face, and the process was mostly accomplished in silence. The ticking of the clock and the scratching of pen on paper did much to accentuate the tension, and it seemed that an event of such momentous meaning in their lives was to pass with little ceremony. But Tomas suddenly and uncharacteristically turned to Fanny and hugged her. She went pink and he, almost immediately embarrassed at his public display of affection, moved away. But the impulsive and unguarded response had broken the ice. The all looked at each other in wonderment and joy, and even James Finn relaxed then and had the good grace to shake the hands of Murad Amrad, Tomas, Utah, James and Nathaniel. To Sonja, Fanny and Hanna he inclined his head, and he smiled at the little girls. They were all now British subjects after all, and as such demanded the respect and courtesy due to citizens of that nation.

As they left the British consul's home, Murad Amrad stopped and looked up at the British flag that crackled and flapped over their heads, the capricious winter wind now fully restored. He stood for a moment underneath it and tried to take in the magnitude of his family's renewed status. They had fled from the Russian Empire in fear of their lives; they had come to the land of Israel, as the rabbi in Bialystok had suggested they might; they had lived with the constant threat of persecution and discovery; Tomas and his family had even sought refuge by giving up their faith. Throughout the past thirty years however, they had remained a strong family unit and built a new life for themselves. But only now was that life secure. Now they were protected by one of the most powerful countries in the world, exempt from the tyranny of the Turkish authorities and inaccessible to the mighty Russian Empire. Under the shadow of this flag they could continue to build a future for themselves, for their children and for generations to come. This was the flag they would now salute as theirs. This was a flag worth fighting for.

Tomas broke into his reverie by touching him gently on the arm.

"Come, Father. Let us go home."

BENI SUEF, EGYPT: 1918

David James put down his pencil and took a deep breath. He'd been writing for a long time and he wished that could be the end of the story, a satisfactory conclusion to a momentous chapter of family history. But there was still a little more to tell. He rubbed his eyes. The shadows in the room still spoke of other times. He had been a young boy again, sitting at his Grandfather Murad Amrad's knee in the shady courtyard of the house in Jaffa. He could smell the tobacco in the long clay pipe his grandfather always smoked. He could feel Murad Amrad's strong hands occasionally pat his head in rough affection.

As one of his youngest grandchildren, David James had benefited from the fact that Murad Amrad had by then been too old to work. Instead he and his grandfather spent many hours together and Murad Amrad would often recount the story of his life. He had considered this story to be his legacy, something infinitely valuable to be handed down to his grandchildren, family history passed down in the age-old way from the old to the young, never to be forgotten.

Fifty years had passed since then. But recently, feeling his time running out, David James had been thinking a great deal about his family roots. He had come to realise that in pushing his family history to the back of his mind for so long, he had denied his children the opportunity to know it. Both his own parents had died before any of them were born, so his children had never sat at their knees and heard them tell their story. Was it too late in the telling he wondered? Would Wilfred and his sisters come to cherish their family history or would they prefer to bury it, much as he had been guilty of doing? He shook his head, picked up his pencil and returned to his writing.

Tomas's friendship with James Finn was somewhat tarnished from then on. Finn hung on as British consul for another year, but eventually his inability to manage his money was the primary cause for his dismissal. Before he left for England, and much as Murad Amrad had supposed, the Foreign Office were forced to intervene in his debts. By managing to lower the rate of interest charged on all his loans, they reduced the final amount he owed by half. They then mortgaged his lands and drew up a repayment schedule with his creditors that compelled James Finn to repay his debts over a period of some years. All this took time however, and James and Elizabeth Finn were forced to remain in Jerusalem for the best part of a further year until all the agreements with their creditors were finalised. By the end of their time in Jerusalem they were, as James Finn had feared, virtually without funds even to buy food. Eventually they set sail for England in July 1863 and the new British consul, Noel Temple Moore, took over his duties.

As Finn's main creditor, Tomas suffered considerable financial loss. But in overall terms, he considered his worth to be vastly increased. As he and Fanny went on to have three more daughters, Lizzie, Fanny and Esther, the family embraced their new status as British subjects with pride and enthusiasm. During the next twenty-five years, natural disasters occasionally afflicted the population of Palestine, very much as they always had done; earthquakes, plagues of locusts, droughts, famine and outbreaks of cholera were just something to be got through. But in Jerusalem, as the population doubled, nothing halted the progress of building work once it was permitted outside the walls of the old city, and New Jerusalem began to take shape. Not only the Russians, but the French, the Germans and the English all added their stamp on the new city, constructing apartments, hotels, orphanages, hospitals and churches, each seemingly more grand in design than the last. The road between Jerusalem and Jaffa was eventually made serviceable for horsedrawn carriages, and the journey became a far more comfortable and safe experience, not only for the increasing number of visitors from all over the world, but for the Galperin family as they travelled between Jerusalem and their property in Jaffa. This they continued to do frequently; while Jerusalem was the city in which they lived and worked, Jaffa was where they came to be together, to celebrate, to rest, or to help with the harvest.

When Murad Amrad died in 1871, a vital connection to the family's past died with him. He had been an old man by then of course, and had not been feeling well for some time. Sheikh Abu al

Khayr had died the year before and Murad Amrad had missed his friend deeply. Perhaps this was the ultimate reason for his demise, or perhaps he was just tired and ready to go. But whatever the cause, he died in his sleep with his beloved Sonja at his side. When the family gathered together at the house in Jaffa to mourn his passing, it was also to honour the head of their family and the man who had led them to a new life. The house never felt quite the same after Murad Amrad's death. But the locals continued to refer to the property as Sheikh Murad's land and, for all David James knew, they still did.

Meanwhile, down the dark corridors of power in the Foreign Office in London, events were set in motion that were to alter the course of the family's future once again. After many years of indecision, the British Government had finalised a plan to reduce the number of Jews in Palestine under their protection. The majority of these were of Russian origin. Many had been in Palestine for several generations. And the fact that there were now more foreigners under British protection in the whole of Syria than there were natural born British nationals themselves had propelled the British Government into action.

Unaware as yet of any threat to their situation, the Galperin's social life in Jerusalem continued to flourish. Their position in the city was elevated when all of Tomas and Fanny's girls made good marriages. Sarah to a German, Anna and Esther both to Englishmen, Fanny to a Maltese and Lizzie to a Frenchman. Tomas would joke that his family had become as multi-national as Jerusalem itself. Nathaniel meanwhile married a girl he had known since childhood and remained in the city. Abraham had returned from Malta in 1865 at the age of seventeen, much to his mother's joy, but he had returned to Malta two years later to take up a teaching post at the Protestant College where he remained. Neither he nor James ever married.

Tomas's business concerns in Jerusalem went from strength to strength, aided to a great extent by James and Nathaniel who worked with him. James specialised in antiquities and Nathaniel in jewellery and gemstones. Both travelled extensively around Palestine and Syria and did much to broaden the family's business interests.

David James had never had much interest in the antique or jewellery trade, however. Maybe it was because his brothers had already established themselves in the business by the time he grew up. But by then Jerusalem had grown as well, and by the 1880s the city housed European shops and diverse innovative commercial concerns. He took a job in the new telegraph office, where communications regarding the proposed new railway line between Jerusalem and Jaffa introduced him to what was to become a life-long passion. During this time he had many dalliances with young ladies about town, but much to the disappointment of his parents, failed to settle down with any of them.

Back in London, the daunting task of sifting through the names of Jews who had been given British protection since the 1840s, and of sorting out who remained eligible for such protection, was slow. But in 1889, the name of Tomas Galperin finally came to light. Against his name was the information that he and his family had been Russian Jews, that they had converted to Christianity in 1858, and that they had been awarded British protection in 1861, only months before Finn was dismissed. The Foreign Office requested that Noel Temple Moore provide further clarification as to why Tomas Galperin had merited British protection. From consular records in Jerusalem, Moore was able to inform them that Finn had logged the reason as a case of persecution. "I felt duty bound to afford him British protection," he had written in his report. On further investigation of the case, the Foreign Office had no such compunction and Moore was accordingly instructed to update the records. On 18th June 1889, Moore duly wrote against the name of Tomas Galperin, that British protectorate status had been provided 'for reasons unexplained' and was to be revoked.

Tomas exploded into a furious rage when he received the letter informing him of the British Government's decision. He screwed the paper up and set out immediately for the British consulate where he demanded to see Moore. But he was refused permission and was forced to return home. David James remembered how his father appeared to give up then, his foothold on security and status suddenly whipped away. The British protection that he and Murad Amrad had worked for was now to be denied to his children, and

229

the value of their ill-fated diamond fund reduced to a signature on a meaningless report. He spent days pacing up and down his shop, his pace at first frantic and then slow as he accepted the inevitable. But he had taken on the mantle of someone he wasn't born to be and, with it removed, he was no longer sure of who he really was. One day, three months later, the sound of his footsteps came to an abrupt end, and Fanny found him slumped on the floor of the shop he loved. He had died of a heart attack.

Fanny went back to Jaffa after that, to be with Utah and Hanna, neither of whom had ever married. Nathaniel took over the shop and James divided his time between tending to their land in Jaffa and continuing to trade in artifacts. David James knew there would now be no place for him in what had been their family home. His relationship with all his brothers was strained. He therefore decided to travel to Egypt. Anna and her husband had invited him to visit them in Alexandria, where they lived.

Once there, they showed him as much of Egypt as they could and he became enamored with the vibrant social life of Alexandria and Cairo. On a visit to the pyramids with a party of friends, he was introduced to Maria, the daughter of an Italian doctor and his bohemian musician wife. They fell in love very quickly and he needed no persuasion to stay on in Egypt. After appealing to the British consul in Cairo to safeguard his position in Egypt, David James was granted 'British citizenship for life'. He accepted a job with the British run Egyptian State Railways in Cairo and, a year later, he and Maria were married. When the registrar filled in the marriage certificate, both parties declared themselves as British subjects – Maria had been born in Malta, a fact that made her a natural born British citizen. David James had taken up the mantle of British protection that had fallen from around his father's shoulders, and from then on had given the legality of his family's on-going British status no further thought. He had registered the births of their four children at the British Embassy in Cairo, and had brought them up to believe they too were British by right. And Maria had never questioned it.

EPILOGUE

At the end of World War I, Wilfred returned to England with what was left of his regiment. Shortly afterwards, he took delivery of a package from Egypt. Inside it was his father's letter, which he read with great sadness. David James had died of pneumonia a few weeks after writing it. Wilfred hadn't seen his father for many years, and had long ceased to think of Egypt as his home. But he had been looking forward to their reunion. He had been sent to school in England at the age of ten and, with the exception of a short visit to Cairo before he went up to Cambridge University, his relationship with his father had been conducted through letters. When war had broken out soon after his graduation, he had joined up, and there had been no further opportunity for a return visit to Egypt.

Wilfred glanced briefly at the attached sheets of paper neatly tied with string – his father's family chronicle. The writing was spidery and difficult to read and he felt reluctant to expose himself to any further emotion. He was also in a hurry to make up for lost time, eager to get on with the rest of his life and, as a result, he decided to reseal the package and leave it for a later date, when he had more time.

He finally sat down to read it on an autumnal morning in 1963, and by this time he himself was an old man. He was at his home in Oxfordshire, England, and had just received a letter from the Foreign Office. At a loss to understand fully what the letter conveyed, he remembered his father's account of the family history and decided to see if it would shed any light on the matter. The chronicle had remained sealed for nearly fifty years, and when he pulled the package from among his family documents, he found the sheets of paper were stained brown at the edges and the writing on them faint. Wilfred's hands shook and he struggled to untie the string. Once he'd done so, he sat in a chair at the window in the clear morning light and began to read his father's words. The day passed, and the light outside faded. He got up briefly to switch on the lamp, then returned to his chair and continued to read. And when eventually he reached the end, he was crying unashamedly – for his grandfather, for his father and for himself. He knew what it felt like to no longer be sure of who you were.

The Foreign Office,
October 15th, 1963

Dear Sir
It has come to our attention that your birth was registered in error.
Although your father David James was granted the status of British Protected Person for life, his children were specifically excluded from holding this status. This decision was conveyed to your father in a letter from Sir Evelyn Baring dated 25th April 1890. While it therefore appears that you have no legal claim to British nationality, it has been agreed that you may continue to enjoy passport facilities. It will however be necessary, since it was registered in error, to cancel the registration of your birth, which was effected at the former British Vice Consulate at Suez…